Harry's Children

Sheila. R. Kelly

ISBN: 9798794700886

In memory of my nieces, Joanne and Nicola, whose lives were cruelly shortened by Huntington's disease.

CHAPTERS

Introduction

This is a work of fiction. All the characters are fictitious, except for Arthur Rook and Mrs Jones, who were choir leaders in the 1960s and 70s for the Manchester Girls' choir. I remember these two wonderful people with affection, and I am sure they wouldn't have minded my mentioning them by name.

I have placed one character as a teacher in the Anderson Institute [Anderson High School] in Lerwick. If there was ever a Mr Roberts in this school, I apologise; it isn't the same person.

All the locations are real places in Greater Manchester, South Wales and Shetland.

One:

Who's The Daddy?

"He lied to me! He's been lying to me all my life!" Sian hid her face in her hands, sobbing uncontrollably.

Roberto was mortified. "Cara mia, I am so sorry, I thought you knew." He put his arm around her heaving shoulders.

She pulled away from him roughly. "Don't call me that! I'm not your cara mia. I'm your sister!"

"But that is what I have been trying to tell you. I am not your- what you say – natural brother. Dad is my natural father, but he is not yours. You were born when he was away in the war. He had been away over two years. When he came back he accepted you as his own, and you know he has always loved you, but he is not your natural father."

He put his arms around her again, and, this time, she allowed him to comfort her as she sobbed into his chest.

"So, cara mia, I am not your brother, but I love you, and I want us to be married."

"No, I can't take this in. Please don't mention it again." She replied. "We might not be natural, as you say, but I've only known you as my brother since I met you. Can't we stay like that?"

Roberto's heart sank; he had loved Sian since he first saw her. He had known from the start that she wasn't his true sister; his mother had told him the story of how she met his father and how they had exchanged confidences. They had only spent one magical day together, in Italy, in the middle of the war, but Roberto had been the result of that day's intimacy. Harry, his father, hadn't known of Roberto's existence until eighteen years later, when Roberto turned up in Manchester.

"If that is what you want cara – Sian, but I will hope that one day you will feel the same about me."

Sian didn't answer: she was thinking about the shocking fact he had just revealed. She gazed, unseeing, at the valley spread out below them. The view was marred by all the works that had been going on the last few years. Uncle George had been horrified when he had heard of the plans for another reservoir in the valley in the late fifties. There had been lots of opposition, but the water companies had got their way, and now, in spring 1965, Dovestone reservoir was almost complete. It had changed the beautiful valley dramatically. Optimists hoped that the valley would be beautiful again, once the reservoir was filled with water and the scars on the earth covered with grass. George wasn't so sure.They were sitting on the rocks at Indian's Head, above Greenfield. It was one of their favourite places. They often walked up from Auntie Jenny's house to the trig point on Alphin Pike and then across to these rocks to enjoy the view and breathe in the fresh air of the moors.

But, today, Sian didn't even enjoy the view across to Alderman's hill. She looked a picture of misery. Bob, the young border collie came to rest his head in her lap. He could sense there was something wrong. She stroked his head absentmindedly, the action calming her a little.

"How did I not realise?" said Sian. "I know my age, when I was born, and I know that Dad was away until after the war ended. I must be an idiot!"

She looked up at Roberto, her eyes still wet with tears. "I remember, I must have only been two. I think it was my first memory, because I can't remember anything before that. We were in Uncle Dai's house, though I think it was our house too, then. Uncle Dai was a soldier and I knew my dad was a soldier too, though I don't know how I knew. Mum must have told me."

"Dad walked in and I said, 'Daddy?' and he said, 'yes lovey, I'm your Daddy' then Mum started crying and everyone was hugging everyone else. That's why I've always known – always assumed - that he's my Dad. But why has he never told me? I'm twenty one now; he's had lots of time to tell me. Why has he continued to lie to me?"

"I do not know, Sian. Maybe he has just never found the right moment."

"Well he should have found the right moment by now! I shouldn't have had to find out like this, from somebody else. Oh, I'm sorry Roberto," she could see how upset he was. The tears were shining in his eyes too.

"Sian, I am truly sorry. I should not have assumed that you knew."

"No, it's not your fault Roberto. I shouldn't have lost my temper. I just can't believe how stupid I've been; and I bet everyone else knows. Oh, does Auntie Jenny know? She must do, and Auntie Norma, and oh – Grandma and Grandad! How could they all keep it secret all this time? Come on Roberto; it's time to get this all out in the open, starting with Auntie Jenny!" She stormed down the path with Roberto and the dog in hot pursuit.

She was so furious that she ran through the fields, where Mavis was tending her horses, and just waved to the woman without stopping.

"Don't you want to ride today?" shouted Mavis, as she stared in astonishment at Roberto and Bob chasing after Sian. "Roberto, is everything alright?"

Roberto slowed enough to answer, "Yes, we will speak later; sorry." He bounded after Sian, taking the stile at the top of Dacres Road in one leap. He caught up with her just as she stormed through the back door of Jenny's house.

Jenny looked up from her baking. "Are you ok Sian?" she asked, amazed.

"Ok? I'm furious!" Sian shouted. "Why have you never told me that Dad isn't my real father?"

Jenny wiped her floury hands on a towel. "Oh, that," she breathed.

"Yes, that!" Sian almost spat the words out. "Don't you think I had a right to know?"

Jenny turned to Roberto, who was looking really uncomfortable. "Can you make a pot of tea, lovey?" she asked him. "We'll go and sit in the living room. It's easier to talk sitting down." She put her arm round Sian's shoulder and led her through. George looked up from his newspaper and, seeing Sian's tear-stained face, he stood up quickly.

"Oh, I'll just go and see Malcolm next door. I said I'd help him with his fence." He was out of the door before Jenny could get Sian seated.

Sian was beginning to calm down a little. "Where's Colin?" she asked. She didn't want to upset her little cousin. He was only two; the same age, she realised, as she had been when she first met her dad.

"He's asleep upstairs," replied Jenny, her face relaxing into the look of pure devotion that she always had when she thought of her son.

"That's good; you can concentrate on giving me an explanation." Sian sat on the edge of the chair, refusing to relax.

"Well, it shouldn't be me giving the explanation. It should be your Dad, but, as you've asked, I'll do my best, but you'll have to ask him, too."

"Oh, I will, and give him a piece of my mind!"

"Now, don't forget that your Dad has had a very hard time of it, and I know he thinks of you as his own daughter. He has never treated you any differently from your sisters, has he?"

"Well, no, but he should have told me." She was calming down, and she sat back in her chair as Roberto came in with the tea tray.

"Do you want me to stay?" asked Roberto. He was looking very uncomfortable.

"Of course," Sian replied. "You know all about it anyway. You might as well hear Auntie Jenny's side of the story."

Roberto sat down and looked apologetically at Jenny. "I'm sorry; I only know what my mother told me. I did not realise that Sian was unaware of it. I never would have told her like that."

"I told you Roberto; it's not your fault. I should have been told years ago. Go on then Auntie Jenny. Tell me what you know."

"Well, we didn't know you existed until Harry brought you and your Mum back to Manchester at the end of the war. We had wondered why she had stopped writing to us, or coming up for holidays. It was obvious, of course, when we saw you. You were about two and a half at the time and we all fell in love with you immediately. Your Dad had obviously accepted you and so we, your Grandma, Auntie Norma and I, also accepted you. More than that, we loved you right from the start. Grandad took a bit longer to come around, but you were soon helping him in the garden."

"Oh yes, I remember being in the garden with him a lot when I was little," Sian mused. "But, did Mum tell you what happened? I can't imagine her loving anyone else but Dad. She adored him."

"No, she never said, but I think your Dad knows the full story. I got the impression that someone took advantage of her. You have to remember, lovey, that she was only eighteen when they got married, and just a couple of months later he was sent overseas and he was away for four years. It was very hard for her."

Sian was quiet for a long time after that. They all sat, sipping their tea, lost in their thoughts.

Roberto looked up suddenly as he realised that Sian was crying again. These were not angry tears as before, but silent, heart-rending tears in rivulets down her face.

"Cara mia!" he cried, as he went over to her and kneeled on the floor at the side of her chair, so as to get as close as he could. He took hold of her hands. "I cannot see you so sad. Dad still loves you; you know that. We all love you; your sisters, grandma and grandad, Aunties, Johnny, all of us. There is no need to cry."

"I know, it's just that – oh I don't know. I was so proud of my Dad, I am proud of him; but he's not my real Dad, is he?"

"He is as real as any Dad could be; more real. My Papa, in Italy, is not my real dad, but I love him and I know he cares for me. I am glad that I found Dad, but I'll never forget the man who raised me and taught me how to be a good man."

Jenny could see that Sian was taking in all that Roberto was saying, and that she wasn't needed now, so she went upstairs to her son. When she came down with Colin in her arms, Roberto was drying Sian's tears with his hankie.

"Colin struggled to be put down and ran over to Sian. "Cwying Sian?" he asked. "Sad?" He climbed into Sian's lap for a cuddle, and Roberto went back to his own chair.

"I'm a bit sad Colin, but I feel better now you're here," said Sian, and she gave him a big cuddle.

"Good!" he said, confident that his favourite cousin was alright. "Biscuit Mummy? Please." He turned his blue eyed gaze to Jenny.

Jenny laughed and went into the kitchen to get the biscuit tin.

Sian had been living with George and Jenny since she left school and started working in a shoe shop in Oldham. She had always got on with her auntie, and had spent many weekends at the Greenfield house as a child. Mavis, up at the farm always welcomed her and allowed her to spend as much time with the horses as she liked.

When her cousin Colin was born Sian was proud to become his godmother. She couldn't imagine living anywhere else now, though she knew that space would be a problem as the boy grew, as the little house had only two bedrooms. She didn't worry about that, though, deciding to cross that bridge when she came to it.

It was Wednesday, Sian's half day, so she had been home by lunchtime, and Roberto had finished his postal round early, which was why they had taken advantage of the fine weather to climb up to Indian's head.

Sian was amazed that it was still only 3.45pm. So much had happened and her life, or more precisely, her outlook on life, had completely changed.

"Do you think Uncle George would take me to my Dad's in the car?" she asked Jenny. "I can come back on the bus later. I really need to speak to Dad about this now. Otherwise I know I won't sleep."

"I'm sure he will lovey. I'll go and get him." She got up and went out of the back door.

"I will go with you to Dad's," said Roberto. "You shouldn't be alone on the late bus, and I need to speak to Dad too; to apologise for telling you. He should have been the one to explain."

"Exactly!" said Sian, becoming angry again. "He should have told me years ago. It's not your fault Roberto, and you don't need to come with me. I'll be alright on the bus."

"I know, but I want to go with you. Please do not stop me." He pleaded, gazing into her eyes. Two pairs of deep brown eyes reflected each other. Roberto's eyes were full of love, and Sian couldn't avoid the intensity. Against her better judgement she realised that she did have some feeling for him, but it wasn't the intense love that he obviously felt for her. She mentally shook herself and dragged her gaze away. "Okay, you can come with me, but I do all the talking; understood?"

"Yes," he replied, contritely.

Harry was already at the back door when they arrived. He had only just arrived home from work and had been taking his shoes off in the kitchen. Uncannily, he was aware that Sian was coming, and that she was upset. He was subliminally aware of all his children and knew instinctively if they were in trouble. It didn't matter to him that Sian wasn't his biological daughter; in fact he had almost forgotten, he loved her just as much as his other daughters.

He watched her tearstained face as she came around the corner of the house, followed protectively by Roberto, with George a few feet behind.

"What's wrong lovey?" he asked, but Sian just glared at him and pushed past into the house. Roberto gave a sheepish smile and George came forward and shook Harry's hand.

"I won't stop, Harry," he said. "I know Sian wants to talk to you, I have an idea what it's about, and you won't want an audience. Come over at the weekend if you have time and we'll go up on the moors with the dogs."

"Ok George; thanks for giving them a lift. I'll come over on Saturday." He watched his brother in law get back into his car and then went back into the house.

18 year old Carol was in the kitchen, her grey eyes, so like his own, full of concern. "I'll make a cuppa Dad. I think we

may be having tea late tonight. Auntie Audrey had everything ready for shepherd's pie but she hadn't put the stove on yet because Lynette just woke up, so she's feeding her first. I was just about to put the spuds on but I'll leave them for now. I tried to get the others to go next door, but they know something is happening and they want to be in on it; and maybe they should be. It's about you not being Sian's father, isn't it?"

Harry only wondered for a split second how Carol knew; but then of course she had inherited his gift of being in tune with other's feelings. She was bound to know, even if she hadn't done the maths and realised that Sian was conceived while Harry was away during the war. He smiled ruefully.

"I should have told her, and all of you, years ago; but she has always felt like my own. I could go years at a time without even thinking about it. Well, I'd better go and face the music."

He went through to the living room and looked round at his family, all waiting expectantly. Pamela and the twins – aged 14 and 13 but looking like triplets- were sitting side by side on the settee. Three pairs of deep brown eyes looked up at him, full of intelligence and curiosity.

Sian was sitting in the rocking chair by the fire, Roberto at her side and Flossie, the black Labrador, at her feet. Harry's heart gave a summersault as he looked at her; she was the image of Bronwyn, his first wife. Bronwyn used to sit in the same chair, stroking the dog's head in exactly the same way. For a moment the grief threatened to overwhelm him. He was saved by his youngest child.

Audrey, Harry's second wife, was sitting at the table, feeding their six month old daughter with something smooth that looked like thick tomato soup. The baby looked up and shouted "Dada!" spraying food all over her mother. Audrey just laughed and wiped herself with a baby's bib. Harry's heart overflowed with love for them and for all his children. He felt blessed.

Sian wasn't feeling blessed; She was angry, and she didn't like her Dad smiling foolishly around at everyone. All his children, apart from her! Why should he look so happy, when she was feeling bereft. It wasn't fair!

She glared at him and hissed through her teeth, "You've got some explaining to do!"

The twins and Pamela stared at her in shock, and then, as if all their eyes were synchronised, their gaze swivelled to Harry, to see what his reaction would be.

He looked ashamed. They all looked at Audrey. She looked sad; then they looked at Carol, who was just coming in with a tray laden with teacups. Carol was looking sympathetic. She put the tray on the table and gave the first cup to Sian. "It'll be alright sis," she said, gently.

Sian turned on her. "You knew, didn't you? Did everyone know apart from me?"

"We don't know!" said Nerys. "What secret have we been kept out of?"

Harry pulled a dining chair away from the table and sat facing Sian and Roberto. "I'm so sorry lovey. You are right; I should have told you years ago. It never seemed the right time, and that was when I remembered at all."

"What, what!" shouted Nerys. "You haven't told us what it was that was never the right time. Tell us now!"

"Nerys, you shouldn't speak to your Dad like that," Audrey mildly rebuked.

Nerys was a little taken aback. Audrey never told them off. She had the courtesy to say, "Sorry Auntie Audrey; sorry Dad."

Sian responded; "Dad should be the one who's sorry. What he hasn't told you, and, more importantly, never told me, is that I am not his daughter. Roberto told me today, it wasn't his fault; he thought I knew. His mother had the decency to tell him, years ago, when she told him that *your* Dad was his natural father. I've been lied to all my life!"

Roberto just sat with his head down, saying nothing.

The three young teenagers were flabbergasted! They sat open mouthed, not saying anything at first, then Rosalind said, "Dad, is this true?"

Harry took a big gulp of his tea. "Yes, it is, but first I want to say to Sian," he looked at his eldest daughter. "I have loved you like my own. Right from the first time I saw you, I've thought of you as my own daughter. You are my daughter, in every way, except biologically." His eyes were filled with tears.

Everyone was quiet for a time; it was obvious that the younger girls were trying to make sense of it; Carol was sipping her tea and trying not to cry. Audrey was crying, but trying to hide it. Baby Lynette was oblivious to the drama; she had her mouth open, waiting for the next spoonful.

Sian's anger was cooling a little, turning to sorrow.

She said, more quietly now, "Tell me what happened. How did Mum come to have me when you were away in the war? Oh, how stupid I've been; I should have worked this out years ago!"

"You're not stupid, lovey," said Harry. "There was no reason for you to think otherwise, but you must believe that I didn't set out to deceive you, and neither did your Mum. In fact your Mum had convinced herself that you were mine, even to the point of putting my name on your birth certificate as your father. It was the only way she could cope with what had happened."

"What did happen?" Sian had now relaxed enough to sit back in her chair. Roberto was holding her hand, but she didn't seem to notice.

"Your Mum and Auntie Dilys were going out for the evening when they witnessed a nasty car accident in which a good friend and neighbour was killed. There were two airmen on the way to the pub, they couldn't do anything for poor Mr Jones, but they consoled the sisters until the ambulance and the police came and then they took the girls to the pub." Harry gazed into the distance, remembering what Bronwyn had told him and reliving the anger and devastation that he had felt at the time.

"Both girls had too much to drink. Bronwyn didn't normally drink alcohol at all, and it was brandy they were drinking. She only vaguely remembered what happened next. The airmen walked the girls home, but they had missed their lift back to camp and asked if they could sleep on the floor. Dilys gave them her mother's bed to sleep in; it was still in the downstairs front room. Dilys went to bed, but Bronwyn fell asleep on the settee in the back room. She was dreaming of me and didn't realise that the airman was taking advantage of her until it was too late. The man was ashamed and left the house with his friend before morning."

Harry looked round at his family. All the girls looked shocked. Audrey knew the story; she just looked very sad, and Roberto had been told a version of the story some years before.

"They never saw the airmen again. They found out much later that both men had died when their plane had been shot down."

"Dilys didn't notice that Bronwyn was pregnant until several months later. Bronwyn had never told her what had happened that night, and was so ashamed that she tried to hide it. She told Dilys that she had thought it was me, and, by the time you were born, Sian, she had convinced herself that you were the child of my spirit."

There was complete silence in the room.

Sian had tears streaming down her face, but she said nothing. Carol gave her a hankie and then knelt at the side of Sian's chair, in mute support. Roberto was still on her other side with his arm across her shoulders.

The three younger girls were staring at Harry; trying to take in what he had just told them. Pamela was the first to ask a question.

"How did you find out Dad; did you know nothing about Sian until you came home after the war?"

Harry wondered how much he should tell his daughters. They knew that he and Carol had some sort of gift; where they could often sense how people were feeling, and even sometimes seemed to know what they were thinking. In fact all the girls, apart from Sian, he thought, ruefully, were aware of each other no matter where they were at the time.

They didn't know about the dreams though. He looked at Carol as if to ask her what he should say. She looked up at him and smiled. He heard her voice in his head.

"Tell them you dreamed about Sian's birth and afterwards; just enough to explain; but not about my dreams or about Mymie." Harry smiled back. He didn't stop to wonder how Carol could speak directly to his mind. She had been doing it, on occasion, since she was quite young.

He thought about it for a while, and then said, "I've always had very clear dreams, and sometimes my dreams have come true. I dreamed about your Mum even before I met her; so, when I did meet her, I knew she would be my wife."

"I dreamed about her a lot while I was away in the war. In my dream I saw you being born, Sian. I couldn't believe it at first, didn't want to believe it, but the dream was so real; it had to be like the ones I had had before; the ones that had come true."

Sian was staring at him in disbelief. "You saw me being born, in a dream; are you kidding me?"

"No, I wouldn't lie to you about that. I dreamed about you often over the next two years while I was away, and I came to love you, just as I had with your Mum; so when I saw you for real when I came home on leave, I already thought of you as my daughter."

Sian pulled away from Roberto and launched herself at Harry. "Oh Dad!" she sobbed.

Harry held her close and stroked her raven curls. "You'll always be my daughter; never forget that,"

"Course she will," said Nerys. "And you'll always be our sister too!"

"She is our sister, silly! We've got the same Mum," said Pamela.

"Yeah, well that's what I meant, and don't call me silly!" Nerys retorted. Rosalind giggled and, suddenly, the atmosphere was lightened. Everyone began to laugh and the girls came over to hug Sian. It became one big round of hugging and laughing. Baby Lynette was bouncing up and down in her high chair, laughing as much as anyone.

Tea was late that evening, but there was plenty for everyone. Fruit cake and cups of tea followed the shepherd's pie, and the conversation moved on to other topics.

The twins and Pamela were now in the third year of secondary school, though not at the same school.

Pamela was at the Grammar School and the twins were at Brookdale Park Secondary Modern, the school that Harry and his sisters had attended. Although the lessons at the two schools differed in many ways, there was one subject that they all loved – music.

The twins were excited about a visitor to the school that day.

"We had the inspector for music at school today," said Nerys. "His name is Mr Rook, and he has a choir – the Manchester Girls Choir, and he asked everyone in our choir if we would like to join. They have rehearsals every Friday evening at Moston Fields School. Can we go Dad? We can get the number 7 bus from Church Street."

Before Harry could answer, Pamela piped up, "That's near my school; I pass it to get the bus home. Can I go too, Dad?"

"I don't see why not," said Harry. "What time do you have to be there?"

"Seven o'clock and it finishes at eight thirty," Said Rosalind.

"Well, that'll give you time to have your tea," Audrey said. "I'll make sure it's ready in good time for you."

"You can go on the bus and then I'll pick you up in the car at nine," said Harry. He was immensely relieved that the subject of Sian's parentage seemed to have been forgotten; at least for the present.

He was surprised that the younger girls hadn't asked more questions about his dreams. He found it difficult to explain how he was able to somehow travel to a distant place in his dreaming state. He knew that he had to have a strong emotional connection with the person in his dream and, in fact, he had only dreamed in this way about Bronwyn. Well, that was apart from when he was visited in his dreams by his distant cousin, Mymie, who seemed to be even stronger in the gift, and on occasion by Carol. He suspected that Carol was stronger too. She seemed able to purposely visit his dreams, and speak to him, when she wanted to, whereas he had no conscious control over it.

Sian and Roberto were getting ready to leave. "I don't want to leave it too late," said Sian. "I've got to be up early for work in the morning."

"I also have to be up early," said Roberto. He was a postman, based in Manchester, and living with his uncle in Ancoats, though he was hoping to get a transfer to Oldham soon, to be nearer to Sian. He hadn't told anyone about this plan yet; he was waiting until he was certain.

"I'll run you both home in the car," said Harry.
"It'll saving you waiting for buses."

"Are you sure Dad?" asked Roberto. "Do you not have any homeworks to mark?"

Harry smiled; his son was always so thoughtful. "No, son, I've got a free evening for a change. Come on, I'll enjoy a drive out."

He kissed Audrey and his younger daughters goodbye, noticing that Rosalind was looking at him strangely. It seemed as though she wanted to tell him something and, as he smiled at her, he got a very definite feeling that she also was a "dream walker" as Mymie called it, and that she wanted to talk about it. "I'll see you later lovey," he said to her, conveying the meaning that he understood. She smiled gratefully and he knew that she also understood.

Well, fancy that! He thought.

Sian and Roberto were quiet as Harry drove to Ancoats, but Sian became more talkative after they dropped Roberto off.

She was pensive at first but, as they were passing through Failsworth, she blurted out, "Roberto wants to marry me!"

Harry wasn't surprised; he had gleaned as much from the events of the evening, but he had also known for a long time that Roberto's feelings for Sian were much more than brotherly, though he was unsure of Sian's feelings; she had never been as easy to read as her sisters.

He was silent for a moment as he decided how to react. Sian was looking at him anxiously as she waited for him to speak.

"Well, lovey," he finally said. "Now that you know he isn't your brother, how do you feel? There's nothing to stop you marrying him, if you love him."

"That's the trouble; I don't know how I feel. I told Roberto not to mention it again. I've always thought of him as my brother, ever since we met him in the ice cream shop. Well, ever since he told us ..."

Harry noticed her preoccupied look as she remembered that first meeting in Granelli's. He smiled.

"I remember what you said that day. Before Roberto shocked me by saying he thought I was his father..."

Sian blushed fiercely. "Oh no, don't remind me!" she cried.

"Well, you need to think about it. Before you thought he was your brother, you said he was 'gorgeous'. So you must have been attracted to him then."

"Well, yes, and I still think he's gorgeous, in a brotherly way though; and he's gentle, and kind and thoughtful....." she drifted off and looked out of the window. They were going up the long hill through Werneth. The stone houses looked mellow in the evening light, but Sian wasn't really seeing them; she was deep in thought. Harry said nothing, but just concentrated on his driving, allowing her to get things sorted out in her mind.

They were passing through the centre of Oldham before she spoke again. "We couldn't get married anyway, even if I wanted to," she added hastily. "I may not be your natural daughter, but you are named as my father on my birth certificate, and Roberto is your natural son."

"That's true," replied Harry. "Or it would be true if Carla had put my name on Roberto's birth certificate, but she was married to Alberto when Roberto was born, and he wanted to be named as Roberto's father. That's why his surname is Granelli."

Sian just said, "Oh." She was silent again and Harry left her to her thoughts. She needed to sort out this whole family conundrum in her own mind.

They were both quiet again for some time as Harry drove through the gathering darkness. They were in sight of Jenny and George's house when Sian spoke again.

"So, supposing – just supposing that I wanted to marry Roberto . . . I'm only saying hypothetically . . . I don't want to marry him, but – if I did, what would you think?"

Harry smiled. "I would think that you had both really thought it through, and, if you were both happy, I would be very happy for you."

"Oh, right," she replied, slowly.

They were at Jenny and George's gate. Sian got out of the car and just said, "Bye Dad," absentmindedly.

"Bye bye lovey, tell George I'll be over on Saturday."

Sian just waved as she made her way to the back door.

Harry had such a lot to think about on his way home that he hardly noticed his surroundings at all.

Two:

Singing and Dealing with Bullies

"Is this the right door?" whispered Rosalind

"Why are you whispering?" said Nerys, in a loud voice, designed to annoy her sister. "Course it's the right door; it's the only one that's open anyway, and we saw another girl going in this way."

"You don't need to shout Nerys; I can hear you!" Rosalind retorted.

"It is the right one; a girl in my class is in the choir, and she told me," said Pamela, ignoring her sisters' bickering. "The senior choir should be in this room on the right, but we will be in the juniors for now, until we're fifteen. That room should be just round to the left."

As they reached the open door to the classroom on the right they could see several older girls sitting in a semicircle, chatting. Mr Rook was also in the room and he came to the door to welcome the new girls.

The twins recognised the music inspector from his visit to their school. He was a kindly faced middle aged man with thinning grey hair.

"Hello girls; you are from Brookdale Park, aren't you . . . oh, I didn't realise that you're triplets; how lovely!"

Nerys laughed; she loved it when they were mistaken for triplets. "No, me and Rosalind are twins. Pamela is ten months older, and she goes to the grammar school." She indicated her older sister. "She's the brainy one, but she's got no common sense, so we have to look after her."

Mr Rook laughed as Pamela said, "Hey, cheeky!"

"Come along, I'll introduce you to Mrs Jones, she leads the junior choir." Mr Rook led them round the corner to another classroom, where there were about twenty girls surrounding a woman with shiny black hair tied into a bun at the nape of her neck. She had an infectious smile and blue eyes that twinkled as she looked round at everyone.

She caught sight of Mr Rook bringing in the new girls. "Triplets, how lovely!" she cried, as all the other girls turned to stare at the newcomers.

"That's exactly what I said, but I was wrong," chuckled Mr Rook. "These are the Roberts girls; twins and an older sister who just happens to be identical. I'll leave you to work out who is who. Enjoy the choir girls!" he said, as he left the room.

Mrs Jones scrutinised the three girls for a while, and then said, "No, I can't tell which of you is the older one. You're going to have to tell me."

As usual it was Nerys who did the talking. "I'm Nerys, and this is my twin, Rosalind. She's the shy one. Pamela is ten months older," she pointed to Pamela, "She's not shy but she can be a dolly daydream at times. I'm the noisy one!"

"I can see that," said Mrs Jones, with a wry smile. "Why don't you three sit at the end of the front row here? I'm putting you with the sopranos for now. You'll gradually find out where your voice fits best in the choir, but I expect that you'll be quite comfortable with the high notes. I'll soon realise if you are struggling. We don't do auditions here. If you enjoy singing we are happy to have you."

"We love singing," Nerys spoke for all three of them, as they took their seats.

There followed an evening of unalloyed pleasure for the girls. They lost themselves in the joy of learning new songs and blending their voices with the other girls.

At the end of the session they walked out in company with Wendy, the girl who was in Pamela's class at school.

"You never said that you have twin sisters," said Wendy. "And also how alike you all are. It's amazing!"

"Well, it's not amazing to me. I get so fed up of being told that I'm identical to these two. I like being just myself at school."

"That's not what you said when you first passed for grammar school!" retorted Nerys. "You wanted to give up your place and go to Brookdale with us."

"Well, I was just a kid then. It was fun all dressing alike and confusing people. Now I like people to know it's me."

Rosalind looked hurt. "Don't you like being our sister now?" She had tears in her eyes.

"Course I do, silly. I wouldn't be without you two dafties. Just sometimes I like people to know it's me without them saying 'which one are you?' So that's why I don't say anything at school." She put her arm around Rosalind as they walked out of the school gate.

"You've got a sister in the upper sixth, haven't you?" asked Wendy. "She doesn't look anything like you."

"Carol, yes; She's the only one who looks like our dad, apart from our baby sister, that is. It looks like she'll be like dad."

"Blimey, how many sisters have you got?"

Nerys giggled. "There's six girls and two boys, only the boys are men, and they are a half brother and a step brother. Our eldest sister, Sian, is twenty one. The littlest one, Lynette is a half sister, cos we lost our mum through illness and then Dad married Auntie Audrey, but she's not a real auntie, but she's lived next door forever and she helped look after us when Mum was poorly. So Auntie Audrey is Lynette's mum, but our dad is her dad too." Nerys took a deep breath after imparting this information and gave a big grin at the amazement on Wendy's face.

"There's Dad!" shouted Pamela quickly, before Wendy could ask any awkward questions. The familiar green Ford Cortina was parked on Moston Lane. Harry was standing at the side of it, waving.

"Where do you live, Wendy?" asked Rosalind. "We could give you a lift, if it's not too far."

"It's not far; I usually walk it. I live at the top of St Mary's Road, just after the turn off Nuthurst Road."

"Oh, we can easily drop you off there, can't we dad?" said Pamela, as they reached the car.

"What's that lovey?" Harry asked.

"We can drop Wendy off on St Mary's Road."

"Yes, that's no bother. Jump in the front Wendy; the others can sit in the back. It'll stop them arguing about whose turn it is to sit in the front."

"Aw Dad, it was my turn!" cried Nerys.

"Well, it's Wendy's turn now, but you can get in the front when we drop her off."

Nerys began to complain. "Aw, but . . ."

"Oh, shut up Nerys, you're showing us up!" retorted Rosalind.

Nerys was so surprised that her normally quiet twin had shouted at her, that she just got into the back seat without saying anything else, though she had a sulky expression. Pamela gave Rosalind a sisterly smile.

Rosalind looked at her dad's face in the mirror; he was smiling too. She felt good.

Harry drove up Moston Lane, on to Nuthurst Road, crossed the wide expanse of Lightbowne Road and then slowed for the approach to the turn into St Mary's Road. "How far down is your house?" he asked Wendy.

"It's just after the turn, Mr Roberts. The third one on the left, with a bay window; the red front door. Thank you for the lift," she added as he stopped outside her house.

"You're very welcome," Harry replied.

Nerys was unnaturally quiet as she got into the front seat, but she soon perked up when Harry asked the girls if they had enjoyed the singing.

"It was great!" they all said it in unison, and then started to giggle.

"We've brought home the music sheets of the songs we learned. Mrs Jones wants us to know them off by heart when we go next week. We can practice them together," said Pamela.

"So the house is going to be full of music?" Harry laughed. "I'll have to get some ear plugs!"

"We don't sound that bad Dad," said Rosalind.

"Only kidding lovey; I'll enjoy listening to you, and I'll bet Auntie Audrey will play the piano for you if she gets time."

The piano was next door, in Audrey's parent's house. She had left it there when she and Harry got married, as his house was so full of children; there was little room for the piano.

Audrey didn't mind going next door to practice her piano. It gave her an excuse to see her mum every day, not that she needed one, and her mum could play with baby Lynette while she listened to the music.

"It'll be great to sing with Mum," said Pamela. She had been very close to Audrey since she was a newborn, when Bronwyn was unable, or unwilling, to care for her; so it came naturally to her to call her stepmother, Mum. They thought the world of each other; even the arrival of a new baby sister hadn't weakened the bond they shared. The other girls all called Audrey, Auntie, but they all loved her.

"Is anyone hungry?" Harry ventured, knowing what the answer would be.

Three voices cried, "Starving!" as Harry laughed.

"We'd better stop at the chippy then," he replied.

They arrived home bringing the fragrance of fish and chips with them. Audrey had the kettle on already and soon had a pot of tea made. They all sat round the fire eating their fish and chips out of the paper. It was only when they sat back, replete, that Audrey asked how the choir practice had been.

"It was great, Mum," said Pamela. "We learned three songs, and we have to know them off by heart by next week. Will you play the piano for us sometime?" She gave Audrey the music sheets to look at.

"I'd love to do that. If the weather's bad on Sunday you won't be going hiking, so we could do it then, and we can make time after school one or two days too."

"Aw thanks Auntie Audrey," said Nerys, "You're the best!" she leaned across to kiss her. Audrey was pink with pleasure. She loved being with the girls.

Carol came in just then; she had been next door, talking to Johnny. "Chips; did you get any for me?"

"I put yours in the oven," said Harry. "They might be a bit dry now, though. I didn't know you would be that long."

"Oh, they'll be ok. Johnny and I were having a heated discussion about the Vikings."

"I thought your subject was English," said Nerys. "What do you know about the Vikings?"

"I'm doing history A level too, as well as English language, literature and French, which you would know if you took any notice. Anyway, I was talking about the Vikings rampaging and pillaging, and Johnny said there was a lot more to them than that. "

"Oh, what did he say about the Vikings?! Asked Rosalind; she was very interested in history.

"Oh I don't want to talk about that now. Tell me how your choir practice went."

Harry and Audrey smiled at each other as the three sisters vied with each other to tell Carol about the choir. Harry felt a pang of grief as he thought about how proud Bronwen would have been if she could see her girls now, but he wasn't sad for long. There was too much love in the family for sadness to persist. He counted his blessings.

The girls never missed a choir practice throughout that spring and into summer. Harry was there every Friday to take them home and always gave Wendy a lift to her house.

That was until one Friday in June, a few weeks before the twins' fourteenth birthday. Audrey had a heavy cold and baby Lynette was teething. Harry arrived home from work to find his wife almost in tears and the baby with two red spots on her cheeks and her eyes red from crying. Harry's mum, Alice was cooking the tea, but she looked really tired too. The girls were trying to help, but they just seemed to be getting in the way. Harry remembered that Carol was going to a friend's house after school. She would have had everyone organised if she had been there.

Harry took over; "You girls get yourselves ready for choir practice," he said, and they gratefully escaped up the stairs.

He took the baby into his arms and she snuggled into his neck. "Audrey, you can sit by the fire and put your feet up." She sank, gratefully, into the rocking chair.

He carried Lynette into the kitchen. "What can I do to help, Mum?" he asked.

"I've nearly finished now lovey," she answered. "Just sit at the table there and talk to me. The girls have set the table in the living room, so it'll only take me a tick to finish off and dish up. Tell me what's happening at your school; there's always something interesting your pupils get up to."

Harry laughed. "We were reading 'Pied Piper' by Nevile Shute; you know the one, where an old Englishman makes his way through France at the beginning of the war, picking up several children on his way?" Alice nodded.

"We got to the part where the old man was letting the children splash in a stream, when two English soldiers in a lorry offered them a lift. They were also trying to get to the coast. The children rushed to get their clothes on and all

34

piled into the lorry. This is the bit where my class all shrieked with laughter. 'It was only when they had travelled several miles that the old man realised they had left Sheila's knickers behind!'"

Alice chuckled. "Why the word 'knickers' in a book makes kids laugh, I'll never know. After all, we all wear them."

"Exactly, but I couldn't help laughing along with them. The laughter was infectious!"

"Well, tea's ready now lovey. You call the girls down and I'll dish up. Then I'll go and give your dad his tea. Ours is ready in the oven. Shall I come back later so you can go and pick the girls up? I think Audrey will be going to bed early and you may need help with Lynette."

"No, it's ok Mum. The girls can come home on the bus for once. It'll still be daylight when they finish."

The girls were quite happy to get the bus home after choir practice; it was a novelty for them. As they got to the bus stop, Wendy set off to cross the road.

"Aren't you getting the bus with us?" Nerys asked.

"No, in the summer I usually walk across Broadhurst fields. It's not far, and I can save the bus fare to get sweets on a Saturday."

"We'll go with you then," said Pamela. "We can get the bus at the stop outside your house. We've just missed the number 7 anyway, so we'd have twenty minutes to wait for the next one."

Everyone agreed and they crossed to the fields together.

They'd just crested the slope on to the field when they saw three boys coming towards them.

"Oh no!" breathed Wendy.

"What's up?" Nerys asked.

"Tony Wilkinson; he's obnoxious, and his mates aren't much better. Maybe we should go back to the road and wait for the bus."

"No, why should we? We've got as much right to be here as they have. We'll just walk past and ignore them."

"You don't know what he's like; he can be really nasty. . ."

It was too late anyway; the boys were approaching fast. The girls looked at the tall, gangly lad in the middle. He had an evil grin on his acne-scarred face.

"Well, if it isn't Wendy Pendy! I bet you're really pleased to see me, aren't you? And who's this?" he eyed up the three sisters. "Triplets, triple the fun then!" The look on his face made their skin crawl.

Nerys made a brave attempt to confront him and his henchmen, who were just standing there, grinning. She herded the other three girls away to one side and stood between them and the boys. "You leave us alone, you big bully! My brothers would make mincemeat of you!"

His laugh sounded like a donkey neighing. "Your brother's not here though, is he? Come on, show us your boobs." He moved right up to Nerys until their faces were almost touching and she took an involuntary step backwards.

Her voice was shaky as she said again, "leave us alone." Making him laugh even more.

Before Nerys knew it, Rosalind; quiet, timid Rosalind, had stormed forward and placed herself between her sister and the boy. Her eyes flashing, she hissed, "You are despicable; go away, back to your cesspit!" Her eyes bored into his and it was obvious he found it hard to look away.

His face paled and his spots stood out against his ashen skin. It was his turn to take a step back and he finally managed to take his eyes away from hers.

"Come on lads, they're not worth bothering with, they've got no boobs anyway!" At that he turned and walked rapidly away; his bemused mates followed him, occasionally looking back at the girls.

"How did you do that?" Nerys was staring at her twin as if she had grown another head!

"I don't know. I just got really angry and thought it was the right thing to do. I thought about Dad, and how he always says that you should face down the bullies. I felt as though Dad was with me."

"I know how she did it," said Pamela. "Rosalind's like Carol and Dad; she can make people do what she wants them to, well, at least when she's angry."

"I've never done anything like that before, have I?"

Nerys laughed. "No, cos you've never got angry before. I don't think I've ever seen you angry. You usually leave it to me to kick up a fuss, and then I get into trouble!" She saw Rosalind's face drop and quickly said; "only joking sis. You're usually too quiet and shy to get into trouble, but I'm glad you got angry tonight. Thanks for saving our modesty!" She gave Rosalind a big hug and Pamela joined in.

Wendy was just standing there looking flabbergasted, her shocked gaze going to each sister in turn. She didn't speak until Pamela took her arm and said, "Come on Wendy; we'll miss the next bus if we don't get a move on."

Wendy allowed herself to be led away and then finally said, "What just happened?"

"Oh don't worry about it. This kind of thing happens a lot in our family," said Pamela. "Our Dad, and our Carol have this thing; they just glare at someone who's being horrible and the person just calms down, or apologises, or just walks away, just like that lad did. It seems that Rosalind can do it too. I wish I could."

"Me too," said Wendy.

"Me three," said Nerys, and they all laughed.

They got to Wendy's door just as the bus turned into St Mary's Road. The three sisters ran to the bus stop, a couple of doors along, and waved goodbye to their friend. They swarmed up the stairs, singing their favourite song, making the conductor smile as he gave them their tickets.

Harry was waiting at the back door when they arrived home. His anxious gaze rested on Rosalind's face as he asked, "Are you all alright?"

Nerys was the one to ask, "How do you always know what's going on? It's weird!"

Rosalind spoke, "I told you Dad was with me." She looked up at Harry and said, "Thanks Dad."

"You did it all yourself lovey. I'm glad you are all ok, but I think, in future, if I can't pick you up I'll ask Johnny or Roberto to meet you."

"That'd be great!" Nerys had a big smile on her face. "We can show off our handsome brothers to the other girls." She had already forgotten about asking Harry how he knew what had happened. Harry and Rosalind shared a relieved smile. They found it virtually impossible to explain what they did by instinct, so they were glad that they didn't have to.

Three:

A Change of Name and a Journey

"Good morning masturbates . . .oh sorry, Mr Bates!"

The trio of adolescent boys giggled as they saw Johnny Bates' face turn a deep red. He glared at them and said a gruff "good morning," as he passed them in the school yard.

It wasn't any use punishing them, or even complaining to the headmaster. Most teachers had to put up with derogatory nicknames, usually only said behind their backs, but these three youths had been trying to push him into losing his temper ever since he started at the school last September.

He was the history teacher at a secondary school in Oldham. The school had a very good reputation, which was why Johnny had been delighted to be offered the post. This was his first job since he left university, and he had been hoping that it might be a job for life; now he was not so sure.

He was thinking about a post that he'd seen advertised, as he made his way to the staff room; the only drawback was the distance it was from his home.

He was very close to his family. He lived with his grandparents, and next door were his mother and stepfather and four of his stepsisters, and, not least, his adorable baby half sister. If he moved away from Manchester he wouldn't be able to see them every day, as he did now. He would miss them.

He was tempted though. He had always wanted to travel, and this would be a beginning; also, he would hardly admit this to himself, it would get him away from a difficult situation.

As he entered the staff room he shrugged off his mixed feelings and prepared to get on with his day. Judith, the girls' PE teacher smiled at him.

"Hello Johnny, isn't it a lovely day?" Her smile was hopeful as she took her bag off the chair next to hers so that he could sit there.

And there was another reason to move away. Judith was a lovely girl. She had blonde hair tied in a ponytail and intense blue eyes; in fact everything about her was intense.

Johnny had made the mistake of taking her to the pictures once. Since then she had behaved as though they were courting. She hadn't actually gone as far as asking him for another date, but he knew it was only a matter of time before she did. She had already changed her dinner time duties so that she and Johnny both supervised the second sitting in the dining room, and, no matter how late he left the school at the end of the day, she would be waiting by the gate so that they could get the bus together.

It wasn't that he found her unattractive; in fact she was very pretty. He just didn't have any deep feelings for her. He sighed as he sank into the chair next to her and wondered how he could put her off without hurting her feelings.

You're a coward, Johnny Bates, he told himself. *You don't know how to put off this girl, and you don't know how to tell another girl how strongly you feel about her.*

And there it was; the difficult situation that wouldn't go away. He looked across at Judith's eager expression and made a decision.

His decision was cemented when he got to his classroom, where he was teaching a fourth year class. They were waiting in an unruly bunch outside the door, the hated trio at the front, grinning inanely. He definitely heard the whisper, "wanker!" as he made his way past them. He gritted his teeth as he led them into the room.

He had intended spending this lesson leading the pupils in an enactment of a Viking raid. He had costumes and a cardboard cut-out of a longboat ready, but he changed his mind. He felt sorry for the majority of the class, who looked disappointed when he told them to read the chapter on Vikings in preparation for a test the next week, but he was adamant; he had something more important to do.

He spent the time drafting an application letter for the post he had seen advertised, and, in his break time, he wrote it out neatly and signed it 'John Roberts'. That was the other thing he was determined to do. He would speak to his Mum and Uncle Harry tonight about changing his name.

Harry, Audrey and Carol were sitting quietly in the living room. Audrey was knitting and the others were reading. They had been watching 'Coronation Street' which was a favourite with the whole family, but now the television was off, the other girls had gone upstairs to play records on their Dansette record player and baby Lynette was asleep.

Johnny came in through the kitchen; the back door was always unlocked until the last person went to bed.

"Hello lovey, have you had a good day?" Audrey asked, though she could tell immediately that there was something on his mind.

"Not bad," he lied. "There's something I want to tell you, though, and I don't know how you are going to take it."

Carol studied his face. "Shall I go upstairs?" she asked, thinking that he wanted to talk in private.

"No, it's alright; everyone will need to know eventually anyway, but thanks Carol,"

"Sit down son," said Harry.

Johnny had a lump in his throat, hearing Harry call him 'son'. It wasn't the first time by any means; Harry had treated him like his own son for as long as he could remember. Johnny had never met his own father, who had been killed in the war, but he had never felt the lack. Harry had always been there for him.

He didn't know how to start, so he decided to just come out with it. "Mum, Uncle Harry, I want to change my name to Roberts. Then I'll have the same name as the rest of the family, except for Roberto, of course."

It all came out in a rush, and he felt foolish. He hadn't told them the main reason for wanting to change; he was too embarrassed.

Carol and Harry seemed to understand his feelings, but Audrey looked upset. "You're not ashamed of your father,

44

are you Johnny? I know your grandfather and Uncle had been in prison, but your father was a good man."

"No, it's not that . . . " he started, but Carol spoke up for him.

"I know what you mean Johnny. Your Mum is called Roberts and your grandparents that you live with are called Kerr. I bet you are always being asked why you've got a different name. I think it's a great idea. You've always been a big brother to me; now you'll be even more my brother."

Johnny wasn't sure if he wanted to be more of a brother to Carol. Deep in his heart he wanted something very different, but he doubted whether Carol would ever see him in that way. This was the other awkward situation that he wanted to escape.

Harry was aware that Johnny's reasons for changing his name weren't that simple, but he decided to go along with Carol's reasoning.

"Well I'm happy for you to change your name to ours," he said. "I'm sure it will make life easier, but what about school, won't it seem strange going in next term with a completely different name?"

"Yes lovey," said Audrey. "Surely that will be difficult?" She was already coming round to the idea.

"Ah, well, there's something else; I've given in my notice today. I'm leaving at the end of term. I've never settled at the school; the headmaster isn't approachable and the other staff members aren't that friendly. I want to make a completely new start."

Again Harry was aware that Johnny had over simplified his reasons, but felt that the young man was entitled to keep some things to himself. "Have you thought about what you will do next?" he asked.

"Er, yes; I don't think you are going to like this," he looked at his Mum. "You know I've always wanted to see more of Great Britain? Well, I've applied for a job in a school in Lerwick; in the Shetland Isles. I may not get it of course, but it's what I want," he urged them to understand. "If I don't get it I may have to take a temporary teaching post somewhere else. But I really do want to move away, at least for a while." His gaze travelled from one to the other as he tried to gauge their reactions.

Audrey had tears in her eyes. "Johnny, that's an awful long way away. Can't you get a post a bit nearer, Yorkshire, or North Wales?"

"This was the only post advertised for a history teacher Mum, well, apart from posts in the cities. London are always advertising, but I wanted somewhere quiet; countryside, fresh air. I'll keep in touch of course. Now you've got the phone it'll be easy to talk to you, every day, if you like. That's if I get the job."

Carol rescued him again. "Shetland? That's amazing. We have a distant relation who lives there. In fact I was thinking of visiting her during the summer holidays. She's called Mymie and she's in her seventies. She's grandma's second cousin, or something like that."

Both Johnny and Audrey looked amazed. Audrey looked at Harry. "I didn't know you had other relations Harry. You've never spoken of this lady; Mymie? That's an unusual name"

Harry looked at Carol, wondering how to explain.

Carol was the one with the answer again. "She got in touch with us not long ago." Carol didn't say how Mymie had got in touch; she just quickly continued. "Apparently she is the last of the line in Shetland, but she knew that she had cousins in Manchester. Somehow she found Grandma's address. I think she is quite a clever old lady. Anyway, I was intrigued and I've been corresponding with her. Grandma's been in touch too, of course."

Harry breathed a sigh of relief that he had spoken to his mother about Mymie quite recently. Although Alice didn't have the same 'gift' as Carol and Harry, she understood it, and she was also intrigued to discover that she had a relation in Shetland.

"I know what," said Carol. "If you have an interview during the holidays I can travel up there with you and visit Mymie at the same time. That way you'll have company on the journey."

Sheila. R. Kelly

Johnny was lost for words. He loved being with Carol but he was finding it increasingly difficult to hide his true feelings from her. It didn't help that Roberto and Sian were obviously in love. He was sure that the family would think he was just copying them if he declared his feelings.

No, it was better if he put some distance between himself and Carol. He couldn't turn down her offer of company though, if he got an interview. It would look strange; so he would have to grin and bear it for the time they were together, but after that, he could settle into his new life. He could make new friends, and maybe even get a girlfriend.

"That'd be great Carol," he replied. "It will be like a holiday and the interview won't seem as daunting."

Audrey was still tearful. "Are you sure this is what you want lovey? Surely you'll miss being with the family; everyone will miss you, that's for sure." She pleaded with her eyes.

"I may not even get an interview Mum, and if I do, I may not get the job. But if I do, I'll be home during all the school holidays, and I'll phone regularly. It won't be so bad, you'll see."

Harry went over to his wife and put his arm around her. "We have to let Johnny live his life lovey. I'll be here, and the girls will keep you busy; and you'll enjoy Johnny so much more every time you see him." He turned to Johnny. "I hope you get the job Johnny. It could be just what you need and, if you don't settle there, you can always come home."

The first week in July found Johnny and Carol on the train to Aberdeen. They had never been further north than the Lake District so, after the train left Carlisle, they spent most of their time looking out at the scenery and commenting on what they saw. The gentle hills and dales of lowland Scotland were similar to Lancashire, but somehow different. "It has a definite Scottish feel, I think," said Carol.

Edinburgh was very impressive, with its castle and Arthur's Seat and stately buildings. Soon after this they were crossing the famous Forth Bridge. They both gasped in awe of the bridge itself and the lovely view down the firth to Bass Rock. They were fortunate that they had a very clear day for their journey, and the views kept getting better as they travelled further north. They crossed another two firths, almost as impressive as the firth of Forth and the railway hugged the coast. The sea was blue/green and sandy beaches alternated with rugged cliffs and deep coves. For eyes used to the flat beaches of Blackpool and Southport the scene was enchanting.

The time passed very quickly and it seemed that very soon they were emerging from Aberdeen Station. They had time to explore a little of the Granite City before they had to make their way to the quay where they would board the ferry. They left their luggage in a locker at the station and made their way uphill to Union Street.

The buildings of grey granite were quite impressive, especially on the sunny side of the street, where the stone seemed to sparkle. They had a look in the shop windows but didn't see anything they wanted to buy, at first. They wanted to get some Shetland gifts for the family. Carol was thinking of knitted socks or gloves, as Shetland was famous for its knitting. Johnny was too concerned about his interview to think about gifts.

"I'd like to get something for Mymie, though I don't know what she likes." Said Carol. "I've got her a box of embroidered hankies, because everyone likes them, but I wish I could think of something, I don't know, a bit more special."

"But you don't really know her, only from letters," Johnny didn't know about the dreams and so, of course, he didn't realise that, in actual fact, Carol knew Mymie as well as she knew her family in Manchester. "She probably won't expect a gift anyway."

"I know, but even so I'd like to get her something nice."

They were just passing a large stationers when Carol suddenly remembered. "I know, Mymie said, er, wrote that she likes doing jigsaws. Let's go in this shop and see what they've got."

Johnny didn't seem to notice Carol's slip of the tongue; he just said, "Ok, sounds like a good idea."

The shop had a good selection of jigsaws and Carol soon saw one that she liked. "Look at this one Johnny; it's a lovely picture of an English country cottage. I expect it's different to Shetland houses. It's only five hundred pieces, so it won't be as difficult as a bigger one."

"Yes, it's quite pretty," said Johnny absentmindedly. He had seen something that interested him. He picked up a book on Scottish history. "I think I'll get this one."

Carol looked at the book and laughed. "It had to be history for you Johnny!"

After they paid for their purchases they realised that they were hungry. They had finished their sandwiches on the train hours ago, so they went into the nearest cafe.

"I know we said we'd have our tea on the ferry, but that's over two hours away," said Johnny. "We could have tea and cakes now, to tide us over."

"Good idea," agreed Carol, eyeing a display of delicious looking scones.

The scones were enormous, and came with jam and cream, and the tea was hot and strong; just as they liked it. They left the cafe with a satisfying feeling of fullness.

They found a street that led downhill, back to the railway station, where they picked up their cases and made their way round to the quayside.

The St Clair was easy to see, as it was the biggest ship there, and people were already making their way up the gangplank. After checking in at the office they joined the queue and were soon on board.

They had booked a two berth cabin, as the journey north took all night. They wouldn't arrive in Lerwick until 8 o'clock the next morning. Their cabin was quite low down in the ship, but it did have a porthole, and was equipped with a tiny shower room with washbasin and toilet, so they would have no problem getting ready for bed later. They left their luggage in the cabin and went to explore the ship.

After they had climbed steep stairs and wandered along several corridors, they sat for a while in the bar area near the front of the ship and watched as it made its way out of the dock area and into the open sea. Immediately they felt the increased movement, and Carol began to feel a little queasy. A lady sitting nearby noticed that Carol had become very pale. She leaned across and said, "You can get a peerie tablet for the seasickness dear. Just go to the counter at the top of the stairs."

Carol thanked her and smiled; the lady sounded so much like Mymie, she was obviously a Shetland lady. Johnny offered to go for the tablet. He seemed perfectly alright. He came back with a glass of tonic water from the bar.

"The purser said that tonic water is good too, if you're feeling sick. You can take your tablet with it. He also said that you'll feel better if you go out on deck for a while"

Carol took the drink and the tablet gratefully. She was annoyed with herself for feeling seasick. She was a practical person who could deal with most situations and was rarely ill. "Sorry Johnny, I'm spoiling our trip," she said.

"No, it's not your fault. Lots of people get seasick; it can happen to anyone. Anyway, you'll soon feel better when that tablet begins to work. Then we can go for something to eat."

"Oh, don't mention food; let's go out on deck," she said, finishing her drink.

"Take your coat dearie," said the pleasant lady. "It'll be cold out there."

They had left their coats in the cabin, so Johnny went down to get them while Carol waited near the door to the outside deck. She was glad of the rush of cold air each time someone opened the door and was eager to get outside as soon as Johnny returned.

They leaned on the rail and breathed in the sea air, watching the waves and the gulls soaring around. Despite the cold wind it felt incredibly peaceful, and Carol gradually began to feel better.

"i never realised how cold it can be out at sea, even on a lovely sunny evening," said Carol, watching the sun, which was still fairly high in the sky.

Johnny nodded. "We've never been this far from land. Even on Swansea beach the wind doesn't get this cold. It's a nice cold though; refreshing. Shall we walk around the deck, at least as far as we can go?"

"Good idea, and then I think I might be able to eat something."

After they had eaten they returned to the bar area and met the kind lady again. She now had a teenage girl with her. "Come and sit with us and tell us why you are visiting Shetland," the lady invited. "By the bye, my name is Maggie and this is my daughter, Kirsty."

They introduced themselves and began by telling her about Johnny's interview."

"Oh, I hope you get the job Johnny. Kirsty here was at the Anderson Institute, She left after last term. It's a grand school"

Johnny smiled at Kirsty and asked what she hoped to do now that she had left school, but she didn't answer, in fact she hadn't spoken at all, and just stared at her hands folded in her lap.

Carol decided that Kirsty must be very shy, and changed the subject in an attempt to make her feel more comfortable.

"I've come up with Johnny because I am visiting a relative in Levenwick. She is a second cousin of my Grandma.

"Oh, I know a few people in Levenwick; what is her name?"

"Mymie Tulloch," Carol replied.

"Oh I know her. She used to be a teacher in the primary school in Lerwick. She taught me when I was a peerie lass. She's a lovely lady, and very bright and active for her age. She must be mid seventies now, but she comes up to Lerwick every week on the bus and does a bit of shopping, though they have a good shop in Levenwick that sells most things."

"i'm looking forward to meeting her. We've been in contact for a while now and she is a very interesting lady." Carol replied.

They sat together chatting for a long time, Maggie giving them lots of information about Shetland and suggesting so many places to visit that there was no way they could see them all in the week. In any case, Johnny had his interview and Carol wanted to spend time with Mymie, but they were grateful to Maggie for the information, and for her natural friendliness.

All this time Kirsty never spoke a word, but Maggie didn't make any excuses for her, or try to force her to take part in the conversation. Johnny felt that this showed what a good mother she was. In his limited experience as a teacher he found that too many parents tried to push their children into uncomfortable situations, which didn't help their social development at all.

Both Johnny and Carol were becoming very tired, having to suppress yawns. They had had a long day travelling, so they made their excuses and went down to their cabin.

"What did you think of Kirsty?" Asked Carol as they made their way down the stairs. "She seemed very subdued; do you think she was worried about something?"

"I just thought she was shy," Johnny replied.

"Yes, maybe" But Carol thought that there was more to it than that.

When they reached their cabin, Carol said, "You use the bathroom first; you look exhausted."

She sat on the bottom bunk, musing, until Johnny came out, wearing his pyjamas. He climbed into the top bunk and sleepily said, "Goodnight."

"Goodnight Johnny," she replied, but he was already asleep. She smiled, remembering all the times they had shared bedrooms as children. He had always had the ability to fall asleep immediately, wherever he laid his head. It seemed that he hadn't grown out of it.

Four:

New Friends and a Problem Solved

When she emerged from the bathroom, Carol realised that she was now wide awake, and something was bothering her, though she didn't know what it was yet.

She sat on the bunk and tried to concentrate on her feelings. What was it? She looked at her watch; it was nearly midnight! At this rate she wouldn't get any sleep and she would arrive in Lerwick looking like a zombie.

Finally she managed to identify the problem. Someone was in pain; someone on the ship. She needed to go and investigate, if only for her own peace of mind. She looked down at her pyjamas, decided they were substantial enough, and put on her coat and shoes. Remembering to take the key to the cabin she set out to discover who was in pain.

The corridors and stairs were very quiet. When she got to the main public deck she saw that there were several people asleep across the seating. They must have decided not to go to the expense of a cabin. Anyway, they all looked very comfortable, so she continued to search.

Her feelings took her to the door to the outside deck. The person in pain was out there. She ventured out and she could see a figure leaning over the rail at the far end. Maybe they were seasick? As she approached the figure, though, they began trying to climb over the rail, in danger of falling overboard!

Oh no! She thought; her heart was pounding with alarm. She rushed forward to grab the back of their coat and pulled. The person uttered a deep sob and collapsed at her feet. It was then that she recognised Kirsty.

"Oh Kirsty, whatever's the matter? Nothing can be that bad, surely."

The girl didn't answer at first , but sobbed uncontrollably as Carol hugged her tightly. They sat there together on the deck for a long time, Carol allowing Kirsty to cry herself out. Eventually the sobbing eased and Carol was able to lead her into the warmth of the bar.

There were only a few people still drinking near the bar, so Carol led Kirsty to a table that was the furthest away. "Shall I get you a tea or a coffee, or brandy even?"

Kirsty raised her tearstained face and said, "Just water please."

Carol went over to the bar, hoping that the girl wouldn't run away, but she was still there, hunched up, when she returned with two glasses of water.

She waited until Kirsty had taken a few sips and then said, "Do you think you can talk about it?"

"I don't know; you'll think I'm a terrible person. I am a terrible person. You should have left me to go over the side!"

"You're not a terrible person. Nothing can be that bad, but it can help if you talk about it. If you can't tell your mother about it, I'm a good listener."

"I've done something shameful. I don't know what to do!"

Carol now realised what the problem was. "You're having a baby, aren't you?"

Kirsty burst into fresh tears and nodded. "You see how shameful I've been? My mother will never forgive me!"

"What about the father?" Carol asked.

"He's gone!" Kirsty said, bitterly. "It was just the once, and then he'd gone down the 'sooth mooth' He wasn't a native, you see."

Sooth mooth?" Said Carol in puzzlement.

"Oh, sorry, it's what we call people who are not originally from Shetland. They are 'sooth moothers' You see, they arrive via the sooth mooth of Bressay sound. Thats the area of water between Lerwick and the island of Bressay. All the ships from the south {she pronounced it 'sooth'} come into Lerwick that way, and go back that way."

"So he knew nothing about the baby?"

"No, it was at Up Helly Aa. He came up for that, and then he was gone again."

"Up Helly …?"

"Sorry, I forget that you don't know everything about Shetland. We have a viking festival every year at the end of January. It goes on all night, and everyone takes part, in one way or another. Hundreds of people come up from the south. He was the cousin of one of my friends. He was lovely, very handsome, and he seemed so kind. He kept asking me to dance, and then, later in the night, we went out for a walk, and we ended up at his cousin's house. It wasn't far from the hall where we were dancing. There was no one else at the house. Everyone was still partying. I'd had a few drinks, though my mother didn't know that. She was busy looking after our visitors. He, I suppose he talked me into it, but I shouldn't have let him!" She sobbed.

"It's not your fault Kirsty. I take it he was older than you?"

"Yes, he said he was twenty one, but I think he was older than that. I was fifteen then."

"Then it was definitely all his fault. He took advantage of you, flattered you and gave you drink. He knew what he was doing. It was a despicable thing to do. Anyway, your Mum will know that it wasn't your fault when you tell her.

"She won't understand. She'll hate me!"

"I'm sure she won't hate you, but what I am sure about is that she would never recover if she lost you. She would be absolutely devastated, wouldn't she?"

Kirsty looked up at Carol in wonder. "I never thought of that; I just thought that she'd be better off without me, without the shame, but she would be alone. My Dad ran off when I was little, and it's just been the two of us since then. She'll be ashamed of me though, and how will she show her face to her friends?"

Carol shook her head. "She'll be upset at first, but she will forgive you. She loves you. And she'll love the baby, once she gets over it; and you'll love the baby too."

"She might want me to have it adopted."

"Well, I don't know her well enough to say, but I imagine she will want to keep her first grandchild close; what do you think?"

"Her grandchild; it will be her grandchild," Kirsty breathed in wonder. The tears were still shining on her eyelids, but she gazed out of the window, at last thinking of this baby as a real person.

Carol gave her time to take it in, and then said "Are you ready to tell her now?"

""Now, you mean right now?"

"What better time is there? She needs to know, and it'll be just you and her in the cabin, away from everyone else."

"Oh, alright, but, will you come with me Carol? I'll feel better if you're there."

"If you want me to, yes, I'll come with you."

"You won't tell her what, you know, what I tried to do?"

"No, I don't think she needs to know that. Just say you were walking on the deck to clear your head, and I was also out for some air."

They made their way down to the cabin, which turned out to be on the same corridor as Carol and Johnny's. Kirsty opened the door with her key and Carol stood back to allow her to wake her mother first, but they were surprised to see the light on. Maggie was sitting on the lower bunk, fully dressed.

"Where have you been all this time Kirsty? I was just coming to look for you. I was so worried."

"I'm sorry Mum; I thought you would be asleep. I was walking on the deck and I met Carol."

Maggie hadn't seen Carol until that moment. She looked puzzled and said, "Hello Carol, is there something wrong?" She looked from one girl to the other.

Kirsty looked pleadingly at Carol. She obviously didn't know how to start.

Carol spoke: "Maggie, Kirsty has something to tell you, and she asked me if I would come with her. Is that alright?"

Maggie was looking increasingly anxious. She took Kirsty's hands. "Sit here on the bunk with me dearie." She looked around. "Carol, will you be comfortable on that suitcase? It's quite sturdy." Carol nodded and sat down.

Kirsty was crying again and still finding it very difficult to speak.

"Come one Kirsty, you can tell me anything, you know that. Nothing is so bad that you cannot share it. I know that you haven't been yourself for a while. That's why I suggested the shopping trip. Whatever it is, we can deal with it."

Kirsty blurted it out then. "I'm having a baby!"

Maggie reared back as though she had been hit, but she didn't shout or cry. She just said, "I thought it must be that, but I didn't want to believe it. You're just a child yourself, and I didn't even know that you had a boyfriend!"

"Kirsty sobbed even harder at that. "I don't have a boyfriend, it was just the one time, at Up Helly Aa, and then he was gone."

Now Maggie really did look shocked. "Kirsty, you must be over five months pregnant, how did you hide that from me? Oh, I wish you had told me sooner. You must have been terrified!"

"I didn't know what to do Mum; I was so ashamed, and I refused to believe it myself for a long time."

Maggie hugged her daughter tightly and now they were both crying. Carol just sat quietly and waited for them to get over it.

Eventually Maggie sat back and said, "I thought you were still having your monthlies. I bought you the pads and thought you were using them."

"I took them to school and left them in the toilets for other girls to use."

"I see, well, at least you didn't waste them." She found a box of tissues and they both dried their eyes. "You're not showing yet," she commented, looking down.

"Oh, I, er, borrowed one of your girdles," Kirsty confessed, and she pulled down her trousers to show her mum and Carol the tight garment.

"Well you don't need to wear that any more; the poor mite will be squashed! Does anyone else know about the baby?"

"No, I've been very careful, and I made excuses not to do sports the last few weeks at school. I'm not sure that the teacher believed all my excuses, but she let me off anyway. Even Sarah doesn't know, and it was her cousin, you know, at Up Helly Aa …"

For the first time Maggie looked really angry. "Oh yes, I remember him; thought a lot of himself. He was at least twenty five! Did he know you were fifteen then? He broke the law, you know!"

"He may have known, because he knew that Sarah and I were in the same class, but Sarah was already sixteen then."

"Whether he knew or not, it was still despicable of him. He took advantage of you!"

"Carol said the same." Kirsty sniffed.

Maggie looked across at Carol. "Thank you so much Carol. It was so lucky that you were out on deck at the same time. Kirsty obviously needed someone near her own age to talk to. I'm so glad you were there; but you must be really tired now, look at the time! You need to get to your bed. Shall we meet up at breakfast?"

Carol said that would be lovely, and she hugged both mother and daughter before going to her own cabin. She opened the door quietly, and saw that Johnny was still fast asleep. She got into her own bunk and soon fell into a deep sleep.

She sought the comfort of Mymie's voice and, as she expected, Mymie was with her in a heartbeat. "Hello Carol; you are on the St Clair? You seem a peerie bit agitated."

"Yes I'm on the St Clair, but I've only just got into bed. I've been helping a girl with a problem, but I think she is going to be alright now. I won't give you any details, because you may know her, but I'll ask her in the morning if I can share her problem with you. I know you will be sympathetic. Johnny and I are fine though. I'm really looking forward to meeting you in the morning. Johnny is meeting up with the headmaster, who has arranged accommodation for him. I'll get the bus down to Levenwick."

"You won't need to get the bus, my neighbour, Andy has offered to take me up to the ferry terminal, so I can meet you, and he'll give us a lift home."

"Oh, that'll be lovely. What a kind man!"

"We all help each other whenever we can. Andy loves my apple pies," she laughed. "Well I'll see you in the morning dearie. Sleep well."

"Thanks Mymie, and you."

Johnny woke Carol at 7am. "Come on sleepyhead. You need to get up if you want breakfast before we dock. There's some lovely views through the porthole, I can't wait to get up on the deck where there's bigger windows."

Carol sat up and said, sleepily, "You go ahead Johnny. I'll meet you in the dining room when I'm ready. If you see Maggie and Kirsty, sit with them. They were so friendly last night."

"Ok, I can get more information about Shetland from them. See you soon."

They had breakfast with Maggie and Kirsty, who smiled shyly. Johnny commented on the lovely views. He was blissfully unaware of the incident in the middle of the night.

They were passing the island of Mousa, which lay close to Sandwick. Maggie talked about the iron age broch on the island, telling Johnny and Carol that it was the best preserved of its kind. Apparently there were many ruined brochs across Shetland and some other parts of Scotland. "It's a pity you can't see it from this side, but if you get time while you are here, take a boat trip from Sandwick to Mousa. You can get a close look at the broch, and there's plenty of wildlife too."

Carol was pleased to sense that Kirsty was a lot less miserable. Mother and daughter sat close together and the love radiated between them. The sight of them was almost as good to Carol as the views from the windows.

As they approached Lerwick they passed between two grassy headlands. "That's the Knab, on the left, and the island of Bressay on the right." Said Kirsty. They could see through the windows on both sides from where they were sitting.

They had finished breakfast and the crew had already cleared their table, so Carol said, "Maybe we should go and get our bags now, and then we can stand on the outside deck until we dock."

"Good idea," said Maggie. "We'll meet you out there in a while."

It took them only a few minutes to get their things together and go up the steep stairs one last time. They handed in their cabin key and made their way out to the open deck on the port side, so that they could see the town of Lerwick as they passed. The buildings were mainly of grey granite, in tiers up a steep hill. The busy harbour was full of all kinds of boats. It was windy, but a beautiful clear day.

Maggie and Kirsty joined them as the ship began to manoeuvre into position at the terminal. Johnny had wandered to the far end of the deck, so Carol had a chance to ask Kirsty how she was.

"I'm getting used to the idea now, though it is still scary, just knowing my mother doesn't blame me has made the whole thing less frightening." She smiled at Maggie.

"I wondered if you mind my sharing your news with Mymie? I know she is a caring person, and I feel that she could be a good friend to you. Also I have to admit that I will find it easier if she knows. I won't have to worry about keeping your secret while I am here."

Mother and daughter looked at each other, and both nodded at the same time. "It willna be a secret for long, anyway," said Maggie. "And you are right, Mymie is a caring soul. We dunna mind if she is one of the first to know."

Johnny rejoined them just then. Looking down they could see a few groups of people waiting. "They must be meeting passengers," said Johnny. "I wonder which one is the headmaster?"

"That's him," said Kirsty, pointing to a smart looking man, standing with three other people. "The other three are teachers. I wonder why they are with him?"

"We'll soon find out; the gangplank is being attached," said Maggie.

Carol had caught sight of a white haired lady standing with a tall man wearing a blue boiler suit. The lady was quite tall too; her back was very straight, despite her age. She looked up at Carol with bright intelligent eyes, and smiled.

"I think that's Mymie," said Carol.

"Oh, I thought you were getting the bus down to Levenwick?" Johnny commented.

"Oh, er, Mymie did say she might be able to get a lift from a friend. Didn't I tell you?"

"No, I don't think you did." Johnny was looking quizzical, but he didn't get time to ask more questions, as the announcement to disembark came.

As they reached the bottom of the gangplank, the headmaster came forward and said, "John Roberts? Pleased to meet you." He looked beyond Johnny, saying, "There should be two more applicants on the ship. I don't suppose you got to know them last night?"

"No, I'm sorry sir, I didn't realise …"

"That's alright; at this time of year the ferries can be pretty full, and I didn't tell any of you that other applicants would be on the same ship. Ah, I think this is one of them; Miss Smith?"

The woman looked to be about forty, with dark brown hair pulled back into a severe bun. She came forward to shake the headmaster's hand. He introduced her to Johnny, and looked around for the third applicant. A young woman was coming towards them. She walked confidently up to the Headmaster, shook his hand and introduced herself as Miss Jones.

"Good, we are all here. Three of my staff have offered to accommodate you for the two nights you will be here." He led them to his colleagues.

Carol and her friends had held back while the introductions were going on. Johnny turned to Carol and said, "I'll meet you tomorrow afternoon at the Market Cross, as we said. I might know something by then. I'd better catch up with them." The headmaster was already marching away with his charges.

Carol gave him a quick hug. "Good luck." Her smile gave him confidence.

She now had time to turn her attention to Mymie, who had courteously stayed back until the headmaster had finished his greeting. Mymie smiled and held out her hands and grasped Carol's. Her touch was firm and warm. "How lovely to meet at last," she said.

Carol was looking into grey eyes, the exact colour of her own and her Dad's. "I would have known you anywhere," she said, and they both knew that it wasn't just her looks, but Mymie's whole being that was so familiar. Carol recognised a kindred spirit; someone so completely like herself and her Dad that her heart soared. She was going to love this week with Mymie.

Mymie turned to the man at her side. "This is my good friend and neighbour, Andy, who's giving us a lift."

Andy shook hands with Carol, and then said, "I see you've made some friends already. Hello Maggie, I haven't seen you for a peerie while. This must be Kirsty?"

Carol was amazed to sense that there was an attraction between Andy and Maggie, but she didn't think that either of them realised, although Maggie was blushing as she spoke to him. "Hello Andy. How are you keeping?"

"I'm fine, working my croft; looking after my sheep and hens, selling my eggs. I do a lot of handyman work too. It keeps me busy. Are you still working at the Gilbert Bain?"

"Yes, I like doing the cleaning at the hospital. Everyone is so friendly."

"What about you Kirsty, are you still at school?"

Kirsty pulled her coat further around herself and looked embarrassed. "No, I left last term. I haven't decided yet what I want to do, but my mother says there is no rush. I'm taking a break from studying for now."

Andy seemed a little taken aback by this, but he didn't comment; he just said, "Can I give you two a lift? It's on my way and there's room. Three of you will fit on the back seat."

"That's kind of you Andy; we were going to walk, it's not that far, but the case is heavy. We did quite a lot of shopping in Aberdeen," Maggie laughed.

They all piled into Andy's car, a Land Rover that was so muddy it was difficult to tell its colour, and he drove round to Maggie's house, just half a mile away, in Lerwick. Maggie turned to Carol as they got out of the car. "I hope you'll have time to come and see us before you go home.

Come for tea and home bakes one afternoon, you too Mymie; and bring Johnny, if he doesn't mind sitting with four females."

"That'd be lovely," said Carol. "Have you got a phone?"

"Yes, we've only had it a few weeks. Here's the number." She gave Carol a slip of paper from her handbag, "I keep a few of these in my bag; it saves writing the number out if anyone asks."

"I'll phone you when we've made plans. It'll be lovely to see you again."

They soon left the town and were on the road south. It was seventeen miles to Levenwick and the road was single track, so, every so often, Andy had to stop the car in a passing place to allow another vehicle to pass. Carol didn't mind how long it took, as she was entranced with the views. As they reached the crown of the first hill - Andy said this was Upper Sound - there was a wonderful view on her left, across to the island of Bressay. The island was green and hilly, with houses here and there, and a white lighthouse at the south end. "How lovely!" She exclaimed.

The road meandered through fields where sheep were grazing. Single storey houses were dotted about, sometimes in groups. The road passed through an area called Cunningsburgh, where there were several houses. Carol was delighted to see a burn here with masses of primroses on its banks. There were also lots of different wild flowers along the edges of the road.

"I'm surprised to see primroses so late in the summer, we see them in May and June. I expect your seasons are later here?" Mymie nodded her agreement.

"You have so many wild flowers here. We don't have so many around Manchester, even Daisy Nook, which is the nearest bit of countryside to us, doesn't have this much variety," said Carol.

"You like wild flowers then?" Mymie asked. "We'll have to have a walk down to the beach and on to the cliff edge. We have sea pinks and blue squill there. It makes a pretty picture in the summer."

"That'd be lovely," Carol smiled.

The road took them through Sandwick from where, Mymie explained, the boat trips to Mousa departed, and then they made a deep turn inland, where the road skirted another burn. "This is Channerwick, and that road on the right takes you to Bigton, on the west side. Just after this bend in the road we drop down into Levenwick," said Andy. "Not long now."

Carol gasped with delight as the road took another turn and they were looking down on almost a full circle of a bay, bordered by two headlands and with a beautiful crescent beach on the south side.

"That's Levenwick beach," said Mymie. The furthest headland is Noness, which extends from Sandwick. The nearer headland is the Taing. It's easy to get to from the beach. We can have a walk down there later, as it's such a fine day."

Carol just nodded. She was speechless with admiration for the beautiful scene. Mymie smiled. She had lived here all her life, but she was familiar with the effect that Levenwick had on visitors.

Andy stopped the car in a wide passing place. On the left, below sloping fields, was the spectacular beach. On the right, higher up the hillside, Carol could see a house, just visible above a dense hedge of wild rose. A low wooden gate opened on to a path up to the house. Mymie led the way through a garden that was densely packed with flowers, mainly lupins, masses of oxeye daisies and clumps of white and purple flowers that Carol didn't recognise.

"What a lovely garden!" Carol exclaimed.

Mymie laughed. "Andy wouldn't agree with you. He can't understand why anyone would want to grow something you can't eat."

"Well, it's a waste of good growing space for food," said Andy, who was following, carrying Carol's suitcase.

"You'll have to see Andy's garden while you're here," said Mymie. "His vegetable garden is a wonder to behold."

"I'd love to." She turned to Andy. "My Dad is of the same mind. His garden at the back is all vegetables, though he has a small lawn at the front."

They were approaching the house entrance, which was via a small porch. Carol was amused to see a dog leaping up to see out of the window.

"That's Bess," Mymie explained. "She's a border collie, but she's useless at herding sheep, which is why she was given to me. She's a wonderful companion. She goes everywhere with me, except when I go to Lerwick." As she opened the door, the dog came bounding out, dancing around in excitement.

"You'd think I had been away a week, wouldn't you?" Mymie laughed as she patted the dog to calm her.

"My Dad's first dog was called Bess," said Carol. "She passed away just before the war. He still talks about her. Although we've had other dogs since, she still has a special place in his heart."

"I know he has a love of dogs, as I do, and you too, I can tell."

"Yes," said Carol as she knelt to stroke the dog.

"Well, come in, come in. Are you staying for a cuppie Andy?"

"No thank you Mymie; I have jobs to do, and I'm sure you two will have lots to talk about. Will I come over to take you to Lerwick tomorrow afternoon Carol? It will be no bother. The bus takes such a long time."

"That's really kind of you Andy. If you're sure you have time?"

"I have to go anyway to get a few things. I might as well go in the afternoon. I can get all my jobs done in the morning. It'll be nae bother to drop you at the market cross and pick you up later. Do you ken where Johnny will be staying after tomorrow night? I was thinking he could stay with me, as Mymie doesna have the room. I would like fine to have him; he could come and go as he pleases."

"That's very generous of you Andy. I think he was going to book into a bed and breakfast, as he's just staying with one of the teachers tonight and tomorrow. He's already looked into hiring a car for the rest of our visit, so that we can see some of the out of the way places. I'll tell him of your offer; I'm sure he'll be delighted."

Andy said goodbye, leaving Mymie to show Carol around the tiny house. It was a mixture of styles, the front part consisting of a modern kitchen and bathroom with a flat roof. The central part was the original house, a living\dining area with a bedroom to the right. Another bedroom had been added to the back of the house at some time. This was Mymie's bedroom. She showed Carol into the other bedroom, which had a single bed with a small table at the side and a solid looking wardrobe.

"This was my bedroom when my parents were alive, but I keep it for guests now. Not that I have many, but I'm hoping that will change in the future. I'm thinking of putting a double bed in here; there's plenty of room. Do you think that Harry and Audrey will come up at sometime? I would love to see them."

"I'm sure they will. Dad speaks very fondly of you; he's always grateful for your wise advice. Now it's so much easier to travel, I expect they'll come soon, especially if Johnny gets the teaching job. Aunty Audrey will miss him terribly."

"And what about you; will you miss him?" Mymie's clear grey eyes looked into Carol's as if she was seeing into her soul.

For the first time with Mymie, Carol felt uncomfortable. "Of course I'll miss him. He's been like a brother to me my whole life. It'll be strange not seeing him come in through the back door. He's always treated our house as his own." She turned away to look at the lovely view through the window. "I will miss him," she said again.

Mymie smiled knowingly. It was obvious to her that there was more than sibling love between them, but she said nothing. They needed to work that out for themselves.

"Come on, let's get that cuppie. I've got some fruit cake, or would you like a sandwich? It's nearly lunch time."

"Just the cake and a cup of tea will be lovely," said Carol as she followed Mymie into the kitchen.

The kitchen assaulted all her senses at once. The Rayburn in the corner was giving off comfortably warm heat and a wonderful savoury smell, while her eyes were drawn to the large window over the sink, which boasted a view of the whole of Levenwick Bay, the white sand dazzling against the blue-green of the waves. The green fields were dotted with ewes and their lambs; gulls soared overhead. She was drawn to this lovely sight, leaning over the sink to get a better look.

Mymie smiled affectionately while she placed the kettle on the hob. "I love looking out of that window too. I was amazed, when this extension was first built, to see the view framed in it. All the other windows in the house are smaller and set deep in the walls. Although I'm used to the view, I love to see the changes that the weather brings. The sea can be a wild thing, with waves crashing over the rocks out there; or it can be as still as a lake - though that's rare - and when there is a full moon there are lovely reflections on the water. I couldn't live anywhere else."

"I can understand that," said Carol, reluctantly turning away from the view. "I never thought that I could live anywhere else but Manchester, but I'm not so sure now."

She sat down at the kitchen table and said, "What's cooking? It smells delicious!"

"Oh it's just a casserole I put in this morning to slow cook for our tea. We'll have it about five o'clock. I'm sure you'll be ready for it after we've had a walk over to the Taing."

She placed a large wedge of cake in front of Carol. "The tea will be just a peerie minute," she said, as she poured the boiling water into the teapot.

Carol smiled. "I love that word, peerie, though I can't pronounce it like you do. It just sounds so right. I hope you'll teach me some other Shetland words while I'm here."

"If you like, I will," said Mymie as she poured out the tea.

After they had their tea and cake they set off for a walk down to the beach with Bess running ahead. Carol marvelled at the way Mymie was striding out down the track. She looked so strong, and so much part of the Shetland scene, with her patterned jumper, long black skirt and walking boots. She looked a lot younger than her seventy five years.

Carol was glad that she wore her stout walking shoes, as they got down to sea level and continued along a sandy path to the beach. There was no one else around; they had this beautiful beach to themselves as they walked along the water's edge and the dog ran in and out of the waves.

"Doesn't anyone else come to the beach; no children making sandcastles?"

"There are not so many children biding in Levenwick at the moment. The older children like to get the bus to Lerwick when they are not at school. There are a few families with younger children. They will come to the beach, but not as often as you would think. Some people will bring their dogs for a run. It's a good place, away from sheep, and some people like to collect shells or pretty stones for crafting or for their gardens. I like to pick up a pretty stone if I see one. We have so many lovely beaches, you see. There's a large one close to Lerwick, and Quendale is not far from here and it's an even bigger beach; and the ayre at Bigton, on the west side, is very beautiful. You and Johnny must visit it while you are here."

"What is the ayre?" Asked Carol

"Its a stretch of sandy beach that has the sea on both sides. It's also called a tombolo. You can walk across it to St Ninian's Isle, which is also well worth a visit."

"It sounds wonderful."

"It is; now, shall we walk over to the Taing? We just have to walk up the grassy slope over there, past the burial ground and over to the rocks. You can see the open sea from there. There's a flat rock I like to sit on and watch the waves, and there are often seals on the rocks below."

"Oh yes." Carol was keen to see as much as possible, so they set off up the slope, Mymie managing it easily.

After a short walk up the incline they came to the edge of the grass. It wasn't so much a cliff, rather a series of rocks gradually going down to the sea. The waves were crashing over the lower rocks. Mymie led the way down to a flat rock just below the grassy area. There was enough room for them both and the dog to sit down. Immediately they were out of the wind. Carol had ceased to notice the wind until then, but she was well aware of the lack of it. It felt really warm sitting there and she was able to look around in comfort.

At first she was fascinated by the waves crashing over the rocks. It seemed that each wave was bigger than the last, and she worried that the next one might come right over where they were sitting. Mymie knew what she was thinking. "The waves won't get up this far; not today, anyway. When there is a very high tide and an easterly gale, the waves will come right over the top, and you can easily see them from the house. I never get tired of watching the waves. When I was young I would stay here for hours. My mother had a bell she would ring at the door to tell me to come home, though I could only hear it clearly if the wind was from the west."

Carol was enthralled.

"I wonder what happened to that bell?" Mymie mused, then she saw something. "Look, there are seals on the rocks below!"

Carol gazed where Mymie was pointing, and she eventually saw the grey forms on the rocks. There were about six of them, only slightly lighter in colour than the rocks they lay on. They stared back up at the humans, looking comfortable, despite the waves occasionally splashing over them. "Oh, how wonderful!" She watched the seals with pleasure. She wondered what other amazing sights she would see in this magical place.

Five:

The Origin of the Gift

After their evening meal, Carol and Mymie sat by the fire drinking tea. Carol had seen Mymie so many times in her dreams, sitting in the same chair, looking so reassuring and always giving wise advice; it didn't feel as if it was the first time she had sat there herself, she felt so at home.

Mymie understood. "I feel the same; as if you had sat there talking to me all those times. That's the wonderful thing about being a dream walker. We are always there for each other; you, me and Harry, and now Rosalind too."

Carol's eyes widened. "So you know about Rosalind? I wasn't sure, but she scared off three bigger boys a few months ago, and that's something that Dad and I have both done in the past. I wasn't sure how it was connected to the dream walking."

"Oh yes, it's all part of the same gift, that, and being able to understand animals; but it's unusual for two siblings to have the gift. That's why there are so few of us."

"Do you know where the gift originated?"

"Oh yes; the story has been passed down through the family for hundreds of years. You know that a lot of we Shetland folk are descended from the Norse people?"

Carol nodded, her eyes alight with interest.

"Well, in ancient times in Norway there were people with what were thought of as magical gifts. Some of them were myths, particularly those who were thought to be shape shifters, or berserkers. They were said to take on the essence of animals during a battle, but I imagine it was just the adrenaline rush. According to the sagas, no one was ever seen taking the shape of an animal."

"Other gifts were genuine though. They were thought to be gifts from the gods. Some people had great strength, some could see into the future, some were even said to be able to change the future. Dream walkers were rare even then, and I think that the ability to sense the feelings of others, and to communicate with animals may have been separate gifts at first, but the people with different gifts would marry each other and, over time, the gifts were combined in their descendants."

"Our ancestor was a young man called Haki. It was the early 900s. He was from a fairly wealthy family, and his father also had the gift. A much wealthier cousin, Bjorn, valued Haki's gifts and offered to foster him when he was quite young. It was common for children to be fostered by relatives in those days. Haki was happy to live with his cousin, because he had a premonition that Bjorn would travel overseas and he wanted to go with him. You see, Haki had been having a dream about a girl since he was very young."

"Just like my Dad!" Carol exclaimed.

"Exactly; When Haki was a teenager his cousin Bjorn fell in love with a beautiful young woman, Thora; but when he asked for Thora's hand in marriage, her father refused. So they planned to elope. Bjorn got a ship well prepared with stocks of food and furs, and he had a crew of twelve men. They set off to sail to Dublin, but it was the wrong time of year, autumn. They were met with stormy seas, and they only got as far as Shetland when the ship was damaged. They managed to land on Mousa, where they moved all their possessions into the broch. Nobody lived in the broch at that time, but there was a family living in a small, thatched croft house on the island. This family were frightened of the Norsemen, but Haki used his powers of persuasion to put them at ease and the two groups of people got along well during that winter."

"And the girl Haki had been dreaming about was one of that family?"

"Yes; she was called Jemima, Mymie for short, and Haki recognised her at once."

"So you were named after her?" Carol smiled.

"Yes, there has been a Jemima in every generation of the family since then."

"The Norsemen stayed on Mousa through the winter and repaired their ship, but, when they were ready to move on in the spring, Haki wanted to stay with Jemima. Bjorn was sympathetic, as, of course, Haki's situation was the same as his own. He didn't want to lose his gifted cousin, and he tried to convince him to bring Jemima to Dublin, but Haki said his destiny was in Shetland. Bjorn finally agreed to let him stay."

"What a wonderful story," Carol was enchanted. "But how did our branch of the family come about?"

"Well, throughout the years, one child of each generation inherited the gift, just the direct descendants of Haki. Often brothers and sisters had a close affinity with each other, but only one child would be a dream walker. That was until my grandfather and his brother were born, in 1847. They were identical twins and they both had the gift. Their parents were amazed, as it had never happened before."

"My grandfather, George, didn't dream about his future wife, as she was a local girl, Andrina. He had grown up with her. My great uncle Andrew, though, dreamed about a girl from childhood and, when he was eighteen, he left Shetland and travelled down to Manchester. He got a job in a cotton mill, where he was noticed by the foreman as being very bright, and he could also read and write, which was rare. They put him to work in the office, which he enjoyed. He didn't earn much more than the general mill workers, but it was enough for him to rent a terraced house and to ask his girl to marry him. She was called Alice, and she also worked in the mill. He talked to his brother in dreams on a regular basis; so, of course, this was also passed down through the family. Though, for some reason, he never gave my grandfather his address. The family just knew that it was somewhere in Manchester"

"Andrew and Alice only had one child, Annie, who was your great grandma Davies. She was born the same year as my father, Andrew. He was a dream walker, but he didn't use that part of his gift until I was an adult, to contact me when I was away. He was very good at sensing people's feelings, and he could always diffuse an awkward situation by talking an angry person out of their anger. He had a great affinity with animals. He would go out in the night to see to a ewe that was having a difficult birth. From the time I was about ten years old I would awake and go with him to the ailing ewe, she had woken me too."

"So like my Dad, though it was mainly dogs with him, and me." Said Carol. "I didn't know that great grandma Davies had the gift; Dad never said; and grandma too?"

"Well, that's another strange thing. As for your great grandma, she must have had the gift, but used it very little. Her husband had been her next door neighbour since they were children, so she didn't dream walk, but I know she also had an affinity with animals, and the reason I know, I will tell you about after I've made another cuppie." She went into the kitchen to put the kettle on, and Carol followed her to help.

When they were settled by the fire again Mymie continued. "Your great grandma Davies had four children; your grandma Alice and great uncle Tom, and two other boys. The eldest, George was named after my grandfather, and the second one, Andrew - always known as Andy - was named after his grandfather."

"It was Andy who had the gift. His gift for dream walking was very strong. We had lost contact with the Manchester family when my great uncle Andrew died. I had discovered I could dream walk and I was reaching out when Andy detected me. I was ten years old. We became great friends, although we never met each other. He told me lots of things about the family, including his mother's way with animals. Then he was killed in the Great War. It was terrible; I felt him leave me. Just like Harry felt his brother leave him when he was drowned."

Carol gasped. "I didn't know that. Dad never said! I can understand why though. I'm aware of all my sisters; it would be horrible to not feel their presence ."

"Yes, and what was worse, I lost my love, my fiancé, in the same battle;" she looked down at a ring bearing three tiny diamonds on her left hand. "I didn't have the same connection with him that I had with Andy, but I knew that he was gone. His parents lived in Levenwick; where Andy lives now, and they didn't get the telegram telling them that their son had been killed until weeks later. I had to keep it to myself all that time, because, how could I tell them that I knew?"

"What about my other great uncle,George?"

"He was killed in another battle a year later. I only found out from Harry a long time after. Harry's great grandfather hadn't told his daughter about the gift, as it seemed she hadn't inherited it, and I don't think that he told her anything about Shetland, so the two sides of the family lost touch, until Andy discovered me. When he passed on I thought I was the last one. It felt very lonely"

Carol was crying now. "That must have been terrible for you. How did you cope with all that grief?"

"By keeping busy; I went to Aberdeen and trained to be a teacher. That was when my father contacted me in his dreams. I got a job at the primary school in Lerwick and I used to stay there during the week, and just came home at the weekends, to save the long journey. My father was a great comfort, until he too died, in 1925; my mother died soon after. If I hadn't discovered Harry, I think my life would have been dreary."

"Oh Mymie, I'm so glad you found us!"

"So am I dearie, so am I," she replied, fervently.

Carol continued, "I've realised that I can't just walk into anyone's dream; not that I'd want to; it would be a terrible intrusion, but I am able to come to you, or to Dad, whenever I want to. I haven't tried to contact Rosalind."

"That's true; we can only see people we are emotionally attached to. I don't know how it happens that we dream walkers can see the person we will meet in later life; just that it happens. I only observed William after he had left to go to war, though I couldn't speak to him like I spoke to Andy, and like I can speak to you and Harry."

"Isn't it strange about Grandma though? She passed on the gift to Dad without realising that she, too, had the gift. Do you think it had anything to do with uncle Andy dying?"

"I don't think so; I said earlier that it was very unusual for two siblings to have the gift, but then, as far as I know, our ancestors had small families. My father and your great grandma were both only children. My grandfather and his twin had no other siblings. Your great Grandma broke the pattern by having four children. The story that was passed down the generations only mentioned the person who was strongest in the gift. Maybe more of them had the gift, but didn't pass on the gift, or didn't use it; Definitely Andy was very strong in the gift, but your grandma, not as strong, didn't realise she had it. I know that she felt the passing of your uncle Billy, and so did her mother.

"I didn't realise that either," said Carol. "Now that I think of it though, Grandma is very perceptive." She sat back and yawned.

"I think it's time for your bed," said Mymie. "You've had a long day."

"Yes I think you're right. Goodnight Mymie."

"Goodnight dearie. I will not call you in the morning. You don't need to be up early."

Carol awoke to the sound of the sea. Her window was slightly open and bright sunlight was peeping through the curtains. She looked at her watch; it was ten o'clock. She couldn't remember when she had slept so well. She made her way to the bathroom and noticed that Mymie was in the kitchen as she passed. There was a wonderful smell of baking.

She washed and dressed quickly and joined Mymie in the kitchen. "That smells delicious. Is it your famous apple pie that Andy likes so much?"

"Yes, I've made three; one for Andy, one for us and I thought I would come with you to Lerwick and take one for Maggie and Kirsty." She placed a steaming bowl of porridge in front of Carol and offered honey or jam. Carol tucked into this hungrily.

"You should have woken me up. I could have helped."

"You needed your sleep, after all the dramas of yesterday, but if you'd like to help, you could take Bess down to the beach while I prepare the meal for tonight. I thought we could invite Andy."

"That'd be lovely; you're so kind."

"I'm enjoying cooking for more than myself." Mymie replied.

Carol walked swiftly down the hill with the dog. It was a cloudy day, and windy, but quite clear. She could see the waves crashing over the further headland, and tried to remember the name of it, but her head was so full of the impressions of the previous day, she couldn't think of it. She didn't worry about it, but just enjoyed the sights and sounds and smells. Bess was enjoying the smells too; she investigated every tuft of grass and clump of wild flowers.

She saw Andy working in his garden and waved to him. He shouted that he would see her later, and turned back to his work.

They spent about an hour on the beach, Carol looking for pretty shells and pebbles, and Bess running in and out of the waves.

She found an almost complete sea urchin shell and several small pebbles that she thought Mymie might like for her garden. Eventually Bess came up to her and sent an image of her water bowl. "Of course, you can't drink sea water, can you? Come on then, let's go back." Bess wagged her tail and set off for the path back to the road.

Mymie had the kettle on, and sandwiches made for lunch when they got back. Carol gave her the pebbles, but kept the sea urchin for herself. "Oh, and I've got something for you in my case. I forgot all about it yesterday." She went into her bedroom and brought the jigsaw and the hankies.

"I got the hankies on Newton Heath market, but I saw the jigsaw in Aberdeen and thought you might like it."

"The hankies are really pretty, and I enjoy a good jigsaw. Perhaps we can start it together tonight?"

"I'd like that."

Andy came for them at two o'clock. I thought you'd like to look at the shops before you meet Johnny at four," he said. "I have quite a few things to do, so it will give me plenty of time."

The journey to Lerwick was just as interesting to Carol as yesterday's. "I don't think I'd ever get used to seeing these lovely views," she commented.

"It's not so great when it's pouring rain and blowing a gale," said Andy.

"I expect you're right," she agreed.

When they arrived in Lerwick, Andy dropped them off on the promenade, just near the Market Cross. "I'll see you at Maggie's, about five o'clock," he said.

They waved to him and set off to explore the shops. "I'd like to get some traditional knitted socks or gloves for the family," said Carol.

"Well, we can look at them in the shops and make a note of the prices, but I have a friend in Bigton who knits them for the shops, and she'd like fine if you buy them from her, as the shops pay her very little for her work. We could go there tomorrow or the day after, as It's on the way to St Ninian's isle."

"That's a lovely idea!" Carol was delighted.

They wandered up the Street arm in arm. Mymie explained that it was called Commercial street, but everyone just called it 'Da Street'. She said hello to so many people as they went along that Carol thought that Mymie must know everyone in Shetland; but then, she thought, she couldn't walk along Church Street in Newton Heath without speaking to several people. She imagined that the population of the whole of Shetland Mainland was similar to that of Newton Heath.

As it neared four o'clock they made their way back to Market Cross and saw that Johnny was already there, talking to another young man. There was an air of excitement emanating from him. He gave a beaming smile as they approached.

"I got the job!" He said. "I felt sure that one of the women would have been chosen, but it seems I've got what they want."

Carol gave him a hug. "That's great news. I'm so pleased for you."

"Oh, this is Angus," He introduced the other young man. "I'm staying at his house. He teaches maths and PE."

Angus said hello and stood back while they chatted about the job. He seemed a little shy.

Carol told Johnny about Andy's offer of accommodation. "It means you'll be near us and we can more easily explore; you'll love Levenwick!"

"That's really generous of him. I need to stay in Lerwick until tomorrow morning. I'm having a meeting with the Head at nine o'clock, that should only take half an hour, and then I'm picking up my hire car. So I'll see you later in the morning. Please thank Andy for me."

Mymie gave him directions to her house, and then they left him to enjoy the rest of the day with his new friend.

They made their way up one of the steep lanes that led from Da Street, and across to Maggie's house.

Maggie and Kirsty were poring over a mail order catalogue when they arrived. "We're ordering things for the baby," Maggie explained. "It's a shame I didn't know when we were in Aberdeen; we could have bought a few things while we were there; It's alright dearie," she said to Kirsty when she saw tears threatening. "It's good you've told me now."

"We've got you something from 'Peerie Moots,'" said Mymie, and she brought two small parcels out of her basket. Kirsty opened them to find two tiny nightdresses in one, and two baby vests in the other.

"Oh they are lovely , thank you so much!"

Carol laughed. "Mymie told me what 'Peerie Moots means; Little children. I love that, it just sounds so right!"

"Are you staying for a cuppie? I'll put the kettle on," said Maggie, without waiting for an answer.

"Make one for Andy, too. He's coming here to pick us up. Oh, and here's an apple pie for you," said Mymie.

"Oh thanks Mymie, that's lovely." Maggie went to make the tea and Mymie followed her to help. The two girls sat together, looking at all the baby things in the catalogue.

"Have you and your mother come to terms with the fact of the baby now?" Carol asked.

"Yes, it's amazing that, just over a day ago I was dreading it; but now that my mother knows, and she doesn't blame me, I'm actually looking forward to having my own peerie baby. I just don't know how to tell my friends."

"Why don't you get them all together and tell them all at once? That way they'll all hear the true story, instead of it being passed from one to the other. If they are good friends they'll all stand by you. Anyone who speaks badly of you doesn't deserve to be your friend, and you can just ignore them. Some older people may disapprove, but I'll bet that most people know someone who has had the same trouble. It's far from unknown. Once you have your baby in your arms, you will be so full of love that you won't care about what anyone else thinks."

"Carol, you are so wise, and yet you're not much older than me, are you?"

"I'm eighteen, and I am one of a very mixed up family of eight children. We are always sorting out each other's problems; though none of us has had a baby yet, that doesn't mean it will never happen."

"Eight of you? My goodness!"

"Yes, though three of them are half siblings, and Johnny is my step brother, although he's been like a brother to me all my life."

"Oh, I wish I had a sister like you."

"I could be your penpal foster sister if you like?"

"Would you? That'd be lovely."

"Alright; as soon as I get home next week I'll write to you. I love writing letters. You have to reply though."

"I will."

Just then there was a knock at the door, and Andy came in, saying "Aye aye!"

Carol was surprised that he came in without being invited, but Kirsty wasn't surprised, and Maggie just shouted from the kitchen, "Aye aye Andy, are du wanting a cuppie?" So Carol realised that this was the norm in Shetland. She quite liked the idea.

Andy sat down on the settee and said "What are du girls up to?"

Kirsty quickly shut the catalogue so that he didn't see which pages they were looking at, and said, "just looking through the catalogue."

Andy gave her a strange look, but then said, "I imagine du girls are into the fashion?"

Kirsty just nodded, and Carol changed the subject. "Did you get everything you wanted Andy?"

"I did; it was mainly chicken feed I needed but I got a fair few things for the garden and some wood for shelving. I've been wanting to put shelves up for a peerie while."

The two women came in at this point and the conversation turned to home bakes . "I could never offer just a bare cup of tea," said Maggie. She turned to Kirsty. "D'you ken when we went to see my auntie in Aberdeen? She made the weakest tea you ever saw, and nothing to eat with it!"

Everybody laughed, and Carol said, "I've never thought of it before, but my grandma and aunties always have cake to offer with a cup of tea, but it's not the usual thing in Manchester. Most people will say 'd'ya wanna brew?' but, mainly it will be just a cup of tea."

The conversation carried on in this vein, but Carol noticed that Andy had become very quiet, and she sensed that Mymie noticed too. They didn't stay too long, as Mymie wanted to get back to finish preparing the evening meal.

Andy remained unusually quiet in the car, and, when they got to the house, he just went to build up the fire in the living room while Mymie and Carol were busy in the kitchen.

It was after the meal, when they were all sitting by the fire that Mymie said. "Come on Andy, spit it out; you've got a bee in your bonnet about something!"

He said nothing at first, but looked from Mymie to Carol and then back again, then he blurted out, "That girl is pregnant; it's a disgrace!"

Carol was angry. "She's not 'that girl' she's . . . !" but Mymie silenced her with a look. She sat back and let Mymie do the talking.

There was no anger coming from Mymie, just infinite patience. She sat forward in her chair and looked into Andy's eyes. "Look at me Andy," she said, gently, though her voice was compelling. He looked into her eyes and seemed mesmerised.

"Andy, Kirsty was badly used by a man who should have known better. The disgrace isn't hers, but his, and she needs support from all her friends. As a strong man you can be an immense support to her and her mother. People will listen to you; they look up to you. With you on her side she will have a much easier time in the coming months."

Andy took a deep breath and sat back in his chair. "You're right, of course, Mymie. That peerie girl needs a man at her back. Her father was useless. Yes, I'll be a friend to her and Maggie."

He finished his tea and said, "I must be going. Lots to do. Bring Johnny down to my house when he arrives tomorrow. Goodnight ladies and thanks for the meal." He left as if in a dream.

Carol was impressed. "That was amazing Mymie! I can only do that if I'm angry."

"You only did it when you were angry because you didn't know you could do it; but, if you put your mind to it you can do it in a gentle way; in a way that achieves results without making people fear you. You can't make people do what is against their nature, thank goodness, that would be a terrible abuse of your gift, but I know Andy is a good, caring man. He only spoke like that because it was the way we were brought up in the past. It was always thought to be the woman's fault if she became pregnant. We know better now. Andy just needed to hear what he already knew deep down."

Carol thought about the time when she was four years old; she had forced a bigger girl, who was bullying her sister, to back down. That girl was always fearful of Carol afterwards. "You're right Mymie; it can make people fear you. I've learned a lot today. Thank you."

"You're welcome dearie. Now, shall we have another cuppie and start that jigsaw?"

Six:

Exploration

Johnny arrived at Mymie's house at ten thirty the next morning. He was standing, gazing at the view when Carol went to greet him at the door.

"It's beautiful, isn't it?" Carol asked. It was another dry day, although windy, so they had a good view of the beach and the headlands.

"It is," Johnny breathed, and continued to take in the lovely scene.

Bess came out to greet the newcomer; she danced all around him until he took his eyes from the view and bent down to stroke her. "She doesn't bark," he commented.

"No, I haven't heard her bark, though I'm sure she could if she needed to. She'a a very contented dog," said Carol.

"Are you coming in, or are you going to stand there all day?" Said Mymie. "I haven't had time to ask you about your new job."

They all went into the kitchen and sat round the table. "Well, I had a good meeting with the Head this morning, he had looked through all my certificates, and he was puzzled about my change of name, because, of course, my certificates are all in my old name. He was ok though, when I explained about my mother remarrying and my wanting to have the same name as the rest of the family."

"I start the new term the second week of August; they have different summer holidays here," he explained to Carol. " So I'll only have three more weeks at home before I have to come back."

"But you're not sorry you've accepted the job?" Said Carol.

"Oh no, I'm looking forward to it, but I will miss the family. Angus has offered me a room in his house, at least for the first year. He's single, but he's getting married next year. He has a phone, so I'll be able to phone home every week, and I'll go home for Christmas and Easter, and probably half term too."

"So you've got it all sorted out laddie?" Said Mymie.

"Yes, it seems like it. Oh, I forgot to say, I phoned home last night to tell Mum and uncle Harry the news. They sent their love, to both of you."

"Oh that's lovely," said Carol. "I bought three postcards yesterday ; I haven't written them yet, I'll do it later and post them tomorrow. There's one for your Mum and my Dad, and one each for your grandparents and mine.

"I never thought of postcards," said Johnny.

"Well, your mind has been full of the interview. We can send them from both of us anyway."

"That's a good idea, thanks."

Mymie smiled at the two young people. "Shall we have a cup of tea now, or shall we go down to Andy's and see if he has his kettle on?"

"Let's go down to Andy's, and then Johnny can drop off his bag, and we can go out for the rest of the day," said Carol.

They went out to Johnny's hire car, taking Bess with them this time, as they weren't going to the town. Johnny drove the short distant downhill to Andy's house, which wasn't far from the beach.

Andy was in his garden as usual, and he waved to them as Johnny parked the car in the space next to Andy's.

His large garden was neatly set out in rows of vegetables on one side of the path. The other side housed a large hen house, and about thirty hens were scratching about in the ground. There was a high wire fence around this side of the garden. "That's to keep the hens away from my veggies," said Andy. As he shook hands with Johnny.

"My Dad would love to see your garden," said Carol. "He likes to grow veggies but not this many, and his garden has never been this free of weeds."

"He's a teacher though, isn't he? He maybe doesna have as much time for gardening as I do."

"That's true, and he doesn't have as much land. Grandad helps him out a lot; he's retired."

"Aye, well, shall we go in? Have you all got time for a cuppie? I'll show Johnny his room, and then I've got something to show all of you." He said this shyly, as though he was unsure of their reaction. Carol was intrigued.

Andy's house was similar to Mymie's, in that it was one storey, but it was a different shape, as rooms had been added at different times over the years. His main room was kitchen and living room combined, with the Rayburn stove and the sink at one end, and a large, solid looking table already set with teacups and a tin of biscuits. The other end of the room had a settee and two wooden rocking chairs around an open fire. There were two doors off this room, leading to the two bedrooms. A small bathroom had been added at the entrance to one of these. "That's my bedroom," he said, and led Johnny to the other room. "You'll have to come through the house when you need the bathroom, I'm afraid."

"That's ok; the room is perfect," said Johnny. "It's kind of you to let me stay."

"I like a peerie bit of company now and again. Now, come and let me show you what I've found."

In the corner by the settee was something bulky covered by a grey woollen blanket. "I want to know what you think before I clean it up," he said, as he lifted the blanket. It was a baby's wooden crib, covered in dust, but otherwise in very good condition.

"It's beautiful," breathed Carol. "It's very old, isn't it?"

"Yes, it's been in the family for years. My great uncle made it for his son, William - oh, I'm sorry Mymie, I didna think!"

Mymie had tears in her eyes, but she smiled. "It's alright Andy. It's a lovely thought. You want to give it to Kirsty?"

Carol and Johnny were wondering about the connection between Mymie and the crib. She explained. "My love, the boy who was killed in the great war, was William, the first baby to sleep in this crib. Other babies slept in it later; it was passed around family and friends. The last time I saw it William showed it to me and said that our baby would be the next one to use it."

"Oh Mymie!" Carol cried, and gave her a hug. She couldn't say anything else, because she also had a lump in her throat and tears in her eyes.

"Now that's enough!" Said Mymie, firmly. "There's lots of happy things to think about. Andy, when you've cleaned that up Kirsty will love it. It's a beautiful thing, as well as being just what she needs for her baby's first months. Now, what about that cup of tea?"

They discussed plans for the next few days while they drank their tea. They decided to go down to Sumburgh Head that day, as the morning was almost over, and to Bigton and St Ninian's Isle the next day, if the weather held out. "You canna plan too far ahead, with our fickle weather," said Andy.

Andy wanted to stay working on his garden, but Mymie went with them to Sumburgh Head. They first stopped at Levenwick shop to buy pies and chocolate to eat while they were out. Mymie had brought a large flask of tea so they wouldn't get thirsty.

When they left the main road at Sumburgh, they were able to take the car up a long, winding track to a rough parking area with a fantastic view. Looking north they could see all the ins and outs of the coastline, and the vast expanse of the sea to the east. They then walked up the zigzag track to the lighthouse, with Bess leading the way. All along the way they could look down on deep coves and rugged cliffs containing the nests of thousands of seabirds.

At the top, where there were several buildings, they looked over a stone wall to the cliffs and grassy slopes of the southernmost tip of Shetland Mainland. Here they saw puffins showing off their multicoloured bills. "Aren't they cute?" Said Carol. "They're a lot smaller than I imagined."

"Most people say that when they first see them," said Mymie.

They spent a long time watching the birds and the seals that were basking on the rocks below. They found a sheltered spot and sat down out of the wind to have their picnic.

They took their time ambling back to the car, stopping to look at wild flowers and trying to identify the land birds that were flitting among the tussocks of grass. They recognised a wren, although it seemed bigger and darker than the ones at home, and Johnny thought he saw a wheatear.

It was teatime by the time they got back to Levenwick. Andy had offered to cook for them, so they arrived at his house looking rosy and windblown and feeling happy.

"That was wonderful!" Johnny exclaimed. "I never knew there were so many different seabirds, and all crowded together on those rock shelves; You are lucky to live in such a scenic place, and teeming with wildlife!"

"Aye, well, it's fine in the summer. The winters can be wild, but I wouldna live anywhere else," said Andy.

"No, me neither," said Mymie.

They had a contented evening of conversation and laughter. Andy had a dry sense of humour; Carol was reduced to breathless giggles several times. It was ten o'clock when she and Mymie and the dog set off to walk back. Johnny offered to take them in the car, but they refused, as it was still light and it was less than half a mile. Carol enjoyed the evening walk.

They woke next morning to a still day and a deep blue sky. The absence of wind seemed strange to Carol. She stood in the garden feeling the warmth of the sun on her bare arms and looking at the calm sea. Mymie joined her. "Make the most of it, for it isn't often like this," she laughed. "It's a good day to go to St Ninian's Isle. We'll make sandwiches for a picnic."

They were just finishing packing two bags with food and flasks when Johnny came to pick them up. They were soon ready to go, and Bess was delighted that she was being allowed to go with them again.

"Have you got your purse?" Said Mymie. "We'll visit my friend Ina on the way back and see what knitted goods she has."

As they approached Bigton Mymie spied her friend in the field next to her house, so she asked Johnny to stop so that she could speak to her.

"Hello Ina; will you be in this afternoon? My friend wants some socks and things to take home."

Ina came down to the field edge to speak to her. "Yes, I'm here all day, come any time. Are you going to St Ninian's?"

"Aye, we'll see you this afternoon then."

Ina waved them off and went back to her sheep.

Shortly after, they rounded a bend and they got a wonderful view of St Ninian's Isle and the ayre, Carol had thought that she couldn't see anything more beautiful than the view of Levenwick Bay from Mymie's house, but this view took her breath away, and she could sense that Johnny felt the same. A bank of pure white sand led to a small island, blue/green wavelets lapped each side of the pristine beach.

They continued along a track and parked in a wide area above the ayre. Bess jumped out and ran down to the ayre as soon as the car door was opened. "She loves it here," said Mymie, "but I can only bring her when I get a lift from someone."

They took out the bags and a blanket and followed the dog down to the sand. By this time Bess was running from one wave - washed edge to the other. It was as if she was trying to understand why the water was on both sides. They laughed at her antics.

They walked the length of the ayre and selected a smooth area at the far end to spread the blanket. They all sat quietly for a while, just drinking in the atmosphere. It was incredibly peaceful. The only other people on the beach were a group of children who were paddling in the shallows near the middle of the ayre. They were far enough away that their voices were just a distant echo. "They must be local, as there are no adults with them," said Mymie. "At one time I would have known whose family they were, but I've lost touch a little since I retired."

After they ate their picnic, Mymie suggested that Carol and Johnny go and explore the island with the dog. "There's the ruin of an old chapel up there; a hoard of treasure was found there in 1958. I'll just sit here and enjoy the warmth of the sun," she added.

They set off up the path, Bess leading the way. They felt a slight breeze as they reached the top of the path, but it was still quite warm, with a cloudless blue sky. They soon found the chapel, and spent an enjoyable time investigating all the nooks and crannies, and speculating what life must have been like there all those years ago.

Bess was particularly interested in one corner, where there was a gap in the low stone wall. She started scrabbling at the earth there and whining. "Whats the matter Bess?" Said Carol, as she went over to investigate. The dog sent her a vision of kittens. "Cats, up here?" Carol couldn't imagine why a cat would have kittens up here. Nobody lived on the island. She crouched down, trying to see, but it was a deep dark hole.

She turned to Johnny. "If there are kittens here, where is the mother? She should be guarding them."

"Let me try," said Johnny. He was taller than Carol, but very slim. He was able to get his arm down the hole. He emerged, carrying a dead kitten. He tried again, three times. The fourth kitten, a tabby, was still alive, but only just. Its eyes were open, so it wasn't newborn, but it was thin, and, although it opened its mouth, it was too weak to cry.

"I think they've died of starvation. I wonder if the mother was a feral cat; do they have feral cats here?"

"This is deja vu," said Johnny. "Do you remember when you found that baby rabbit in Wales?"

"Oh yes, and my cousin Gwynneth adopted it! Well, the mother has obviously not been here for quite a while, so we'd better take her down to Mymie."

"What about the others; we can't just leave them here."

"Put them back in the hole and we'll pack it tight with small stones and this sandy earth."

When they were satisfied with the makeshift grave, they returned to Mymie, Johnny carrying the kitten inside his shirt.

"Feral cats are unusual here, but not unknown," said Mymie. "We'll ask Ina if she knows of anyone losing a cat recently. I wonder if the kitten would drink some of this warm tea? There's just a peerie bit left in the flask." She poured the tea into one of the plastic cups and dipped her fingers in it. After a little persuasion, the kitten began to suck her fingers. The tea was sweet, so the kitten got a little fluid and nourishment. It gave a tiny meow when all the tea was gone. They all smiled.

"I wonder what happened to the mother?" Said Carol.

"Probably a bonxie got it." Said Mymie.

"A bonxie, what's that?" Johnny asked.

"It's the Shetland name for the great skua. A big brown bird with a white flash on its wings. They will peck out the eyes of a new born lamb if the ewe doesn't protect it. A cat would be easy game if it didna run fast enough. Generally they steal fish from other seabirds, but they are not averse to grabbing a weak animal"

"Oh, the poor cat!" Carol stroked the little kitten, as if to compensate for the loss of its mother.

"Shall we go to Ina's now, and see what she can do for this peerie cat?'

They were soon back at the car and travelling to Ina's house. Johnny parked on the verge by the gate and they all trooped up the path through Ina's field. The sheep looked at them curiously, but Bess ignored them. "That's why she is useless as a sheepdog," said Mymie. "She doesn't seem to have the herding instinct, but it does mean that she's very safe among sheep, and she makes a very good companion."

Ina's door was open, and Mymie led the way in, shouting, "Aye aye!" As she entered.

"Come in, come in," said Ina. "I have the kettle on, so I hope you are in need of a cuppie." She led them into a kitchen/living room, similar to Andy's. There was a little girl of about four years playing on the rug. "This is my granddaughter, Catherine. Her mother has gone to Lerwick for the day."

Catherine smiled shyly, and then jumped up when she saw the kitten that Johnny was cradling in his hands. "A peerie cat; Lovely!" Johnny handed the kitten to her and she sat back on the rug with the kitten in her arms.

It didn't take them long to explain where the kitten came from. Ina was intrigued. "I dunna ken of anyone who's lost a cat, but there is a farm down towards Dunrossness that has a few cats wandering around the yard. Maybe it came from there? Anyway, the main thing is that this peerie one has got a chance now. Wasn't Bess clever seeking it out?"

Bess looked up at the mention of her name, and Carol and Mymie exchanged a significant look. Ina didn't need to know exactly how they found the kitten. Ina started to rummage in a cupboard. "I think I have a baby's bottle here that I use for orphan lambs. It may be too big for the kitten, but we can try." She found the bottle and washed it out, warmed a little milk on the Rayburn and added sugar. She handed the bottle to Catherine and said,"See if you can get him to suck."

Catherine had fed lambs before, so she knew what to do. The tiny kitten struggled to get the teat in its mouth, but persevered, and was soon sucking.

"She's a fighter," said Carol. "I'm pretty sure she is a girl." She didn't say that, to her, the kitten emanated a female personality, but Ina didn't question how she knew. She just got busy with tea and home bakes.

They all settled with tea and cakes. Ina had picked up her knitting and her fingers were a blur as she worked a pattern into a sock without looking down. Carol was engrossed watching the intricate pattern emerge , until she realised that Ina had asked her a question.

"What are you going to do with the peerie cat?"

Why Ina had decided that she was responsible for the welfare of the kitten, Carol was unsure, but she pondered the question. "I hadn't really thought about it, but, If no one here wants her, I'll take her home to Manchester. There's always room for another animal in our house."

"I want her!" Catherine piped up.

"Oh, I'm not sure what your parents will think of that," said Ina.

"Oh Granny!" She pouted. "We can keep her here then, and I can come over and feed her every day."

"Catherine, dearie. She'll need a lot more care than just feeding at first. She may not make it anyway."

"No, don't say that!" Catherine began to cry, holding the kitten tight to her chest.

Mymie intervened. "Why don't I take her home for a peerie while. I'm good at looking after sick animals, and Bess will help me. She'll need feeding during the night too, and I can do that, because I don't need a lot of sleep. Meanwhile, Catherine, you can ask your parents if you can have her when she's bigger, and you can visit her whenever someone can bring you over to my house. What do you think of that?"

Catherine thought about it, and everyone in the room was willing her to agree. "Yes, I think that will be alright.' She finally said. "I'm sure my mother and father will let me have her though. I'll come over every day!"

"I doubt if you can go every day," said Ina, thinking that Mymie wouldn't want her there so often. "but I can take you sometimes, and your mother will whenever she has time. Thank you Mymie, if you're sure you don't mind the extra work."

"I'll enjoy it," said Mymie. "Just like Carol's side of the family, there's always room for another animal in my house."

Having dealt with the problem of the kitten, and the tea and cakes finished, Ina took them into another room to show them her knitted items.

Carol gasped, there were literally dozens of jumpers, scarves, socks and gloves, all in brightly coloured shetland patterns. "Oh they're lovely!"

"You can have any of these. The shop just takes whatever I've got, unless, sometimes, I make things to order."

Carol and Johnny had an enjoyable time choosing socks and gloves for their large family and imagining the delight they would give. They paid half each of the ridiculously small price that Ina wanted for them. "Are you sure that's all you want?" Said Carol, when Ina mentioned how much.

"It's more than I will get from the shop for them, and I'm glad you are so pleased with them."

In the end she accepted the extra that they offered, and everyone was satisfied.

After Catherine finally gave up the kitten into Carol's care, they set off home. It had been another tiring, but happy day..

Carol was disappointed the next morning to find that she couldn't see the lovely view from her bedroom window. It was foggy.

She joined Mymie in the kitchen. "We often get a foggy day after a lovely still, warm day like yesterday. It brings in the haar, the sea fog. I think we will have to stay home today. I don't want to leave the kitten just yet, though she seems to be doing well." She looked across at the dog's basket. The kitten was lying snuggled up to Bess, who was looking proud of herself. She had taken on the role of babysitter and was really enjoying herself.

Carol was happy to stay with Mymie; she was so interesting to talk to and she learned such a lot about Shetland life.

Johnny came over in the morning to say that he was going to stay at Andy's for the day; he was helping him to put up shelves. Johnny had learned a lot about woodworking from his uncle Bobby, so he was a great help, and Andy told them later how much he had enjoyed working with the young man. Mymie invited the two men to come for their evening meal.

Mymie took the opportunity of doing some washing, and Carol was impressed that Mymie had a twin tub washing machine. "You're more advanced that we are, Mymie," she said. "We thought we were very modern when we had the old gas boiler taken out and got a Parnall washing machine, complete with electric wringer; so much easier than the old mangle by the back door!" She laughed.

"Oh yes, I still have our old mangle round the back of the house, but I love the spinner on this washer. I can hang things on the pulley on wet days and they don't drip." She pointed to the device over the rayburn stove.

"Oh we have one of those in our kitchen, but we call it a rack. I think I like the word 'pulley' better though"

"Oh yes, I can see that the wooden poles that go through the metal holders are like racks. I suppose the word 'pulley' comes from the ropes that we use to raise and lower it. So we've both learned something new today."

They worked in harmony all morning, and, after lunch, they looked at photographs of Mymie and her parents from when she was young, and some group pictures of Mymie and her pupils at the school.

"I think I'd like to be a primary school teacher," said Carol. "I haven't decided yet, because I also think I'd quite like to teach English, like my Dad. It is my favourite subject."

"Well, there's plenty of time," said Mymie. "You've got three years at university; you're studying English, aren't you? And then I expect you'll do a teacher training course. You'll likely discover by then what type of teaching you'd like to do."

"Or, you may decide to get married and have your own children." Mymie felt the distress from Carol immediately. "I'm sorry, you have reservations about marriage?"

Carol knew that she couldn't hide anything from Mymie, so she told her something that she hadn't even discussed with Harry, who knew her better than anyone. " I don't think that marriage is for me, Mymie. It hasn't been discussed openly at home, but I know that my mother's illness is hereditary. Any one of us could have inherited it. I don't want to pass that on to a child. I'd rather not have any children, and that would be a hard thing to tell a possible husband. Besides, I have never had a dream about a future husband, like Dad dreamed about Mum, great uncle Andrew dreamed about my great grandma and Haki dreamed about Jemima. I don't think I am meant to get married."

"But you also know that I didn't dream about William and Your Grandma Alice never dreamed of her love; because they were close by. Maybe you haven't dreamed about your love because he has been close by all your life."

"No, there isn't anyone like that." But Carol felt very uncomfortable because she knew that Mymie sensed something that she, Carol, had been unaware of, until now, that is.

She repeated, "No, no; there isn't anyone." But her heart felt heavy as she said it.

To change the subject, Mymie said, "Shall I make another cuppie and we can do a peerie bit more of the jigsaw?"

Carol thought that was an excellent idea, and the conversation turned to other things.

Later in the afternoon they went out into the garden to dig up some potatoes [tatties, Mymie called them] and turnips, [neeps] for their meal. A large joint of lamb had been cooking in the oven all day. It would go well with neeps and tatties, mashed together with a generous lump of butter.

A very enjoyable evening followed; the four of them sat around the fire talking of the differences, and similarities, between Shetland life and life in Manchester. There was lots of laughter and a few misunderstandings; They all agreed that people were basically the same wherever you lived.

There were four days left of their visit, and the weather was kind, in that it didn't rain, although it was windy and cloudy.

On the day after the fog, Carol and Johnny had a boat trip to Mousa. Mymie stayed at home to look after the kitten and to be in for a visit from Ina and Catherine.

Mousa was the place Carol most wanted to see, after hearing the story of Haki. Boat trips went from Sandwick on fine days in the summer. It was a short trip across the sound to the island.

The ancient broch was impressive. They were able to go inside and up the stairs that were set within the massive walls. They stood at the top, taking in the view and imagining what it must have been like to live here.

They had a walk around the small island and saw one or two ruins of much smaller dwellings. Carol wondered which one Jemima's family had inhabited.

There were a large number of seals on the beach on the east side of the island, and they were able to get quite close for a good look at them. The seals had a good look at the humans too.

As they were sitting on the jetty, waiting for the boat to return, Johnny said, "It's been a lovely day, hasn't it? What do you think of Shetland?"

"I love it. At first I thought it was a bit bare, with the lack of trees, but it's so full of wildlife, and the sea and the sky are so changeable. There's always something new to see; and the people are all so friendly. I don't think I'd ever get bored here."

"Do you think you could live here?"

"I don't know; I'd miss the family so much, but I'd like to come here often. Are you thinking of your job, and whether you can settle here?"

"Yes, I suppose I am, but I've decided to give it a good go. In my mind I've decided to give it five years. I'll miss you . . . and Mum and the rest of the family, of course." He looked into her eyes, and Carol was disturbed by the depth of feeling that she saw, and sensed from him.

She was feeling very uncomfortable, so she looked away and said, "Here's the boat now." They stood on the jetty with the handful of people who had also taken the trip, and the moment had passed.

The next three days flew by so quickly. They explored more of the south mainland and, on the Sunday, they went to chapel with Mymie and met more of her neighbours.

They saved their visit to Maggie and Kirsty for the last day, as they would be boarding the ferry in the early evening, and Johnny had to return the hire car.

They drove up to Lerwick in two vehicles, as Andy wanted to go with them, to take the cradle and to bring Mymie back home after she had seen them safely on to the ferry.

Maggie and Kirsty were pleased to see them and absolutely delighted with the cradle. Andy had cleaned and polished it until it shone and he had managed to get a piece of foam rubber for a mattress. Mymie had made a cotton cover for it and it fitted perfectly.

"I hope you dunna think it's too old fashioned," he said.

No, it's beautiful!' said Kirsty. "And Mother has already knitted a quilt. We just need cotton sheets for it now." She sat by the cradle, stroking the smooth wood and smiling. Carol was happy to see her so contented. She was a completely different girl to the desperate character she had met on the ship just over a week before.

When they were all sitting comfortably , drinking tea and eating Maggie's delicious home bakes, Carol and Johnny told of their explorations of the south mainland and how much they had enjoyed themselves. Maggie and Kirsty loved the story of the orphan kitten.

"Oh the poor peerie thing!" said Kirsty. "It's good you were there that day; it's like fate. Is Catherine going to have her?'

"Yes, her parents said that she can have the cat when she is big enough to eat solid food, as long as she looks after her.' Said Mymie "She has already given her a name, Ninian. I told her it was a boys name, but she was determined that it was the right name for her, and I suppose it is."

"Oh yes, it sounds just right." Kirsty turned to Carol and said, "You always seem to be in the right place at the right time. I wonder how you do it?"

Andy and Johnny looked confused, but the women didn't enlighten them, and the conversation turned to other things.

They stayed until it was time to go to the ferry. Maggie and Kirsty waved from the door, telling them to come back soon.

Parting from Mymie was tearful for Carol. She had so loved being with her cousin and learning the family history, but she was looking forward to going home too. They hugged each other tightly.

Johnny shook hands with Andy and thanked him for his hospitality. "Any time laddie. You repaid me well with those bonny shelves. I would never have got them looking so good. If you want a weekend away from Lerwick any time, you'll be very welcome. We could go fishing."

"I'd love that," said Johnny.

The journey home was uneventful. Carol took a seasickness pill as soon as they boarded the ship, and they both slept all night in the cabin. The train journey wasn't as pleasant on the way south, as it rained the whole time and they could see very little of the views. They spent most of the time reading, and Carol was aware that the easy relationship that she had enjoyed with Johnny for as long as she could remember, had become strained. She didn't want to ponder on the reasons why, so she lost herself in her book; she was good at that.

Harry and Audrey were waiting at Victoria station for them. Carol gave her Dad a big hug. Though the holiday had been wonderful, she was glad to be home.

Seven:

An eventful Autumn

Harry and Audrey decided to go up to Shetland with Johnny when he went to start his new job. Mymie had invited them to stay with her, now she had a double bed in the spare room.

Carol offered to look after Lynette and supervise the other girls, though Audrey at first wanted to take Lynette with them. She didn't know whether she could part with her baby daughter for ten days, but Carol persuaded her.

"I'll enjoy looking after her," she said. "And both grandmas are here to help. I'll make sure the girls help with housework and such. Besides, Lynette wouldn't enjoy a long car journey. Just go and enjoy yourselves. You'll love Shetland." She finally convinced them.

They drove up in the car, as Johnny had a lot of baggage. Harry had refurbished a wireless for him and the two grandmas had made a colourful patchwork quilt for his bed. As well as all his clothes he had dozens of books. There was hardly room for Harry and Audrey's case.

They journeyed at a leisurely pace, staying the night in a B&B north of Edinburgh, and stopping several times between there and Aberdeen, arriving in plenty of time to board the ferry in the evening.

Angus was waiting to greet them in Lerwick the next morning. Harry and Audrey were very impressed with this quiet young man. They had tea and biscuits at his house while Johnny was putting all his things in his room, and then they left him to settle in, promising to call again on their last day. They drove down to Levenwick on a clear, windy day.

"Carol didn't exaggerate how beautiful it is here," said Harry as he drove through the meandering roads of the south mainland. Audrey just nodded and smiled as she admired the passing scenery.

Mymie was waiting at the top of her garden path with Bess at her side. She was all smiles as she welcomed them, and Bess sent Harry an image of Carol stroking her. She knew that he and Carol belonged together. "You're a very clever dog," he said, which set her tail wagging.

They had an idyllic week with Mymie, exploring all the places Carol had told them about and making friends with Andy. Harry spent a happy half day helping Andy in his garden while the two women went over to Bigton to visit Ina and Catherine and, of course, Ninian, who was quite a big kitten now. Audrey was glad that Harry had taught her to drive. She could appreciate how invaluable the car was here. Buses were few and far between and the single track roads made for slow journeys.

In Newton Heath Carol was managing quite well, though she could have done without the twins' practical jokes and Pamela's moodiness. The first couple of days Lynette kept looking for Audrey, saying, "Mama, Mama?" But Carol usually managed to turn her attention to other things. She organised games and read all the favourite fairy tales, showing Lynette all the colourful pictures. They went out every day, even if it was raining, usually taking Flossie, the Labrador. Brookdale park was the favourite place to go. They went to the market on Wednesday and Saturday, and even managed a walk to Daisy Nook on one glorious day. All four girls went, with their baby sister in the pram and Flossie on the lead, pulling them up the hills. They had Vimto and toasted teacakes at the wooden hut opposite Crime Lake, and they picked some early blackberries. They were all sunburned and exhausted when they got home.

Carol hadn't forgotten her promise to write to Kirsty. She sent her a long letter, telling her about all the adventures she was having with her sisters. She sent the letter in a parcel containing knitted items from the grandmas, who had sympathised with the young girl's dilemma when they heard the story.

The whole family, including grandparents, Dorothy, Fred, Alice and Bill, were waiting at the gate when Harry and Audrey arrived home in the evening. The girls had taken it in turns to watch for them driving down Amos Avenue. Lynette nearly threw herself out of Carol's arms when she saw her parents, shouting, "Mama, Dada, Mama, Dada!"

Audrey took the baby from Carol and smothered her with kisses. "Oh I've missed you lovey!" She said, with tears of joy in her eyes. "It's been a lovely holiday, but I'm glad to be home."

"Me too," said Harry.

"Come into our house," said Dorothy. "I've got the kettle on."

"Of course you have, Mum." Laughed Audrey.

Dorothy's living room was crowded, but they all managed to sit somewhere with a cup of tea in one hand and a generous wedge of cake in the other. Everyone was eager to hear about the holiday.

Harry began. "I was expecting to see a frail old lady, despite Carol's description of Mymie, but, apart from the white hair, she was like a woman many years younger. I commented on the fact that she had once said that she was so happy to get in touch with us because she didn't get out so much. I was amazed when she explained that, at that time, she had broken her leg chasing after one of Andy's ewes that had escaped and was in danger of running onto the road! Apparently the break had taken a long time to heal, so she was housebound for quite a while. It was during that time that she found our side of the family.

"How did she find you?" Asked Dorothy. She and Fred knew a little about the gift that some of the family had, but they didn't know that they could communicate in dreams.

Harry wondered what to say without actually telling a lie. "She didn't actually say," he said. "She likes to keep some things to herself. She contacted me when Bronwyn was very ill, and we have been in contact since then." He didn't say how Mymie contacted him, but Dorothy seemed satisfied with his explanation. She went on to ask what they had done, and seen, in Shetland.

Audrey took over. "Oh, it's, so lovely there Mum. Wherever you go you are near the sea, and it's a lovely blue/green, not like at Blackpool, and so clear. When we were on the beach at Levenwick, I could see right down to the bottom. It wasn't very warm though, and most of the time it was windy, but I didn't mind that. We had missed most of the nesting seabirds too, as they had gone back to sea, but we saw lots of seals, and, one day, we saw a whale!"

The conversation went on for a long time, with Carol adding bits of information and the younger girls asking lots of questions. It warranted another pot of tea and more cake, brought from Alice's house. It was bedtime when they all reluctantly separated. Lynette had been asleep for ages, and everyone was smothering yawns.

Life settled down for a while after the trip to Shetland. Johnny phoned twice a week to tell them how his job was progressing. He generally spoke to Audrey and Harry, but Carol was often in the room and was eager to speak to him. She didn't admit, even to herself, how much she missed him, and she didn't tell Harry that she had begun to dream about Johnny. However, her days were very busy in preparation for starting at university in September. Her A level results came out at the end of August and she had achieved good grades in all her subjects.

Pamela and the twins went into the fourth year of school at the beginning of September. The twins were pleased to be back at school, where they had lots of friends, but Pamela wasn't happy at all. Her friend, Wendy, had moved away and changed school, and, now that Carol had left, she felt very lonely there. She became increasingly moody at home and Harry was beginning to worry about her. He voiced his feelings to Audrey one evening when the younger girls were at choir practice and Carol was upstairs listening to records.

"I wonder why Pamela is so unhappy?" He said.

"It could be her hormones," Audrey replied. "I remember feeling very down when I was her age. I'm ashamed to say that I accused Mum and Dad of not loving me, that they only cared about their sons, which was so ridiculous. Mum was very good about it and reassured me that I was well loved. I got over it in time."

Harry was surprised. "I can't imagine you feeling like that. You always seemed so contented."

"Well, I always played the part of the good little girl if there was anyone else around. My bad moods were all for my parents, I'm afraid."

"So, if that's the case with Pamela, what can we do?"

"I'll have a chat with her, and maybe take her to town for some shopping; spoil her a bit. It's her birthday soon, and we'll be having the usual party, for Lynette this year too. It's hard to believe that she'll be a year old. Pamela can help me to choose a present for Lynette too.

"It's your birthday too, lovey. We now have two multiple birthday parties in the year." Said Harry, giving her a kiss.

"Oh, my birthday doesn't matter. I'll be forty three!"

"It matters to me lovey. You deserve to be spoilt too."

"You can buy me a vacuum cleaner. I'm fed up of cleaning the carpet with the Ewbank!"

"I'll buy you a vacuum cleaner lovey, but that's not a birthday present. Isn't there anything else you'd like?"

"I've got you and the children. I don't need anything else."

"If you're sure lovey." But Harry decided there and then to get her something special for her birthday. She was so generous and loving to all the family and she never asked for anything for herself. He would ask Carol to help him choose something.

Audrey took Pamela to town the following Saturday and they chose a new dress for the party. Audrey also got a good idea for a surprise present for the girl. They got a 'TinyTears' doll for Lynette, though Audrey thought that Lynette was a bit young to appreciate the 'real tears'. Pamela was delighted with it though. Audrey chuckled, thinking that Pamela might play with it more than her sister did. Although she was ten months older than the twins, Pamela seemed a lot younger at times, but Audrey didn't mind; she thought the children were all growing up far too quickly.

The day of the party arrived and Dorothy's house was full of the extended family. Alf and Norma, Bobby and Susan and Jenny and George were all there with their children. The only one of Harry and Audrey's children who wasn't there was Johnny, but he had phoned earlier to wish Pamela a happy birthday. She was delighted to be the recipient of a special phone call from her big brother, and she passed on some news from him to Carol. Kirsty had given birth to a baby girl and they were both well. Carol was pleased to hear the good news, and planned to phone Maggie the next day.

Among Pamela's presents was a very pretty watch from Audrey and Harry. She had thought the dress was her present, so she was doubly delighted.

Lynette seemed pleased with Tiny Tears but she much preferred the miniature piano from Dorothy and Fred. By the end of the day everyone was driven demented by its tinny sound. "I think we'll keep this in your house, Mum!" Laughed Audrey.

Harry surprised Audrey with a gift. He handed her the small package, which contained an exquisite silver locket and chain, delicately engraved with a rose. Inside were miniature pictures of her two children, Lynette and Johnny. "It's beautiful Harry, but you shouldn't have."

"I know, but I wanted to. Carol helped me to choose it."

Sian and Roberto arrived late; they had pink cheeks and bright eyes. They waited for a lull in the conversation before making their announcement. Harry already knew what they were going to say, as Roberto had had a quiet word with him the previous day. "We're getting married!" Sian blurted out, and she held up her left hand, which was now sporting a solitaire diamond ring.

Everyone began to talk at once. Carol went over to her sister and gave her a big hug. "I'm so happy for you; you were made for each other!" Then she kissed Roberto and said, "Well done, brother."

The twins wanted to know when the wedding would be, and Pamela said, "Can I be a bridesmaid?"

No one was really surprised. Even Dorothy and Fred had noticed the growing affection between the young couple since the revelation about Sian's parents back in the spring. Dorothy finally got her turn to congratulate them. "All the best Sian, Roberto. I know you will be very happy."

"We haven't set a date, but we thought about a spring wedding. Now that Roberto is working in Oldham he's going to look for a rented house, preferably in Greenfield, so that we can be near Auntie Jenny."

"But you'll get married at All Saints, won't you?" Said Alice. "It's a family tradition."

Harry had assumed that Roberto was Roman Catholic, but Roberto told him that the whole family had given up religion altogether after the war. Roberto was happy to get married in a protestant church; whatever made Sian happy.

Sian thought about Alice's question. "Oh, well, we haven't discussed it Grandma, but I've been living in Greenfield for six years now, and Colin was christened at St Mary's. I suppose I'd assumed we'd get married there." She looked across at Harry. "What do you think Dad?"

Harry pondered the question. For practical purposes, the majority of the family living in Newton Heath, and Roberto's uncle in Ancoats, it would make sense to have the wedding here, and the reception in the room over the co-op, but it was Sian and Roberto's wedding, so they should be allowed to choose where they got married. He said as much.

"It's your wedding lovey. If you want to get married in Greenfield, then that's ok. We've got plenty of cars nowadays, so it will be no trouble getting everyone there. Have a think about it, but whatever you decide will be fine by me."

Both Alice and Bill were disgruntled, but they said nothing more on the subject. They realised that Harry was right.

The party continued with the usual sing song round the piano and lots of laughter and fun, but Harry had become very quiet. He sat on the settee, deep in thought. Audrey noticed and decided to ask him what was bothering him, later, when they were alone.

When the girls were all in bed and the two of them were sitting by the fire, Audrey asked, "what's wrong lovey? You should be so happy for Sian and Roberto, but you seem so sad."

"I'm angry with myself," he said. "It's something I should have tackled a long time ago, but I've been procrastinating, like I did about my not being Sian's Father. I'm so stupid, because it's going to be so much harder now."

"What is?' She knelt down on the floor next to his chair and cuddled up to him, hoping to give him some moral support.

"Bronwyn's illness is hereditary, which means that one or more of her daughters may have inherited it. I hope to God that none of them are affected, but we won't know until they show symptoms, and then it will be too late. I should have told them; I'm such a coward!"

Audrey didn't understand immediately. She looked puzzled as she said, "too late, how? If one of them gets symptoms, we'll be here to look after her. She'll get all the love and care we can give her, just as we did with Bronwyn. It would be cruel to tell them now, when there is nothing they can do about it. They'd be better living in ignorance, surely?"

"But what about their children? They should all know that they have a chance of inheriting, and therefore passing on the illness to any children they may have. They need to be able to make an informed decision about it. And now Sian and Roberto are getting married. Shouldn't I have warned Roberto that he may have a sick wife in the future?"

"Roberto adores her. It won't make any difference to his decision to marry her. He'll love her and look after her no matter what. You would still have married Bronwyn if you had known, wouldn't you?"

"Yes, of course." He said, immediately.

"Well, there's your answer."

"They need to know though; I hate to spoil their happiness just now, but think how they will feel in the future if one of the girls does have the illness, and I never warned them. No, I have to tell them all."

"Even the twins and Pamela? Surely they are too young to be told. Let them enjoy their youth, then tell them later."

"It's going to be bad news whenever I tell them, There's never going to be a good time. What if one of them falls in love, like Sian and Roberto, and I tell them then. How then are they going to tell their boyfriend? At least if they are forewarned they can decide when, or if, they reveal it. I don't know how they are going to react, but I must tell them"

Audrey's eyes filled with tears. "I can't bear the thought of any of them becoming ill. Our beautiful girls. I wish that you didn't know about it being hereditary Harry, then we could just deal with it when and if it happens, as with any other illness."

"But we do know, so I'll tell them, and I'll tell them what Dilys told me when she realised that Bronwyn had what her father had suffered. She said that her father had a very happy, though short, life, surrounded by the love of his family. She said that none of us knows how long we have, so we should enjoy life as much as possible and be glad that we have a loving family. Not everyone has that."

Audrey took a deep breath. "So true," she whispered, thinking of the sad life that her first mother-in-law had.

Harry kissed her and said, "I'll tell them tomorrow. It's good that Sian and Roberto have stayed over with Mum and Dad. Everyone will be here apart from Johnny. We can tell him next time he's home. It's not something you can say over the phone."

The next morning all the girls and Roberto were gathered in Harry's living room. Dorothy had taken Lynette next door, having been told earlier what was happening.

"What's going on Dad?" Said Sian. She was astute enough to realise that this wasn't a happy gathering. Carol, of course, knew already; she was so in tune with Harry, and she had worked it out for herself some time ago. She sat between the twins on the settee, ready to give comfort wherever it was needed.

"What I am going to tell you all isn't pleasant, and if I could save you from this knowledge I would."

Carol felt Nerys wriggling with impatience. She sensed that Nerys wanted to say, 'get on with it Dad!' But she knew it was too serious, and very hard for their Dad to tell them.

"You know that your Mum had an illness called Huntington's Chorea?"

They all nodded.

"What I have never told you is that the illness is hereditary, that is, it runs in families."

"We know what hereditary means Dad," said Nerys.

"Shush!" Said Rosalind.

"Sorry." Nerys was contrite.

Harry went on. "Your grandfather, your Mum's dad, had the disease too. So she inherited it from him. The doctors still don't know a lot about it, but they told me that it is possible that it could be passed on to one, or more, of you girls. You need to know, because it might affect your decision to have children of your own."

Everyone was quiet, and Harry could sense that they were all aghast at what he had told them.

Sian was the first to speak. "Why did you have to tell us now? Roberto won't want to marry me in case I get it!"

Roberto answered quickly. "Cara Mia, I would love you no matter what, and if, in the future, you do have this terrible thing, then I will care for you." This seemed to satisfy Sian for the time being. She obviously hadn't yet thought properly about the reason Harry had told them. What to do about having children.

But Rosalind had latched onto that part of it. "But what will you do about having babies? There could be a risk to them."

Carol kept quiet. She wanted to know what her sisters thought. She had already made up her mind to avoid having children, or even getting married, for that matter, but she didn't want to influence anyone else. It was up to each of them to make decisions about their own life, and Carol felt strongly that no one should judge what others decided.

Sian looked at Roberto; her love for him shone out of her eyes. "I really want your babies," she said quietly.

Roberto pondered this for a while, and everyone seemed to be anxious to hear his answer. "I see it this way," he eventually said. " You may get this illness, but you may not. If we have no children just in case you have the illness, and then you do not have it, we will have lost all the happiness we would get from having children. If we have children, one or two, and then you do have the illness, we will worry about our children maybe getting it, and maybe they will blame us for having them. But, even in that case, by the time this horrible thing happens, there may be a cure or a treatment. If not in our time, in our children's time."

Harry was impressed with Roberto's reasoning.

Nerys was obviously impressed too. "You're right Roberto. We shouldn't let the possibility of becoming ill in the future affect how we live our lives. I think Dad was right to tell us of our risk though. We all need to make our own decisions about it. If Dad had kept us in blissful ignorance, how would we feel in the future if we got married and had half a dozen children?"

"But, what if we have half a dozen children, knowing our risk?" said Pamela.

"Well, that would be your decision and you would have to live by it. But the one thing you should do is to tell your future husband about your risk" Nerys replied.

"I'd never get a husband then!"

Roberto answered that one. "If he loves you enough, he will still marry you, and you can decide between the two of you what to do about children. If he does not love you enough, he is not worth bothering about."

"Anyway," said Nerys. "You're so gorgeous the lads'll be falling over themselves to go out with you. You'll be able to pick and choose who you marry!"

"Stupid, we all look alike!" Pamela retorted.

Rosalind joined in. "Alike, but not identical; not like we used to be. Yes we are all attractive; sorry to be big headed, but we are. Nerys is right, you are gorgeous."

Pamela was flabbergasted! She stared at the twins as if they had grown two heads! She hadn't noticed the subtle changes that had been occurring, but the twins obviously had, and Harry realised that Carol had too.

Harry was pleased that the girls had changed the subject for the moment. He hadn't noticed what they had noticed, but he looked more closely at them now. To him they were all individuals and he thought they were all beautiful, but he was more aware of the essence of them, rather than the look. He now realised that Pamela's hair seemed more lustrous and her dark brown eyes slightly bigger and more sparkling than her sisters. Her skin was clear and her cheekbones a slightly different shape; the turned up nose slightly less turned up. All these minor differences combined to make her looks outstanding. Of all his beautiful daughters she was the most beautiful. It made him infinitely sad to think that they all had this risk hanging over them. He hoped he had done the right thing in telling them the truth.

Carol knew what he was thinking and she spoke for the first time. "You did the right thing Dad. We needed to know, no matter how sad it makes us. We need to incorporate this knowledge into our lives, but live the best life we can; make the most of the life that you and Mum gave us. Yes, it'll always be at the back of our minds, but we can still enjoy life. We have a lovely family to support us. That's a lot more than some people have."

Nerys laughed, although it was a forced laugh. "Carol, you will make a great teacher. You do a good lecture!"

Everyone else laughed then; it served to lighten the moment.

Rosalind then said, "In the words of auntie Dorothy, why don't we put the kettle on?"

"Yes, you do that," said Carol. "I want to phone Maggie and Kirsty in Shetland to congratulate them about the baby. Is that ok dad? I won't talk for long."

"Yes of course, lovey. We all want to hear about the baby."

The telephone was in the hall, on a small table that had a seat attached. The others could hear Carol's voice, but not exactly what she was saying. They did hear her voice increase with excitement though, and her final words were clear. "That's fantastic, of course I will! I'll see you then; bye."

As she came back into the living room her eyes were bright with happy tears. "Kirsty wants me to be godmother to her baby, and she's called her Carol!"

"That's wonderful!" Said Harry. "When is the christening?"

They're having it the week before Christmas, so that I can go up when I'm on holiday from uni'. Maggie has thought of everything. Johnny has been invited too, so I can travel back home with him"

"Is Johnny being a godfather?" Asked Rosalind, handing a mug of tea to Carol.

"No, Andy is being godfather, but Johnny has been visiting Maggie and Kirsty now and again, so they wanted to invite him."

"Isn't Andy too old to be a godfather?" Said Nerys.

Harry laughed. " He's only 42; younger than me. I think he's got a good few years in him yet!"

Nerys blushed; she looked as though she was going to comment on Harry's age, but then thought better of it. "Oh yes, sorry Dad."

Harry laughed even more. It wasn't often that Nerys was lost for words. He was delighted that the news of the baby and Carol's trip up north had given all the girls something pleasant to think about. He was sure that there would be more questions about Bronwyn's illness in the future, and possibly tears, but, for the present, everyone could put it to the back of their minds.

Carol had settled in well at Manchester University, enjoying the lectures and study groups and making new friends. She was still living at home, as she was only a bus ride away and she loved being with Harry and Audrey and her sisters. Some of her new friends invited her to move into a student house with them but she was adamant, giving the excuse that it was much cheaper living at home.

She liked to be at home at the weekends when, if the weather was kind, they would all go to Greenfield and walk up on the moors with Jenny and George. Colin was now two and a half, and loved being in the carrier on his Dad's back as they rambled along the footpaths. Sian and Roberto were usually with the horses.

On a fine Saturday in late October, Harry and the girls were enjoying a cup of tea with Jenny and George before heading home after an invigorating walk on the moors. Sian and Roberto came in, smelling of horses and looking windswept and sun kissed.

"We've got some news!" Said Sian, excitedly. "We've got a house in Greenfield. A friend of Mavis's owns the house and his tenant is moving out. So we've been down to look at it this afternoon. It's on Chew Valley Road, almost opposite the post office, and it's got a lovely small garden at the front and a yard at the back; and it's got a bathroom. They don't all have a bathroom, you know."

Her delight was infectious. Everyone was smiling and asking questions.

"He's moving out after Christmas. The landlord wants to do a few repairs when it's empty, so he said we can start renting from the first of February." She looked at Roberto and he nodded, allowing her to tell all the news.

"We want to get married on the 12th of February, and we've decided to get married at All saints and have the reception at the co op, like you and Auntie Audrey did, Dad. Of course we have to ask the vicar if he can fit us in on that day. I'm sure he will though, because not many people get married in February." She finished out of breath, and waited anxiously for Harry's response.

"That's wonderful news lovey; the weather may be bad in February though."

"Oh, I'm sure it'll be fine. There can be some nice days in February, but anyway, it won't matter what the weather's like, the day will be perfect."

Harry looked at Roberto and Sian, who were bubbling over with happiness, and he agreed that it would be a perfect day.

Things settled down after this. There were no more events, apart from Christmas itself, which was always a big family affair, starting with the joint birthday party and continuing for several days.

This year there was also Carol's trip to Shetland.

She took two extra days off - her friends covering for her and promising to share their notes - giving her ample time to travel up to Aberdeen by train and catch the ferry to Lerwick in good time for the christening.

She was met at the dock by a very excited Kirsty with baby Carol in the pram, and a very different looking Johnny.

He was sporting a bushy ginger beard and his hair was longer than usual, curling around his ears. He had always been very self conscious about his ginger hair, and had preferred a very short style, almost a crew cut, during his teenage years. It seemed that Shetland had been good for him in the few weeks he had been living there. Carol immediately sensed that he had become much more confident, and strangely, more attractive. Her heart gave a strange lurch as she looked at him.

After she had greeted Kirsty and had a peep at the sleeping baby, she turned to Johnny. "You look like a viking; it suits you," she told him.

"Well, it keeps me warm. The wind up here is lazy, it doesn't go around you, it goes through you!" He laughed. "I stole that joke from Andy."

"Where is Andy? I thought he may have brought Mymie up to meet me."

Kirsty explained. "They are at our house. I said I wanted to meet you, and Johnny offered to walk down with me. They are having a cuppie with my mother."

Johnny took Carol's case, and the three of them set off to walk through the streets to Kirsty's home. The weather was dry but very windy. It was much wilder than the last time she had been here and Carol had to battle to keep herself upright. Kirsty didn't seem to notice it at all, though her baby was well wrapped up and the hood was up on the pram. She chattered animately all the way to the house. Carol was glad the she didn't need to respond, except for short answers; she could hardly catch her breath, and she was grateful when she saw Maggie waiting at the door.

The house felt extremely warm, and quiet, after the noisy fury of the wind. After she gave Mymie a hug, Carol sank gratefully into a chair and accepted the cup of tea from Maggie.

"My word, it's windy out there!' She gasped.

"Oh, it can get a lot more windy than this," said Andy. "I've known it to blow a full grown yow down the hillside. It's from the east today, but when it comes from the west it comes down the hill into Levenwick in such gusts that sometimes even an adult can be bowled over!"

Carol was suitably impressed, gasping at Andy's words, which pleased him no end. He loved to boast about the wildness of the weather.

"We wanted to pick you up at the ferry," said Mymie. "but Kirsty so much wanted to walk down with peerie Carol in the pram, and the weather is dry, so we thought that you would survive."

"Oh I was fine, and it was lovely to see Kirsty and Johnny waiting for me. I'm sure the wind has done me some good; blown the cobwebs away!"

144

The baby started to stir, so Kirsty picked her up and asked Carol if she would like to hold her. Carol was delighted and took the baby from Kirsty's arms.

Baby Carol looked up at her namesake and smiled. Carol examined the pretty face and blue eyes, the light covering of dark hair and the rosy cheeks. "Oh she is so beautiful!' She exclaimed. "You must be so proud of her Kirsty."

"Yes, she is beautiful, isn't she? Of course I think so, as I am her mother, but she is more than that. She is good and quiet - she hardly ever cries - and she is clever. She is less than three months old, but she watches everything, and, when I talk to her, she moves her mouth as though she is trying to say the words. Oh Carol, you don't know how much I love her!"

"I can see how much you love her, and I'm so happy for you." Carol looked around at the others in the room. Maggie was a proud and happy grandmother, Andy was beaming as though he was the baby's grandad and Mymie obviously loved the baby too. Even Johnny had a benevolent smile on his face. It seemed that the baby had brought all these people closer than ever. She was sure that baby Carol would grow up in a happy home, surrounded by caring people. She was so glad that she had followed her feelings when she discovered Kirsty on the deck of the ferry that time.

The christening was a lovely affair, though the weather was horrendous and everyone had to rush from cars to the church and back to Maggie and Kirsty's house.

Carol looked around at all the people enjoying the food and drink that Maggie had prepared. Kirsty's friends and quite a few of their parents, along with Maggie's friends from work, as well as some neighbours, were all relaxed and chatting happily. There was no feeling of disapproval at all. Carol made her way to Mymie's side and smiled at her. "I think you have been spreading your magic, Mymie. I don't detect a single bad thought."

Mymie gave her a conspiratorial grin. "It was worth it to give that lovely, peerie baby a good start in life. "

Carol gave Mymie a big hug. "I love you," she simply said.

"And I, you dearie."

Eight:

An Early Spring Wedding

Saturday the 12th of February was a bitter cold, frosty day, but it didn't spoil the wedding. Sian wore a long sleeved white satin dress and, instead of a veil, she had a hooded cape edged with white fur fabric; the whole ensemble made by Audrey. She had also made the bridesmaids blue dresses. Each sister also wore a blue Angora cardigan, knitted by Alice and Dorothy. Although Lynette was too young to be a bridesmaid, she also had a matching blue dress and cardigan; she looked adorable.

Harry felt proud as he walked his eldest daughter down the aisle. He beamed at all their friends and family, noting that old Auntie Elsie was there in the second row, despite the fact that she had loudly opposed the match. She would never miss attending a family gathering, though Harry felt sure that they hadn't heard the last of her disapproval. She glared at him as he passed.

Roberto was radiating joy as he stepped forward to take his bride's hand. His brother, Carlo, was best man and his Italian parents and siblings were in the front pew, Carla was looking as proud as Harry felt; her husband was smiling, but Harry sensed that he was not so happy.

The reception was held in the room above the co-op as usual. The only difference from previous parties being that the piano had been pushed back into a corner, and there was a disc jockey playing pop records. The Beatles, Cliff Richard and the Rolling Stones were favourites among the young members of the family, though the older ones would have preferred the piano.

After Harry had danced with Sian he moved around the room talking to everyone, making sure no one was left out. As he approached Auntie Elsie and Uncle Tom in their corner he saw that they were talking to the vicar and he couldn't help hearing what Elsie had to say.

"I assume you know, vicar, that the bride and groom are brother and sister? I'm surprised that you allowed them to be married in a christian church!"

The vicar was taken aback by the vicious comment. "I am aware of the unusual relationship that the young couple have." He replied. "They told me all about it when they first came to me about getting married. I have seen their birth certificates and I have spoken to Harry; I've known him for many years and he explained the circumstances of both Sian and Roberto's birth. I am absolutely sure that everything is above board and I am happy to marry such a loving young couple; Happy, as you should be Mrs Davies." At this he walked away.

Harry had to hide a smile at Elsie's outraged expression. It was obvious that she had thought the vicar ignorant of the circumstances and she had hoped to cause trouble. Instead, as usual, she had just caused trouble for herself.

Uncle Tom gave Harry a look of apology and held out his hand for Harry to shake.

"Well lad, Your first ones married. Does it make you feel old?"

"I suppose it does, a bit, Uncle Tom; but mostly I am really happy for them, which, in a way, makes me feel younger. Does that sound daft?"

"No lad, I know what you mean. After our eldest got married the house seemed a lot bigger and I felt that we would have more time to ourselves, but . . ." He looked at his wife, but she was taking no notice of him. He shrugged, and Harry sensed that he was used to being ignored.

"Can I get you another drink, Uncle Tom?" He asked.

"Aye lad, you can," he replied and he gave his wife a look that said 'don't you dare interfere!' Harry gathered that Elsie had taken the hint, because she said nothing, though her mouth was set in a thin line.

Continuing his circuit of the room, Harry stopped to talk to the Italian family. Until two days ago he hadn't seen Carla since the memorable day in 1944 when Roberto had been conceived. He had thought beforehand that he would feel awkward meeting Carla again, and he had especially worried about how Audrey would cope with meeting the mother of his son.

He needn't have worried. Carla's manner with Audrey was so natural and friendly that it seemed like the two women had been friends for a long time. Carla and Alberto were staying in Alice and Bill's spare room, and the rest of the family were in Dorothy's house. They had arrived two days earlier and had enjoyed being shown around Manchester. They had visited Louis and the extended family in Ancoats and were impressed with the thriving ice cream business.

"Harry, you must be so proud of all your daughters," said Carla. "They are all so beautiful, and so friendly. My Sophia loves them already. She has invited them all to visit us, but I hope that they do not all come at the same time!" She laughed. "We would not have room for all of them at one time."

"And I wouldn't be able to afford to send them all at once," laughed Harry. "Maybe they should all be looking for Saturday jobs, so that they can pay for it themselves."

They chatted in this way for a while, and then Harry asked the question that had been at the forefront of his mind. "You don't mind Roberto settling here, do you? I know he only planned to come over for a year initially."

"Oh no, I do not mind. Wherever he is happy makes me happy too. I had a feeling that he would stay here if he found you, though I would not ever have imagined that he would marry into your family. When he was growing up I was interested to see the English side of him - how you say - emerging?"

Harry nodded. "Yes, I agree. As soon as he said that he was my son I felt an affinity with him. I saw how much he looked like you, but he also felt part of me."

Carla smiled, fondly looking across at her son, who was now dancing the twist with all his sisters and his two younger brothers. "He was interested in all things English, even before I told him about you, and he was the best at speaking English in his school. Yes, he was meant to be here." Her husband, Alberto, didn't seem to agree. He turned away to talk to Uncle Louis, deliberately distancing himself from the conversation. Now Harry was sure that Alberto didn't approve of the match, but Carla seemed to be blissfully unaware of this, and so was Roberto. Harry hoped that Alberto would accept it in time.

He continued his circuit of the room and finally reached the table where his parents and Dorothy and Fred were sitting with Audrey. She was looking lovely in a navy and white dress. The DJ had just put on one of his favourite Cliff Richard songs - 'When the girl in your arms is the girl in your heart'. He held out his hands to his wife and said, "May I have this dance?' She blushed as she rose and walked into his arms. They waltzed all around the room while the youngsters stayed in the middle, just moving slowly to the romantic tune. It seemed that waltzing was just for the older generation now, but Harry didn't mind; he was dancing with the woman he loved and his family were happy. What more could a man want?

The young couple weren't having a honeymoon. They had invested all their money in their cosy little house. The older members of the family had been generous with wedding presents, so they had plenty of towels, bedding, kitchen equipment and even a pretty clock for the mantlepiece. All the furniture was second hand, except for the bed, which had been made by Uncle Bobby. His talent with carpentry was legendary. Harry's present was the mattress.

Harry drove them to their new home after the reception, and then returned home to find all the older generation in Dorothy's house, having the inevitable cup of tea. The living room was bursting at the seams, but no one seemed to mind. The youngsters were all in Harry's house, listening to records. It seemed that no one wanted to go to bed yet.

"It was a lovely wedding, Harry," said Alice. "The first of many, I imagine, now the girls are growing up."

"I hope we don't have another one too soon though Mum. I've found it's quite expensive, having daughters. Anyway, I want them to have some fun before they settle down. The twins and Pamela have already said that they'd like to visit Italy. I need to save up for the next big expenditure."

"You and Audrey should come and visit us, Harry. You will be surprised how Cassino has changed since you were there. The town has been rebuilt, and there is a most lovely cemetery for the Polish soldiers up on the hillside. It is good to remember them." Said Carla.

Harry felt very sad, thinking of over a thousand Polish men who had perished in the battle of Monte Cassino. "I think I may like to go and pay my respects to those brave men. As you say, Carla, it is good to remember what they did to keep the world free."

"Come next year, if you can. We would like to have you, would not we, Alberto?" Said Carla.

Alberto was put on the spot. It was obvious to Harry that he would rather they didn't accept, but it was also obvious that he adored his wife and would do anything to please her, so he said, "of course, you must come."

Harry looked over to Audrey. She was smiling at him and he could sense excitement at her thought of visiting Italy. He determined then that he would take her there. She deserved a nice holiday; she was always looking after other people and she had made a wonderful job of bringing up his daughters, especially during Bronwen's illness. The fact that his daughters had grown into mature, well adjusted young women was due in no small part to Audrey's love and affection.

He smiled. "Yes, I think we will try to come over next year, all being well. Thank you Alberto and Carla."

Dorothy was sitting in the corner of the settee, gently nodding off. This seemed to be the cue for everyone to go to bed. Harry was amazed to see that it was after one in the morning. He took Audrey's hands and pulled her up from her perch on the floor. "Come on lovey, time for bed."

Alberto accompanied them next door to get his children, so that Fred could lock up.

In Harry's house the girls had brought the record player downstairs. They seemed to have exhausted themselves, as no one was dancing. Carla and Alberto's two sons were lolling on the settee, humming along to Cliff's song, 'Livin' Doll". Their sister was in the rocking chair and all Harry's girls were sprawling on the floor.

"Come on, time for bed," said Harry. The boys got up immediately; they had seen their father at the door. Sophia said, "Oh Papa, cannot we just listen to one more song?"

Harry had to laugh because, just in the middle of saying this, Sophia gave such an enormous yawn, it was obvious that she was nearly asleep.

Alberto didn't need to speak, he just gave Sophia a look that brooked no argument. She immediately got up and said, "Goodnight Pamela, Nerys, Rosalind and Carol. I have had a good day." Her English was perfect. It made Carol wish that she had studied Italian instead of French.

"Buona notte, Sophia, Carlo and Angelo," said Carol. At least she could say goodnight in Italian. It was a start.

The next day Carla's family and Harry's had been invited to Sian and Roberto's house for Sunday dinner. Harry had suggested that Sian and Roberto may have preferred to have their first Sunday alone, but they were both adamant that they wanted the family there, so they set off early, so that Audrey and the others could help with the cooking if needed. They left Lynette with her two doting grandmas.

They couldn't all fit in Harry's car, so he borrowed Fred's car, and Audrey drove his. Even so it was a tight fit, with four girls squashed into the back seat of one car and three Italian youngsters in the other one.

Sian was panicking when they got there. "Dad, I forgot about chairs; we've only got four, can you go to Auntie

Jenny's and ask her if we can borrow some chairs? Oh, and knives and forks." She was nearly in tears.

"Ok lovey, we'll sort it. It'll still be a squeeze though. We might have to have two sittings."

Alberto offered to go with him, so the two men got back into Harry's car to drive round to Jenny's.

"I'll help with the food," said Audrey. "Have you got enough potatoes peeled?"

"Oh, I'm not sure Auntie Audrey. I've never cooked for so many before!"

"Well, not to worry, we'll soon have it organised. Carol, why don't you take everyone down to the river to feed the ducks, I've brought this half loaf of stale bread. You see Sian, you're not the only one unsure of how much food to prepare. I bought far too much bread last week."

"I will stay here and help, if that is alright?" Said Carla.

"Oh thanks, er . . ." said Sian.

"You may call me Mama if you like," said Carla. "As you are now my daughter in law."

"I would love that, Mama," said Sian. Her tears had dried and her smile was infectious. Audrey and Carla were smiling with her.

Carol marshalled all the youngsters together and they set off for the river. Roberto refused to go with them. He wanted to stay and help his wife with the meal.

The three women set to work in the large kitchen, while Roberto prepared the table. Uncle Alf had acquired an extending table for them. No one knew where Alf got all the second hand furniture and other items that the family needed, but he always seemed to know somebody who knew somebody. This table was ideal for the young couple, as it was just a relatively small square when not extended, but it had two pull out leaves, and then another section that opened out in the middle, making ample room for a large group.

The table would have been wasted in the council houses on Amos Avenue, as they had a small kitchen, and the living room, where most people had a dining table, was just about big enough for a table with two extending leaves, but not the extra bit in the middle.

Sian and Roberto's stone cottage had a square front living room, big enough for a three piece suite and a sideboard, with a small television in the corner. The door from the living room opened into a large kitchen, which had a modern gas stove and sink unit against the back wall, and a kitchen cabinet on the side wall. The stone flagged floor of the room would have been empty without the table and four dining chairs. Now that Roberto had opened out the table and covered it with a white bed sheet for a cloth, the women could admire its size.

"Gosh, it's enormous!" gasped Audrey. "I know Alf said it would be perfect for your kitchen, now I can see what he meant."

"I have not seen a table that big in a house," said Carla.

Sian looked really proud of her table. At least she had something right.

By the time Harry and Alberto came back with four more chairs and an assortment of knives and forks, there was an enormous pan of potatoes and another of carrots on the stove, a large joint of lamb was nearly ready in the oven, as Sian had put it in much earlier, and there was a large dish of roast potatoes too. Everything smelled delicious.

The meal was ready, but the young people hadn't arrived back yet. Harry was concerned. He could sense that something was wrong, but he didn't want to alarm anyone, so he said, "I'll go down and hurry them up. Why don't you five have your dinner first, and then I can have mine with the children when we get back. That should solve the seating problem"

The others agreed that it was a good idea, and Harry set off down Greenbridge Lane to the river. Thankfully, this river was nothing like the notoriously fierce Red River between Newton Heath and Clayton. This was actually Chew Brook, which flowed into the river Tame further down the valley. It was wide and shallow here, and very gentle, except perhaps in times of flood.

He could sense the consternation from the group of young people as he approached them, but he was relieved to also feel that nobody was hurt. He found them just beyond the bridge on the banks of the brook. Everyone was standing in a group around one person who was sitting on a boulder, and looking extremely wet.

"It had to be you, Nerys," said Harry as he took in the scene. "What did you do?"

"She was showing off Dad, as usual," said Pamela. "Standing on a rock in the water and trying to get the ducks to come to her. She was enticing them with a piece of bread, and then she slipped off the rock and landed in the water. Why she couldn't stand on the island, I don't know." They all looked across to the small, wooded island in the middle of the flow. Pamela continued, "Angelo waded in to rescue her before we could stop him."

It was then that Harry noticed that sixteen year old Angelo was also wet, though it was mostly his trousers and shoes. He was shivering violently, so Harry took off his jacket and put it around the boy's shoulders. "Come on, we need to get you back to the house and get you warm. Nerys, you should have known better than to do something so stupid, especially in February!"

"But, I didn't mean to fall in . . . !"

"Of course you didn't mean to; you never mean to do silly things, but you often do them anyway. You need to start growing up Nerys!" Harry was unusually sharp with Nerys, and he knew he was being unfair, but, seeing Angelo shivering had upset him. The lad was their guest and he had failed to look after him.

Sophia decided then to give her opinion. "Uncle Harry, Angelo should not have gone into the water after Nerys. We could all see that it was shallow, and she was not in danger, but he likes to be the brave protector."

Harry smiled at Sophia; she at least seemed to be sensible. "You're right Sophia. We should just be glad that no one was hurt." He turned to Nerys, who was squelching along behind all the others with tears in her eyes and a very stubborn look on her face. "Come on lovey, let's get you warm." He put his arm around her and she gave him a grateful look. She had already forgiven him for shouting at her.

They arrived back in the house just as the others were finishing their dinner. Audrey jumped up from the table in alarm when she saw the dripping teenagers. "Oh no, whatever has happened?" She cried.

Pamela spoke first. "Don't worry Mum, nobody is hurt. Nerys got very wet and Angelo got a bit wet rescuing her out of the water."

Roberto quickly finished his meal and took his brother upstairs to find some dry clothes for him. Sian followed him. "Come on, Nerys," she said. "You can go into the spare bedroom and put some of my clothes on."

Audrey and Carla then took over the organisation of the meal for Harry and the youngsters. Alberto said nothing about the incident, but he gave Sophia and Carlo a look which said that he would be asking questions later.

The meal finished and tidied away, everyone was sitting in the cosy living room, where the fire was blazing merrily. By unspoken agreement, nobody mentioned the water incident, instead they complimented Sian on the meal and talked about the wedding.

"It was a lovely day yesterday," said Carla. "I like the way your family all work together, Harry. The bride and bridesmaid's dresses and cardigans, all made by you, Audrey, and your mother and Harry's mother. You are all artists."

"Oh I don't know about that," said Audrey, modestly. "I've always enjoyed sewing, but my Mum and Auntie Alice are brilliant knitters."

"I agree with you Carla," said Harry. "I'm so grateful that the women of our family are so talented. I can't imagine how much the wedding would have cost if we'd had to buy all those clothes ready made."

"The men are talented too," said Carla. "Your brother, Bobby makes lovely things with wood, and you can repair wireless and television, Harry."

Embarrassed, Harry said, "Oh it's something I learned before the war. It's just a hobby now." He changed the subject. "I believe you are a talented wine maker Alberto?'

It was Alberto's turn to be embarrassed. "It is not a talent, Harry. The goodness of the wine comes from the grapes, and the vines were planted many years ago by Carla's late father."

"Ah yes, I remember the wine that Carlo had made. It is still the only form of alcohol that I enjoy. Beer does nothing for me." He suddenly remembered the outcome of his enjoyment of the wine. He looked askance at Carla and she blushed. She also remembered that it was after she and Harry had drunk several glasses of her father's wine that Roberto had been conceived. Both Alberto and Audrey also noticed the look and realised what it meant. Harry knew that he needn't worry about Audrey. He had told her what had happened and she was secure in his love for her. He wasn't so sure about Alberto though. He hoped that his comment about the wine didn't cause any trouble.

To relieve any pressure, Harry brought Carlo and Angelo into the conversation. "What about you boys, do you enjoy wine making?"

Carlo, the older of the two, replied. "We both help with the grape harvest and the wine making, but I cannot say that I really enjoy it. It is something that we have always done since we were small. I hope to go to university next year to study medicine."

Angelo commented. "Carlo is the clever one; I would like to have a gelato - ice cream shop - like Uncle Louis."

Alberto was obviously proud of his sons. "You will both be very good at your chosen work and you will work hard, like your brother Roberto." He turned to Roberto, who was sitting on the floor with his arm around Sian. "I am pleased that you have worked hard at your chosen work Roberto."

Roberto flushed with pleasure at this praise. Harry sensed that Roberto wasn't praised very often by his stepfather.

"And what about you, Sophia; have you decided what you would like to do when you leave school?" Harry asked.

"I do not know yet. I think I may be a nurse , like my Aunt, or maybe even a doctor, like Carlo, though I do not know if I am clever enough. Sometimes I think that I would just like to stay and work on the farm and in the vineyard."

"There is not enough work in the farm and vineyard for you, Sophia. Your Mama and I are not ready to retire, not for many years," Alberto replied. This obviously a subject that had come up previously.

"I know," she sighed. "That is why I do not know what I want to do."

"There's plenty of time for you to decide though," said Audrey. "You are fourteen aren't you? The same as the twins."

"Yes, that is right."

"Then you can just enjoy your life and leave the decisions until later."

"That is exactly what I say to her," said Carla, smiling. "We mothers know, do we not?"

Audrey agreed, pleased that Carla accepted her role as mother to all the girls. "Shall we have another cup of tea?"

Carol laughed. "Auntie Audrey you are so like your Mum when it comes to a cup of tea! Come on, Sian; we'll put the kettle on in your new kitchen."

While the two girls were in the kitchen, Sian confided in Carol. "I've got something to tell you . . . "

"You're pregnant!" Carol smiled at her sister and gave her a hug.

"How did you know? I only just realised myself; I told Roberto this morning and he's over the moon, but wondering how to tell our parents, because, obviously, it happened before we were married."

"I can see that you're blooming, and I think that Dad knows too. Nothing gets past him, as you know. He'll be sorry that you didn't wait, but he'll be ok. You know Dad, he takes everything in his stride. I think you should tell them all soon though. Otherwise you'll be telling Roberto's family in a letter. Why don't you tell them all now, when they've got a cuppa? That way you'll get the whole thing over in one go. I'll get Roberto in to help with the teas." She said, as she went to get her brother.

Nine:

Life Decisions

Pamela felt intransigent; she knew that was the right word, because she had looked it up. *'unwilling or refusing to change one's views, or agree with something'*

It was nearing the end of the summer term and it was parent's evening at her school. When Mum and Dad got home, she knew they were going to try to get her to agree, but she was going to be intransigent. She was going to do what she wanted to do; not what other people expected her to do.

She was sitting in the rocking chair with her bare feet on the dog's back and her favourite book in her hands. She wasn't reading yet, because she was mentally anticipating the argument she was going to have with her parents when they arrived home from the parent's evening at her school.

Carol, who was sitting opposite, in the other armchair, noted the determined look on her sister's face and she sensed waves of animosity radiating from her. She knew that it wasn't anything that she personally had done to upset Pamela, and it was nothing to do with the twins either. She looked up to the ceiling as several thumps in time with the loud music indicated that the twins were dancing to a Rolling Stones record.

"I hope they don't wake Lynette with all that racket," she said.

"What? Oh, I don't think so," said Pamela, absentmindedly. "She can sleep through a hurricane, that one."

"Do you want to talk about it?'

"What," she said again, this time she looked up at Carol but said nothing more.

"There's obviously something on your mind.Is it anything I can help with?"

"No, I just want to read my book, but you keep interrupting me!"

Carol looked pointedly at the book, which was still closed on Pamela's lap. "Carry on then," she calmly said, and turned back to her own book.

Pamela opened her book and raised it up so that Carol couldn't see her face. She didn't lower the book until, thirty minutes later, they heard Harry and Audrey coming in the back door. As Pamela looked over the top of the book Carol could tell that her sister's dilemma had something to do with the parent's evening. She got up and went into the kitchen.

"I'll put the kettle on," she said. "but you'll have to make your own tea; I promised to go over to Grandma's to help her wind some wool." She gave Harry a meaningful look, so he knew that she was making herself scarce.

Audrey set about making the tea while Harry went into the living room, where Pamela was again pretending to read. Flossie jumped up from under Pamela's feet, upsetting the book in the process. Harry stroked the dog and then sat in the chair that Carol had just vacated.

"Pamela, lovey," he said, gently. "You're not in trouble, but we need to talk about what your teacher has told us."

She picked up the book and glared at him, but she said nothing.

"Miss Booth says that you've lost interest in all your studies, except English, and that your homework has been well below your usual standard. This has been going on for a few months."

Looking down at her feet, Pamela said, "Well, it's all boring!"

"You've never found it boring before; what has changed?"

"I suppose it isn't all boring, but I'm fed up of the teachers, especially the science teachers, telling me what I could be if I go to university. I don't want to go to university, and I don't want to be a doctor. I've told them, but they don't listen!"

"Yes, Miss Booth said that you have the ability to become a doctor, or any other profession you'd like to do, but not if you don't work at it. I know you've always said that you want to be a nurse with the twins . . ."

"But that's just it, no one is listening to me! I don't want to be a nurse, or a doctor, or anything else to do with science. I hate science!" She burst into angry tears.

Audrey came in with the tea just then. She gave Pamela a mug of tea, and then sat on the settee and leaned forward to talk to her. " Don't get upset lovey. We only want you to be happy. Tell us what you would like to do."

Pamela looked up with tears dripping off her lashes. "I want to be a librarian."

The twins, unfortunately, chose that moment to come into the room. "What !" Shouted Nerys. "You don't want to be a nurse at Crumpsall with us; since when?"

"Pam, how can you not want to be with us? We always want to be together," said Rosalind, a little more gently.

"You see Mum, no one ever listens to me!" She looked around at her sisters and Harry, and then down at the dog, who had put her head in Pamela's lap, knowing she was upset. She stroked the dog's head. "Everyone assumes that I want what the twins want, just because we all said we wanted to be nurses when we were about five. Well, I've changed my mind, ok? It is allowed, you know."

"Well I think that's rotten!" Shouted Nerys. And she stormed out of the room, slammed the door and stamped up the stairs. Rosalind just looked sadly at her sister as if she didn't believe what she was hearing.

"Here Rosalind, you have my cup of tea and I'll go and get another," said Audrey, patting the settee to encourage her to sit down. She looked imploringly at Harry as she went into the kitchen.

Harry now leaned forward to speak to Pamela. He had known for some time that there was something amiss, but he had assumed the problem was hormonal. He realised now that he was guilty of not taking enough notice of Pamela as an individual. He had been lumping all the girls together in his mind as if they were one person. What else had he failed to notice? He decided there and then to speak to each girl individually to make sure they were all happy.

"Pamela, are you absolutely sure that this is what you want? You may find it difficult to change your mind later on."

"I am sure Dad; I love reading and I love books. I even like arranging them on the shelves. It is what I want."

"If you become a librarian you won't be able to sit in a corner reading a book, lovey. Do you even know what the job entails? I must admit that I don't really know myself. You might find yourself standing behind a desk, stamping books and telling people to keep quiet."

"Well, er, I can advise people what books to read and, er, I like organising the shelves."

"I think you need to find out a lot more about it before you finally decide. Ask Miss Booth if you can spend some time with the school librarian, I'll ask our librarian, and I think that you should learn what a librarian in a big library does. I'll find out if you can spend a couple of Saturdays at Central Library in town. In the meantime, I want you to work at all your studies, even the science, Pamela," he insisted, as she pulled a face at that. "I imagine that a librarian needs to be knowledgeable in all fields, so don't think that it's an easy job. You can't advise someone on which books to read in a science subject if you don't know anything about science, can you?" His intense gaze unnerved her a little, but she had to agree that his reasoning was sound.

"Yes, I suppose you're right Dad. I will work harder, but it won't make me like science any better."

"That's good lovey. I'll make some enquiries tomorrow."

Rosalind had been very quiet during this conversation. She sipped her tea and looked from her dad to Pamela, tears forming in her eyes."

Harry felt her pain. "What is it lovey? Are you sad that Pamela won't be at Crumpsall with you?'

"Well, yes; we had it all planned. We would get the GCEs we need and we would all be cadets together, until Pam became eighteen and started as a student; then she would be able to tell us everything about being a student, so me and Nerys would be ahead of everyone else when we start as students. It would be so much fun too, to get everyone mixed up about which one of us is which. It won't be half as much fun without Pam," she sobbed.

"Work isn't supposed to be fun, lovey, although it helps if you enjoy your work, as I do. If Pamela just went ahead with nursing so that she didn't upset you, that wouldn't be much fun for her, would it? Anyway, there'll always be fun for you with Nerys around."

"I suppose so," she replied, then looked at Pamela. "I suppose it will be better for you if you can become a librarian, but I'll miss you a lot."

Pamela went over and hugged her sister. "Thanks Ros; will you tell Nerys I didn't mean to upset her?"

Rosalind laughed. "Coward! yes, I'll tell her for you, but you can take my turn with the washing up!"

Everyone laughed at that and Flossie wagged her tail, happy that everyone was ok.

Rosalind went upstairs to talk to her twin. A loud voice was heard, and then Rosalind's quieter voice, calming her sister, and then a long, quiet conversation.

"I think she's appeased," said Harry, smiling.

"Rosalind certainly has your gift for calming people," said Audrey.

"I wish I did," said Pamela. "I'm always rubbing Nerys up the wrong way."

"I wouldn't worry about it lovey. Nerys is great fun, but she is a loose cannon at times too. " said Harry.

Harry looked at his daughter. He loved her so much, but he was disappointed that she didn't want to be a doctor, and he didn't think that she would work hard enough to become a librarian. He was sure that the work she envisaged was that of a library assistant but, if she did that, it would be such a waste of her superb brain. She was definitely the cleverest of all the girls. Even Carol had had to work hard to get her place in university. Pamela would only have to apply herself a little more and she would sail through a university course. It saddened him that she had lost interest in her studies; saddened, and frightened him, as he sometimes got the shivery feeling of foreboding that he used to get with Bronwyn when he thought of Pamela.

169

He could only hope that he was wrong. He couldn't bear the thought that one of his beautiful daughters would succumb to the dreadful disease. So he did what he always seemed able to do; he pushed it to the back of his mind and planned how he could make all his girls happy.

Following up on his promise, Harry spoke to the librarian at his school and found out a lot about the job. Apparently there was a university course - Library Science - that covered everything needed to become a librarian. It was not an easy course, as a librarian, it seemed, needed to know something about everything. Pamela would need good grades in five 'O' Level GCEs and two 'A' levels. He passed the information to Pamela, who seemed undaunted by the prospect of working for her grades. It was obvious that she hadn't changed her mind about becoming a librarian. He could only hope that she would continue to work at her studies.

Miss Booth had organised work experience for Pamela at Central Library, the enormous round building next to the Town Hall in Manchester. She was to spend the last three Saturdays of the summer term there.

She was extremely nervous about going there at first and asked Harry if he would go with her. "I'll go with you as far as the information desk," he said. "But you need to speak for yourself when we get there. It'll be good experience for you."

Pamela pouted at this, but agreed, and the first Saturday found father and daughter on the number 25 bus to town.

Harry didn't like to drive into the centre of Manchester, especially on a Saturday, when the streets were thronged with shoppers and costermongers would be wheeling their barrows to Church Street. Besides, he enjoyed travelling by bus from time to time.

As they entered the imposing foyer, Pamela looked across to the enquiries desk and smiled. Harry felt, rather than saw, the smile, and he looked across to see what had delighted his daughter. There was a young man behind the desk. He looked just an ordinary young man to Harry. He had blonde hair in a Beatles style cut, blue eyes behind black-rimmed glasses and a pleasant smile. He was wearing a pale blue suit, which Harry thought looked a little out of place in a library, but Pamela obviously liked what she was seeing.

"You can go now Dad, I'll be alright. Thanks for coming with me."

Harry didn't know whether to be pleased or worried. It was the most interest he had sensed from Pamela for a long time, but she was still only fifteen and he wasn't sure that she should be interested in boys yet. Anyway, he thought, she can't get into any trouble in a library. He leaned forward to kiss Pamela, but she moved away, saying, "Dad, don't kiss me in here!"

"Ok lovey, I hope you have a good day. See you at teatime." He walked back to Oldham Street for his bus, marvelling how quickly his girls were growing up.

Everyone was around the table at teatime. As they all tucked into generous helpings of shepherd's pie, it was evident to at least three people that Pamela was in high spirits. They didn't need to see the sparkle in her eyes, the heightened colour in her cheeks, or the energy with which she attacked her meal; her happiness was palpable.

As they finished eating Carol spoke. "Well, I think you enjoyed your day at the library, Pamela." It wasn't a question.

"Oh yes, it was fantastic. I knew that was what I wanted to do. Now I'm absolutely sure. I had a great time; I learned a lot, and the staff there are lovely!"

Rosalind gave her a knowing look. "Tell us about the boy then!"

Pamela blushed even more deeply and looked across at Harry and Audrey, who were waiting anxiously for her answer.

"It's no good pretending you don't know what Ros means," said Nerys. "It's obvious that you've met a boy. What's he like, and when are you bringing him home for us all to meet?"

"Oh, alright; he's called Alan McCoy, and he's the nicest person I've ever met. Mrs Barnes, the librarian, asked him to show me round, and he was so good, showing me all the departments and the different kinds of books, and then we had our packed lunches together in St Peter's square. It was such a lovely day." She sighed.

"He starts at the university in September, studying Library science. He's doing voluntary work at the library on Saturdays. He lives in Moston, so he's not far away. He's asked if I'd like to go to the pictures with him next week. I can, can't I Dad?"

Harry was taken aback. "Oh, I'm not sure lovey, You're not even sixteen . . . "

"Oh Dad, I'm nearly sixteen, and there are younger girls at school who have boyfriends."

"Well, I think I'd rather meet him first. Maybe if he comes here early enough to pick you up, so we can talk to him first, and you go to the Pavilion, so that you're not far away." He looked at Audrey. "I think that would be ok; what do you think Audrey?"

Audrey looked at Pamela, her favourite, though she would never admit it. "Oh you are growing up far too quickly, but I think you will be sensible. Bring Alan to see us and then, as long as you go straight to the pictures and come straight back, that'll be ok."

Pamela bestowed her beautiful smile on Audrey. "Oh thanks Mum. I will be sensible, and you'll like Alan, he is so kind."

Nerys had to have the last word. "Does this mean we can have boyfriends too, Dad?"

Harry couldn't help laughing. "Do you have someone in mind Nerys?" He quipped.

"No, but I could start looking. It's no use looking at the lads at school though; they're all minging!"

"Minging, whatever does that mean?" Harry asked.

Rosalind was giggling as she answered for her sister. "It means that they are horrible and not worth looking at. Mind you, Malcolm Smith is quite acceptable!"

"You must be joking!" Nerys replied, "He's a swot; always got his nose in a book!"

"Yes, but it's a very nice nose," Rosalind laughed.

"He hasn't spoken to you, has he? You can't have a boyfriend before I do, Ros!"

"No, he hasn't spoken to me. Does he ever speak to anyone? I wouldn't mind if he did though."

Nerys got a mischievous look in her eye. "shall I speak to him? I could say 'my sister fancies you'"

"Don't you dare! I'll never speak to you again if you do that. Anyway, you just said I can't have a boyfriend before you. I'd rather not go out with a lad from school though. Everyone will be talking about it."

Harry was amused at the way the conversation had developed, but he was also disturbed. His girls were growing up too fast, Audrey was right, and he didn't feel ready for it. He looked at Carol; she would be twenty in December, but she didn't seem inclined to get a boyfriend. He sensed the reason, and it gave him some relief, but also sadness. Carol smiled back at him; she knew what he was thinking.

Just after tea Johnny arrived.

Audrey jumped up and hugged him. "What a lovely surprise! I thought you weren't coming home until

Tuesday." She exclaimed, and then stood back to look at him. "Oh, you still have the beard; I thought you may have shaved it off for the summer . . ."

"I know Mum, you're not sure if you like it, but I've got used to it and all my friends like it."

"Well I like it," said Nerys. "I think you look really handsome Johnny. I'm glad you kept the beard. Have you got a girlfriend yet?"

"Give the lad chance to get through the door before you fire questions at him!" Said Harry. "Have you had your tea Johnny?"

"Yes thanks Uncle Harry. Grandma just asked me that too. I went there first to drop off my case. I'm earlier than expected because I had the chance to car share with one of the other teachers, who was going to Edinburgh; he already had a cabin booked on the ferry, so we were able to share. We took turns driving from Aberdeen to Edinburgh, and then I only had to get the train from there. I would have been home earlier in the day, but I was told that the Manchester train I was hoping to get was going to be full, so I waited for the next one. I had something to eat on the train, so I just need a proper cup of tea now. You can never get a decent cuppa on a train."

"I'll put the kettle on," said Audrey, rushing into the kitchen as though her son's life depended on a decent cup of tea.

Ten:

A Boyfriend, A Baby and Football

The family's meeting with Alan went well, though he was a little overwhelmed by Pamela's sisters, who bombarded him with questions. Harry was impressed with the young man. He was confident enough to look Harry in the eye as he reassured him that he would look after Pamela and bring her home immediately after the film finished.

They arrived back in good time and Pamela invited Alan in for a cuppa. The twins were there with Harry and Audrey. Carol was next door, chatting to Johnny and his grandparents.

"What film did you see?" Asked Nerys.

"It was that new musical, The Sound of Music," said Pamela. "Oh it was so lovely - romantic and sad, but with a happy ending, and all the songs are brilliant!"

"I don't suppose that would have been your choice of film, Alan?" Said Harry. "I imagine you would prefer a western, or something with a bit of action.

"Oh no Mr Roberts; I really enjoyed it. I'm quite keen on music, and the story is based during the war, which I found really interesting. It's based on a true story, apparently"

Harry thought that Alan was just being polite, but he didn't comment.

"I think you and Mum would like the film, Dad," said Pamela. "It's set in Austria; you were there in the war, weren't you?"

Harry gave a sad smile. "It was just after the war ended. We stayed in an Austrian town for a long while, helping to rebuild and settle the local people. They had had a very hard time of it." He was quiet for a while, remembering his time in Klagenfurt; In particular he thought of the little dog he had left there with a farmer and his daughter. A bittersweet memory.

"I'd like to see that film, Harry," said Audrey

"Shall we go on Monday then? We'll be in Greenfield tomorrow, so we would be back too late." Harry replied.

"That'd be lovely."

"Can we go with you Dad?" Nerys piped up. "We love a good musical, don't we Ros?" Rosalind nodded excitedly.

Harry looked at Audrey and she nodded. "Ok, if Carol and Pamela can babysit, we'll all go, but don't forget that you have to be up early for school on Tuesday."

"If Carol wants to go with you I don't mind babysitting," said Pamela. "Lynette never wakes up anyway, and I'll get some peace and quiet to read my book."

Carol and Johnny were talking about football with Fred, Johnny's grandad. "I think England have a good chance in the World Cup this year," said Fred. "We've got a really good team. I'm going to get on to Granada rentals this week to get a better television. This one is much too small for watching a good football match. If England get to the final I think we'll invite everyone round to watch the match. The final is on the 30th of July. So not long now."

"Don't get your hopes up Grandad. There are some really good teams. I think West Germany are favourites to win." Said Johnny.

"Oh I hope they don't win," said Carol. "They'll be gloating forever!"

"Don't worry lovey. I've got a feeling that this year will be our year, just you wait and see." Said Fred.

Harry and the twins and Flossie went to Greenfield the next day. Audrey wanted to get on with some sewing and Carol had an assignment to finish. Pamela again turned down the chance of some fresh air and exercise in favour of reading her latest library book. Harry tried to encourage her to go with them, but she was adamant.

"We'll call on Sian and Roberto first," said Harry as he drove into Greenfield. The baby is due in two weeks, so I don't expect they will be out with the horses. Then we'll go round to see if Jenny and George want to join us."

They arrived just as Roberto was leaving the house, obviously in a state of panic.

"Oh Dad, thank goodness. The baby has started. I have to go over to the telephone to ask for an ambulance to take us to the hospital!"

"I'll take you, it'll be quicker," said Harry; He turned to the twins. "Can you two walk to Auntie Jenny's. You know the way, don't you?"

"Of course we do Dad. Flossie knows the way too." said Nerys, "Can we see Sian first, to wish her good luck?"

Sian was sitting on the settee, looking quite calm. "Are you sure you're in labour?" Rosalind asked.

"Of course I'm sure. The contractions are every five minutes. I'm just having a rest - oh no - here comes the next one!"

Roberto rushed to his wife's side. "Cara mia, what can I do?"

Sian grabbed his hand and squeezed as hard as she could whilst gasping. She finally relaxed and was able to say, "Just get me to the hospital!"

Harry was ready. "Come on lovey, let's get you into the car." Roberto supported her as he helped her to the car and the girls waved them off.

"I hope they get there in time," said Rosalind. "I wouldn't like to have a baby in a car."

"I wouldn't like to have a baby anywhere; too painful!" Nerys replied. "Come on, let's get to Auntie Jenny's and tell her the news."

The girls were drinking tea at Jenny's when Harry got there.

"Here, get this cuppa down you," said Jenny. "Did you manage to get there before the baby arrived?"

"Yes, the nurse took her straight through and Roberto said he'll ring here as soon as he has any news."

"I don't suppose you want to go up on the moors now?" Said George. He looked disappointed.

"Oh, I'm not sure; what do you girls want to do? I don't know how long it'll be before Roberto rings." Harry replied.

Before the girls could reply, three year old Colin piped up, "Aw Daddy, I want to go for a walk; you promised!"

"Well, you and I can go . . . "

"I want Wos and Newis to go too," he whined.

"I'll tell you what," said Jenny. "Why don't I stay here to answer the phone, and you all go for a short walk, say, to the new reservoir and back? It'll only take about an hour.

And it'll be better than sitting around here waiting for news."

"That's a great idea Jenny, as long as you don't mind being the one left behind," said Harry.

"No, I'm fine. Anyway, I can be the one to tell the rest of the family. I won't phone anyone yet. I'll wait for Roberto to ring, so that I've got definite news. In the meantime I'll make a pan of tater hash for when you get back."

"That sounds great; thanks Jenny"

They set off up Dacres Road; the two dogs leading the way. They met Mavis in the field with her horses and told her about Sian. "She won't be riding for a while then," Mavis commented. "She was up here just two days ago, helping me to groom them, but she didn't attempt to ride, though I could see that she would have liked to. Give her my love when you see her. I'll go down to Jenny's tomorrow to find out how she is."

They continued through the field and along the lane to Forty Row. The scene from here was very different from the time when Harry first came here with George and Jenny, when the older girls were very young, and the twins hadn't even been thought of. Then it was a gently rolling valley with a brook flowing through.

Now they were faced by a steep dam, just beginning to be covered by new grass, and, when they followed the lane to the top of the dam, there was a vast expanse of water where the valley used to be.

"It looks a lot better now that they've finished working on it," said Harry.

"Yes, I expect I'll get used to it," said George. "but it'll never be the same for me. I loved this valley the way it was, but I suppose they needed the water. Shall we walk all round it?"

"Yes, it shouldn't take too long."

It was a still, warm day, and Harry thought that the reflections of the surrounding hills and the blue sky in the reservoir were quite beautiful; but he didn't say this to George, who was still missing the scenes of his childhood. He thought that it would take George a long time to see that the area, though different, was just as beautiful as it was before.

They arrived back to find Jenny on the doorstep, anxious to tell them the news. "It's a girl, and they are both fine. Roberto was so happy he could hardly speak. He's coming back on the bus; they wouldn't let him stay once the baby was born so he's going back at visiting time. I've invited him over for dinner. I've phoned Mum and Norma, and they'll tell everyone else."

Harry looked at the clock; it was half past twelve. Roberto would hardly have time to eat before going back for afternoon visiting. "I'll drive down to the Clarence to meet him off the bus," he said. The bus terminus was at the Clarence pub, and it was quite a walk from there to Dacres, so Harry thought that Roberto would be glad of the lift.

Roberto could hardly get into the house quickly enough. Before he sat down he was telling them all, "I am a father; my daughter, she is so beautiful, just like her mother. Oh Sian she is so clever to make such a beautiful baby!"

Nerys was getting impatient. "Yes Roberto, you said she is beautiful, but what does she weigh, and what are you going to call her?"

"Ah, she is seven pounds and six ounces and we will call her Michelle. She is so beautiful!"

"Oh, like the Beatles song?" Said Rosalind. "That's a lovely name."

"Yes it is lovely, but we like the name for itself, not just because the Beatles sing it." Said Roberto.

"Well I think it's a lovely name too, but can we eat now? I'm starving!" Nerys looked at Jenny, who started to laugh.

"Trust you to think of food Nerys, but yes, let's eat, and then we can discuss who gets to visit first."

They stayed at Jenny's until it was time for Roberto to go back to the hospital. Leaving Flossie with Jenny and George, Harry and the twins went with Roberto for the afternoon visiting. They would take turns going in, as only two visitors were allowed at each bed.

Harry gazed down at his granddaughter with tears in his eyes. She was the image of Sian at that age and his heart ached when he thought of how much Bronwyn would have loved this baby. He had to be happy for Sian and Roberto though. He swallowed his tears and smiled at them both. "She is so beautiful and I can see how happy you both are. Congratulations!"

Sian was tired but immensely happy, she smiled sleepily at everything that was said, but Harry could see that she wasn't really taking anything in. "I'll go and let one of the twins come in," he said.

"I'll come with you so that they can both come in together," said Roberto. He gave Sian a kiss as he left her side.

The twins had twenty minutes with their sister and niece, and then they came out so that Roberto could have the rest of the visiting hour, which was over all too soon. They drove back to Greenfield and dropped Roberto off at his house before continuing to Jenny's to pick up Flossie. By the time they got back to Newton Heath it was teatime and Audrey had made tater hash.

"We had that for dinner!" Nerys complained.

"Well, you don't have to eat it; there'll be more for the rest of us," Pamela retorted.

"No, it's alright, I'll eat it." Nerys was always hungry.

"I thought you would," said Pamela, sarcastically.

They all settled down to eat.

"Tell us about the baby," said Carol, after they had eaten and were relaxing with a cup of tea.

"Oh she is absolutely gorgeous!" Said Rosalind. "She's got black hair, like us, and the sweetest little face. We didn't see her eyes, because she was asleep."

"How was Sian, did she seem ok? It's exhausting, having a baby." Said Audrey.

Harry answered. "She was really tired; she could hardly keep her eyes open while we talked, but, as you can guess, she is very happy, and Roberto is over the moon!"

"Aw, I'd love to have a baby," said Pamela, dreamily.

"Well, I hope you wait for a while, at least until you finish your studies," said Harry. "And make sure you find the right man first."

Typically, Pamela didn't answer this comment.

Harry was becoming really worried about Pamela. When she wasn't daydreaming she was immersed in a book, and it was never a school book, but one of her favourite novels. He looked across at Audrey and saw the same worried look on her face. What could they do, though? They had tried talking to her and encouraging her studies. Her grades were good, but Harry knew that her grades could be excellent with a little more application. All they could do was hope she would grow out of this moody, dreamy phase.

Sian was home again and settled into a routine with baby Michelle when all the excitement about the football world cup came to a climax. England were in the final, and everyone in the family was excited, even those who were not usually interested in football.

Fred had got his bigger television and had invited everyone round to watch the match on the 30th of July.

The living room was crowded, but nobody worried about that. The grandparents were in the comfortable chairs and settee and the other adults had dining chairs, some borrowed from Harry's and his parents' houses. The twins and Colin were sitting on the floor with Lynette and Anne, Bobby and Susan's daughter, who was now eleven. Pamela had refused to join them, saying that a book was always preferable to football, even if it was the World Cup final.

The atmosphere was electric from the start. Fred was on the edge of his seat, saying, "Come on England, show them bloody Germans what's what!"

Dorothy nudged him, "Fred, language! There's children here!"

"Oops, sorry love; got carried away."

Harry wasn't the only one to laugh at this. He looked at Bobby and Alf and they were stifling laughs. Susan and Norma gave looks that told them to behave. However, the women joined in the groans and the cries of triumph each time the ball went from one side to the other, and there was a heartfelt groan from everyone when Germany scored the first goal, after twelve minutes.

"I'm sure that was off side," said Bill, though everyone knew that it wasn't. They cheered England on even more, and the England team seemed to react with gusto, and Geoff Hurst scored the equaliser after another four minutes. The younger members of the family jumped up, screaming, "Goal, yes, yes!" Even Dorothy and Alice were sitting forward in their seats, shouting their encouragement.

There were no more goals for a long time then, until Martin Peters scored in the 78th minute. It looked like England had won until, one minute before full time, Germany was awarded a free kick - due to handball, which everyone hotly disputed. It was a 2 - 2 draw.

Fred had his head in his hands. "I don't believe it!" He cried. "Never in a million years was that handball. That referee needs his eyes testing!"

"So, it's a draw," said Dorothy. "Will they have to share the cup then?"

There was unkind laughter from some of the men, but Harry said, "It's a valid question." He turned to Dorothy. "No, they will have to play extra time, and if it's still a draw after that, there will have to be a replay of the match on another day."

"Oh dear," said Dorothy. "I'd better put the kettle on then."

That drew laughter from everyone. Dorothy was always ready for a cup of tea.

During the break before extra time everyone got comfortable with tea and cake, and the youngest children, along with Sian, who was tired, went next door to join Pamela; they had had enough football.

There were screams of excitement when Geoff Hurst scored another goal at 98 minutes. "We've got to have won now!" Shouted Fred.

The all watched avidly as the German team tried in vain to score another goal. It was in the last minute that several fans invaded the pitch, confident that England had won.

Just as the commentator said, "They think it's all over, " Geoff Hurst scored another goal. "It is now," he said, triumphantly, as the whistle blew.

England had won the World Cup!

Everyone was euphoric, dancing about and kissing each other. They hadn't had so much excitement since VE Day!

When Harry, Audrey, Carol and the twins finally went back home, Pamela looked up from her book with a questioning glance.

"We won!" Shouted Nerys.

"Oh, good," said Pamela, vaguely, and turned back to her book.

Eleven:

Summer Holidays

After the excitement and inevitable discussions about the World Cup died down, the family turned their attention to Holidays. Harry and Audrey were going to Italy to spend some time with Carla and her family. The twins were being allowed to travel to South Wales by themselves for the first time. Pamela should have been going with them, but she had been invited to go to Cornwall with Alan and his parents. Harry had been dubious about allowing her to go, as she had only known Alan for a few weeks, but a chat with Mr and Mrs McCoy had put his mind at rest, so he gave his blessing.

Carol travelled up to Shetland with Johnny, who was due back at school at the beginning of August. She was looking forward to a week with Mymie.

The twins, Pamela, and Carol would all be away the same week. Harry and Audrey would experience an unusually quiet house, with Lynette being the only child at home. They took her out almost every day, to the park and to Daisy Nook, and one day to Blackpool, to make up for not taking her to Italy. She was still under two years old, and wouldn't appreciate the long journey, and the sightseeing. She loved having the undivided attention of her parents that week, and it made them feel less guilty at the prospect of leaving her with Carol for two weeks.

Carol and Johnny had booked a two berth cabin again on the ferry. They had been brought up like brother and sister, so they didn't feel that they needed to go to the expense of a cabin each. Though, this time, Carol felt a little awkward. She had finally acknowledged to herself that she had feelings for Johnny, feelings that were more than sisterly. She didn't want to feel like this; she had made up her mind that she wasn't going to get romantically involved with any man. She wanted to concentrate on her career. She gave herself a stern talking to, and determined not to let her feelings show.

She sensed that Johnny was completely relaxed with her on the train and the ship. Perversely, she resented this. She had been aware of his regard for her for years, but her feelings for him had been very slow in development. It seemed that he had given up waiting for a sign that she felt the same. She had left it too late, and she was sad, while at the same time telling herself that it was a good thing.

"Shall I take the top bunk?" Johnny asked, as they entered the cabin.

190

"Yes, I don't mind which one I have," she replied.

Johnny looked at her. "Are you alright Carol? You seem very quiet."

"I've just got a bit of a headache," she lied. "I've taken a seasickness pill; I think I'll just have a sandwich for my tea, and then go to bed."

"Oh, ok," said Johnny. "You won't mind if I stay in the bar after tea then? I might see someone I know. It's amazing how many friends I've got in Lerwick already; everyone's so friendly."

"No, enjoy yourself, I'll be fine."

They made their way up to the cafeteria and Johnny sent Carol to find a table while he got their food. He arrived with a tray, and accompanied by a very attractive young woman, whose deep auburn hair lay in abundant waves around her shoulders.

"This is Rhona," Johnny introduced her to Carol. "She's a maths teacher, and comedian!" He laughed. "Everything's a joke to Rhona."

Intelligent green eyes observed Carol. "Hi, Carol, Johnny's spoken a lot about you. I believe he has several sisters, but you are the favourite."

"Oh, I don't know about that." Carol felt irritated by this remark, but she didn't know why. "I think Lynette is everyone's favourite, being the youngest and adorable."

"That's true," said Johnny. "Lynette is adorable and everyone loves her. I'm lucky to have a big, happy family."

"You must miss them, then; being so far away?" Rhona had seated herself between Carol and Johnny, and leaned towards him, effectively blocking Carol's view of him. Carol was sure that the move wasn't unintentional. She decided to ignore it, and began to eat her sandwich.

"I do miss them, but I phone them regularly, and I spend all the school holidays at home. I love my work here, and I'm so busy that I don't have time to miss them too much."

"Maybe one day Shetland will be 'home' to you; I hope so," said Rhona. Carol could sense the beguiling smile, even though she couldn't see the girl's face. She was amused to see that Johnny leaned away from her so that he could see Carol.

"How is your headache?" He asked.

"It's a little better, now that I've eaten something, but I still think I'll go to bed early." She couldn't bear the thought of spending an evening with Rhona, who obviously wanted to monopolise Johnny's attention.

"Oh, you must go to bed if you have a headache," said Rhona. "It will only get worse, being on a heaving ship."

Carol felt like saying, 'how do you know; you're not a doctor!' But she held her tongue and smiled insincerely. "Perhaps you're right. I'll go now; have a good evening."

Johnny stood up and gave her a hug, which almost reduced her to tears. "I hope you have a good sleep Carol. I'll be quiet when I come in. Night, night."

"Night, night lovey," she said, and saw the love in his eyes. So he hadn't lost his regard for her. Why was she grateful for that, when she was determined to concentrate on her career?

She made her way down to the cabin, feeling very confused. "What is wrong with me?" She thought. She got into bed and lay awake for some time, trying, unsuccessfully, to get her thoughts into order. She finally drifted into sleep, and sought Mymie in her dream.

"Hello Carol," Mymie was there immediately, and just as quickly detected Carol's confused state. "You are in bed early dearie. Were you tired from your travelling?"

"No, yes, er, I don't know Mymie. Not really tired but, weary, in a sense." She laughed. "I'm not making sense, am I?"

"It makes complete sense to me dearie. You are confused about your feelings for Johnny. Tell me if this is right; you think you love him, but you shouldn't love him, because he's your brother, but then he isn't really your brother, but then that isn't really the point. The point is that you don't want to be in love with anyone, because you've made the decision not to get involved with anyone, because, what if you have inherited this disease from your mother. Am I close?"

Carol gave a brittle laugh. "You are exactly right Mymie. You know me better than I know myself; but, what do I do about it?"

"That will be your decision to make but, first of all, do you love him?
"Yes," she answered immediately. "But, are my feelings for him as a brother, or something more? That's the trouble, I'm not sure."

"Well, let's look at it this way; you saw him with another girl tonight; how did you feel about that?"

"How did you know. . . ? Oh, of course, it's written all over me, isn't it? Yes, I was jealous. I didn't want him to like another girl; I was afraid of losing him."

"You wouldn't lose him as a brother. He would still be your brother, even if he got married."

"Yes . . . I see what you mean." She thought about this for a while. "I do love him, and I know he loves me in that way too. I've known that for a long time," she finally admitted. "I still don't know what to do about it though. I don't want to love anybody, not in that way. I want to become a good teacher, and I definitely don't want to have children. If I declare my love for Johnny, he will want to marry me, and then it would only be a matter of time before children came along. How could I deny him the chance to have children?"

"Maybe he doesn't want children either?"

"I find that hard to believe, and I would never be able to ask him how he felt about children, because he would say that he didn't want them, just to please me."

"Then you need to sleep on it, now that you are clear about your feelings, and then make your decision. Whatever you decide, I'll be here for you. You know that."

"Yes, thanks Mymie. I always feel better when I speak to you. Goodnight."

"Goodnight dearie."

Carol immediately fell into a deep, dreamless sleep, and awoke, refreshed at 6 am. She hadn't heard Johnny come into the cabin; he was deeply asleep when she got up. She left him sleeping while she showered and dressed and went out on deck.

It was a beautiful, cool, clear morning. The ship was just leaving Fair Isle behind on the port side and she could see Sumburgh Head in front. She breathed in the sea air and mused on her conversation with Mymie. Her subconscious must have been active while she was sleeping, because she realised that she had made a firm decision. Johnny would remain her beloved brother and she wouldn't breathe a word of her feelings to him. She could do this, she told herself; she was strong and it was the right thing to do. She made her way back to the cabin, feeling resolute.

"Come on sleepyhead; you need to get up if you want breakfast before we dock. I'll go and get a table." She shook Johnny awake.

"Oh, ok," he mumbled. "I won't be long."

In the cafeteria she queued up for tea and porridge and looked for an empty table. She saw Rhona sitting alone. "Here goes," she said to herself, and approached the young woman. "Hi, may I join you? Johnny will be here shortly."

Rhona gave a delighted smile. "Yes, of course Carol. Did you get rid of your headache?"

"Yes thanks, and I slept really well. I expect you enjoyed your catch up with Johnny after the summer break?"

"Oh yes. He was telling me all about your family. He thinks the world of you all, doesn't he? I'm surprised that he wanted to move so far away."

"Well, I know that he wanted to see more of the UK, and he likes wide open spaces. He wouldn't have been happy in a city, and the job in Shetland was advertised at just the right time for him."

"I wonder whether he will stay long term, though," said Rhona, half to herself.

"I don't know; though I do know that he's happy here in Shetland, and we have a cousin here, Mymie, so there will always be someone from the family coming up for a visit. He's made lots of friends here, too."

"Yes, that's true," Rhona replied. "I hope he does stay; he's been a good friend to me. I'm originally from Edinburgh, though I've been at the school for three years now. I was thinking of looking for a job south at the end of last term, but I've enjoyed the past year so much that I decided to stay a bit longer."

Carol sensed that Rhona had sincere feelings for Johnny and, now that she had made her decision, she hoped that Johnny could eventually reciprocate those feelings. She sensed him approaching, although she had her back to the entrance.

"Hi, I'm glad you two got together. Did you sleep well, Rhona?"

"Like a top, thanks. I don't have to ask if you slept well; you told me you can always sleep wherever you are."

"Yes, he always amazes me how he can fall asleep as soon as his head touches the pillow," said Carol. "I wish I could."

"It comes from having a clear conscience," laughed Johnny.

"Cheeky! Does that mean my conscience isn't clear?"

"Joking apart, Carol; you think too much. You have to analyse everything minutely. Just go along with life, accept whatever comes your way, or change it if you don't like it."

"Easier said than done," she replied, "but I'll bear that in mind. Of course that's what you did. You hated the job in Oldham so you looked for something better. Was it a good move?"

"Yes, I've been happy here, despite missing the family."

Rhona smiled hopefully. "So, does that mean that you're planning to stay for the foreseeable future?"

"Yes, I think so. I can't see any reason not to stay." He looked at Carol as if to see if she would give him a reason, but she just smiled.

Rhona got up from her seat then. "I'll have to go down to my cabin. We'll be docking soon. If I don't see you later Johnny, I'll see you at school on Monday. I enjoyed talking to you Carol. Hopefully I'll see you again."

As she walked away, Carol said "Rhona's really nice, isn't she?"

Yes, and she's great fun," he replied.

"She really likes you, I can tell."

"Really? I think she's just as friendly with all the other teachers."

"I'm sure it goes deeper than that. She was delighted to hear that you'll be staying."

Johnny just said "Oh," and watched as Rhona disappeared from sight. Carol felt sad that she had sparked Johnny's interest in Rhona, even though that was exactly what she had intended.

They docked shortly after, and didn't see Rhona in the crowds leaving the ship, but they soon caught sight of Mymie and Andy waving. Andy gave Johnny a lift to Angus's house, where he would be living for another two weeks, and then moving into a flat on Pitt Lane. Angus was now married and, although he and his wife had said that Johnny could stay for as long as he liked, he didn't want to outstay his welcome, and had found the flat just before he went south for the summer.

Carol relaxed after they had dropped Johnny off; Mymie sensed this and gave her a questioning look. Carol smiled and nodded, indicating that they would talk later.

The chat would have to happen much later, as Andy was staying for tea. He was delighted to see Carol, and stayed well into the evening, asking her about the family, and about her first year at university. She was happy to talk about things that she loved, and she was delighted that Andy was so interested.

It was after 10 pm when Mymie and Carol sat down with a mug of Horlicks. "It's obvious that you've made your decision dearie," said Mymie. " I sense that you've decided to keep Johnny as your brother and not hanker after anything more?"

"Yes, Mymie. You are spot on as usual. Do you think I've made the wrong decision?"

"No, it has to be the right decision, because you thought it through and you're sure it's the best thing for both you and Johnny. As I said, I'll be here for you whenever you need me. I think you are a very brave girl. I'm proud of you."

There were tears in Carol's eyes as she moved forward to hug Mymie. "Thanks Mymie, I'm so happy that we found each other."

While Carol was enjoying her break in Shetland, the twins were in Wales with Uncle Dai, Auntie Maggie and their cousins.

Harry had dropped them off at the coach station in Manchester on the Saturday, and made sure they were settled on the right coach, which would take them to Cheltenham, where they would change to another coach to South Wales. They were excited to be travelling alone for the first time. They managed to get the front seat in the Yelloway coach from Manchester, giving them a great view of the countryside. At first they just commented on the views and discussed what they would do and see in Wales; whether their cousins had changed much since they last saw them and if they would still get on with them as well as before. Gradually Nerys became sleepy and eventually dozed off. Rosalind was wide awake and began to take interest in their fellow passengers. Most of the people she could see from her seat at the front were older adults. She thought that she and Nerys were probably the youngest people on the coach. Gradually she became aware that someone was unhappy. Carol and Harry would have understood the feeling. It was a kind of keening, as though someone was crying, but without the sound. It was something that she felt in her heart. She had to discover who was so unhappy. She glanced at the driver; he was intent on his driving, and Nerys was sound asleep. She got up and made her way towards the back of the coach, smiling at people as she passed. She finally noticed a tiny, white haired lady sitting alone. Grief was etched on her face as she looked up at Rosalind.

"May I sit with you for a while?" Rosalind asked. "My sister is asleep so I thought I would look for someone to chat with."

The old lady looked surprised but she said, "Yes, of course," and patted the seat beside her.

"My name is Rosalind, and my sister is Nerys. She always falls asleep when we are travelling, though we are usually in my dad's car. This is the first time we've been in a coach."

The lady replied, "My name is Mrs Doris Watson."

"Pleased to meet you, Mrs Watson," Rosalind replied. "Are you travelling far?"

"Just to Cheltenham, to visit my daughter. This is also my first time in a coach. My husband always drove, I never learned to drive. He passed away six weeks ago." She struggled to say this, and Rosalind realised that this was the first time Mrs Watson had told anyone outside her family about the loss of her husband.

"Oh I'm so sorry; you must miss him very much."

"I do; we were married for over fifty years. I don't think I'll ever get used to life without him. My daughter wants me to move in with her and her husband, but I'm a Manchester lass; I can't see me settling in Cheltenham, especially as my daughter works full time and her children have grown up and left home. I would be alone all day. I'd miss my home, where all my memories are, and my friends."

"I'm a Manchester lass too; I wouldn't like to live anywhere else, though I'd love to travel, but just to visit other places, not to stay long term. Which part of Manchester is your home?"

"Moston."

"Oh, we are almost neighbours! We live in Newton Heath. My Dad knows Moston very well. He worked at a hardware and electrical shop there before the war and he used to do deliveries, first on his bike, and then in a van. It was off Lightbowne Road, I think."

"I know it! Mr Marshall's shop, wasn't it? I think I knew your dad too. He had a dog that went everywhere with him; a golden retriever, I think."

"Yes, Bess was the dog. Of course it was a long time before I was born but Dad still talks about her."

"Yes, I remember the young man and his dog. He delivered to our house many times. We, I mean I, live on Spreadbury Street, which is off Lightbowne Road on the other side. We were sad when Mr Marshall died and his sister took over the house. She closed the shop, you know?"

"Yes, my Auntie Susan took over from Dad when he went in the army. She was furious when the sister closed the shop. She wanted to keep the job open for my dad, but it wasn't to be, and maybe was a good thing in the end, because Dad's a teacher now, and he loves his work."

"How old are you Rosalind? You seem very mature, but I think you look quite young."

"I'm fifteen; I'll be in the fifth year when I go back to school, and studying for O levels."

"Yes, I thought you were young. It's very kind of you to sit and chat with me. The journey won't seem so long."

"Oh I like a chat."

"Even with an old lady like me?"

"Oh yes; you've lived a long life, so you must have lots of things to talk about. I love having a chat with my two grandmas."

"Do they live near you?"

Yes; one lives next door and the other one is just a few doors away. Well, to be exact, Grandma Dorothy isn't my natural grandma, but she is my stepmum's mum, so we always call her grandma. We are a big family, a bit mixed up, but we are all very close." She went on to describe the family. Mrs Watson was intrigued, especially when told about Rosalind's elder sister marrying her step brother.

"Well your family is certainly very interesting. How old is your sister that you are travelling with?"

"Nerys is the same age as me; we're twins. We were the youngest until Dad married Auntie Audrey and we now have a younger sister, Lynette, who's nearly two, and she's a little angel. Do you just have one daughter?" Rosalind asked.

"Yes; we weren't blessed with any more children. I suppose that's why she wants me to move in with her. She worries about me, now that I'm alone."

"But you must tell her how you feel about leaving your home. It'd be a shame for you to move away from everything you are used to, just to stop her worrying about you"

"I can imagine what she will say 'what if you have a fall, or if you are taken ill? I'm so far away from you' I can hear her saying it in my mind."

"Well, what if you had a fall? Your friends and neighbours would help, wouldn't they? Would one of your friends hold a key, so that they could get in, in an emergency?"

"Oh, my friend Violet already has a key, and I have a key to her house. She just lives next door, and we are both widows. And we have lots of good neighbours."

"Well, that'll be your answer. You and Violet look out for each other, and, if you couldn't get to the shops, I'm sure your neighbours would help. Do you have a phone?"

"Yes; I've had it since my husband first became ill."

"Your daughter can always ring you, to put her mind at ease."

"You're right Rosalind, of course. I'll tell her. How did you get to be so wise? "

"Listening to my Dad and my Grandparents, I suppose. I just thought about what they would say. Of course they all have each other, so it's unlikely there'll ever be a reason for any of them to move, but I think that is what their advice would be."

"Well, thanks for coming to chat with me, Rosalind. Look, we are just coming into Cheltenham."

"Oh yes, I'd better get back to Nerys and wake her up. Goodbye Mrs Watson. I'll ring you sometime to see how you are getting on."

"That would be lovely. I hope you have a good time with your cousins."

Rosalind returned to her seat, where she found Nerys awake.

"Where have you been? I was just coming to look for you."

"I've been talking to a lovely old lady. I felt that she needed a bit of company."

"Oh you and your feelings; and did she?"

"Did she what?"

"Need some company?"

"Yes, she said it made the journey go a lot faster. She only lost her husband a few weeks ago and it's the first time she's travelled alone."

"Oh that's sad; I'm glad you cheered her up."

The coach pulled into the depot and the girls were first off. Rosalind introduced the old lady to Nerys as they were waiting for the driver to get the luggage out. A woman came over, looking flustered.

"Oh there you are Mother, I thought I'd missed you. I was sure that the Manchester coach came into another bay. Still, you're here now. Were you ok on the coach? Are you tired? Where's your case?" She didn't give her mother time to answer as she bombarded her with questions. Rosalind gave her a sympathetic look.

Mrs Watson managed to get a word in at last. "Denise, this is Rosalind and her sister Nerys. We've been having a lovely chat."

"Oh hello, that's nice," she answered, quickly, but then immediately turned to the driver to claim her mother's case. "Come on Mother, the car's just around the corner." Without another look at the girls she ushered Mrs Watson away.

"How rude!" Said Nerys.

"Oh well, I think she was worried about her mum. Mrs Watson said her daughter wants her to move down here, but she doesn't want to leave all her friends."

"Well, I wouldn't want to live with her!" Nerys was indignant.

"I think she's going to tell her she wants to stay in her own home. I just hope her daughter listens to her."

Nerys agreed and then, spotting a cafe, she steered Rosalind that way to get a cup of tea. They had half an hour to wait for the Black and White coach to Swansea. It would drop them at the newsagents in Skewen, where Uncle Dai would be meeting them.

The journey to Skewen was uneventful. Both girls fell asleep, but were refreshed and wide awake as the coach dropped some passengers off in Neath. They knew then that they were close, and sat alert, watching for their first view of Uncle Dai. He was waving as the coach pulled to a stop. They jumped off the coach into his arms. "Hello Uncle Dai, it's lovely to be here again!"

The driver got their case out, and Dai gave him a tip.

"Oh we never thought about a tip," said Nerys. "Do you think we should have given something to the other driver?"

"No, he wouldn't expect it from two young girls," said Dai. "But I like to tip a driver when I can. It makes them feel appreciated." The girls were impressed.

"Come on now, your Auntie Maggie has bangers and mash for your tea."

"Ooh lovely; I'm starving!" Nerys exclaimed.

"She's always starving," said Rosalind, and they all laughed as they made their way through to Bethlehem Road. It was only a short walk, and they were soon greeting Auntie Maggie and her five children.

They settled in as if they had never been away, and they spent a wonderful week revisiting all their favourite bays with the two youngest girls, Bronwyn and Dilys, named after their two aunts. They bought rover tickets for the buses. The three eldest children were now all at work, Gareth and Elfed at the steelworks and Gwynneth was a chamber maid at a large hotel in Swansea.

The week was over all too soon and Uncle Dai was putting them onto the coach home. When they arrived in Cheltenham they were delighted to see Mrs Watson in the cafe. She was getting the same coach home. Her daughter was with her, but, when Mrs Watson saw the girls, she turned to her daughter and said, "You can go home now, Denise. You know I don't like long farewells. The girls will keep me company now."

Her daughter obviously wasn't happy at being dismissed in favour of the teenagers, but she kissed her mother and said, "Alright Mum. I'll phone you this evening. Have you got your ticket safe?"

"Yes lovey, you know I have. I'll be fine. Bye bye."

She waved until Denise was out of sight, and then she turned to the girls with a triumphant look in her eyes. "I did it! I told her that I'm staying at home. She didn't like it at first, but I remembered what you said, Rosalind, and I stuck to my guns. She had to agree in the end that I would be lonely in her house while she was at work. She's going to ring me every evening. I told her that once a week would be fine, but she was adamant, so I agreed to that. I love my daughter and my grandchildren, but I have to say that I'm so happy to be going home to my own little house. I can cook what I like and watch my favourite TV programmes." She was beaming, and the girls smiled along with her.

They all got on the coach and they got the back seat so that Rosalind and Nerys could sit on either side of her. They chatted non stop all the way to Manchester, the girls telling her all their adventures in Wales and Mrs Watson talking about her grandchildren.

Harry was waiting at the coach station with the car. He took Mrs Watson home too. Though she said that she was happy to get a taxi, Harry wouldn't hear of it, especially as she only lived in Moston. "It's almost on our way home," he said.

So they dropped her off at her neat terraced house. Her friend, Violet was waiting at the door. "I've got the kettle on, so take your case in and then come in to tell me all about it," she said.

The girls waved and then turned to Harry to regale him with all they had seen and done.

Pamela was already home when they got there. She had also had an enjoyable week down in Cornwall. "We were in a lovely hotel in its own grounds in Carbis Bay, that's near St Ives. My room was at the front, and there was a slight view of the sea between the trees. I even had my own bathroom! Well, it was a shower room, and quite small, but I felt so posh! I wish we had a shower," she said, looking at Harry. "I had a shower every day, sometimes twice a day. It makes you feel so clean."

"I don't know anyone around here with a shower," said Harry. "I don't even know if the council would let us have one. You can get a sort of shower attachment that you can put on the taps of the bath; one of the teachers at our school has one, but she said it's no good for showering yourself; she just uses it to rinse her hair after shampooing. A proper shower would have to be installed by a plumber and goodness knows how much that would cost. I think you'll have to forget that for a while Pamela. Anyway, tell us about your holiday. I don't suppose you spent the whole week in the shower?"

"No Dad, don't be silly! We went on the beach a lot, and swam in the sea, and walked along the clifftops. One day we went to a lovely little place called St Agnes Cove. It was so beautiful! The sea was blue/green and there were lots of waves. We watched people surfing. Alan wanted to learn to surf, but his mum wouldn't let him. She mollycoddles him a bit you know."

"Well he's her only child," said Audrey. "I expect she worries about him a lot."

"He's eighteen though Mum! She'll have to let him make his own decisions sometime."

Nerys piped up. "He'll have to be a bit more assertive then; I bet you boss him about as well."

"No I don't, cheeky!"

Audrey, the peacemaker, said, " Let's have tea now, it's all ready, and then you can tell us more about your holiday, and Nerys and Rosalind can tell us about theirs."

They enjoyed a hearty meal, and then they got comfortable with cups of tea while the girls related their adventures.

Carol arrived home on Monday, looking rosy cheeked and bright eyed.

"Looks like you had good weather in Shetland," said Audrey.

"Yes, we only had one day of rain. The rest of the time it was clear and windy. It certainly makes my cheeks glow!"

Carol went on to describe her week with Mymie, mentioning Maggie and Kirsty and how much baby Carol had grown. Andy had been generous with his time and his car as usual, taking her to see Catherine and Ninian, who was now quite a big cat, and driving her and Mymie up to Lerwick.

"Maggie and Andy seem very close; I sensed romance in the air," Carol smiled.

"Oh that'd be lovely, if they got together. They're made for each other." Said Audrey.

"But they're old, aren't they?" Said Nerys.

"Trust you to say that," Rosalind retorted. "They're only the same age as Dad and Auntie Audrey; and anyway, even if they were ninety, there's no reason they can't get together. There's no age limit on love!"

"Well said, Rosalind. I was just going to say the same," said Carol.

Nerys stormed upstairs in a sulk. Rosalind got up to go after her, but Pamela said, "Leave her; she knows that she was wrong, that's why she went off. She'll soon get over it. I hope they get married. I wonder if Maggie is still young enough to have a baby?" She drifted off into a daydream about babies.

Harry gave Pamela a worried look. Carol, sensing what he was worried about, gave him an encouraging smile and changed the subject.

"Are you both ready for your holiday now? What time do you leave on Wednesday?"

"Oh, we have to be up at 5am," said Harry. "Roberto is going to run us to Ringway Airport and then he is going to have the car while we are away. Then he'll pick us up on the Saturday of the week after."

"I can't wait to get in the 'plane," said Audrey. "I'll be nervous, my first time flying, but what an experience it'll be!"

"I hope it'll be clear, then we'll get some fantastic views, especially going over the Alps." Harry added.

"Oh, the Alps," Audrey mused. "How wonderful!"

oOo

Harry and Audrey arrived in Cassino exhausted after their journey. They had travelled by air from Manchester to London Heathrow, and then to Rome. The train from Rome to Cassino took less than 2 hours, but they were already tired when they left the aeroplane and found their way to the railway station. This last part of their journey passed in a haze of weariness that stopped them enjoying the scenery.

They were grateful to see Alberto waiting for them, and more grateful for his taciturn nature as he drove them up to the farm. Conversation was not his strong point, so they were able to sit back and relax for the twenty minute drive.

Carla and her children were much more noisy. They were standing at the door and welcomed them with open arms, asking them questions about their journey and about the other members of the family.

"Let them get into the house," said Alberto."Can you not see how tired they are?"

"Oh sorry Harry, Alberto is right; come in, come in!" Carla ushered them into the large kitchen and sat them down on the sofa against the wall. The big, wooden table was set for the evening meal, with a large bowl of salad in the middle. There was a delicious smell of food coming from the range. "Chicken and pasta is almost ready Harry; do you remember?" Carla smiled.

Harry was taken back to the month of May in 1944, when the battle of Monte Cassino was finally over and the men had been given some time off to go down to the town from their camp, partway up the mountain. Harry and his friends had rescued Carla's father from a rock fall, and they had been rewarded with a wonderful meal. He remembered how bad the town had looked at that time, almost completely destroyed by bombing. He had been pleased to see, despite his weariness, that it had been rebuilt. He said as much.

"Yes, and the monastery has been beautifully rebuilt," said Carla's son, Angelo. "You must go up to see it while you are here."

"I'd like to," said Harry. "And I'd like to visit the Polish cemetery, to pay my respects."

Alberto said, soberly, "Yes, that is very beautiful also."

"Is there any other thing you would like to see?" Asked Carla.

"If it's possible, we would like to go to the cemetery near Salerno. Audrey's late husband is buried there. I got on to the Commonwealth War graves Commission and they have told me exactly where to find the grave."

"There is a train. You may have to change at Naples. I will find out for you," said Alberto.

"That's very kind of you," said Harry. Alberto seemed more friendly, now that he was in his own environment. Harry was relieved; the atmosphere in the kitchen was comfortable and everyone was smiling.

"Come to the table now, let us eat," said Carla, serving up dishes of pasta and chicken. Alberto opened two bottles of wine as everyone sat down.

The food was as delicious as Harry remembered, and he had two glasses of wine, refusing a third glass, as he was beginning to feel sleepy. He looked across at Audrey; she was struggling to keep her eyes open, and she had only had one glass of wine.

Carla looked at them both and said, "I think you would like to have an early night. Shall I show you your room?"

They gratefully accepted and were soon unpacking in their room. Harry suspected that Carla and Alberto had given up their own room for their guests. It was a large room with a window that overlooked the town. He gazed down at the new buildings, and remembered the devastation that the war had wrought. He felt lucky that he had lived through it all, while at the same time feeling guilty. He had heard of 'survivor's guilt' and told himself that he should live the best life that he could, in gratitude for his life. He had much to be grateful for.

He turned to Audrey, who had just returned from the bathroom. She was looking sleepily beautiful in her new nightie. He took her in his arms saying, "Happy, lovey?"

"Yes; tired but happy. I think we're going to have a wonderful holiday."

The next day Carla and Sophia went with them to the Abbey at the top of Monte Cassino. They were overwhelmed by the size and the beauty of this building. It was built of cream coloured stone that sparkled in the sun and it had an atmosphere of tranquility that belied its history. The destruction during WW2 wasn't the first time that the monastery had been destroyed. In its long history it had been sacked by Lombards, Saracens and the French, and it had been destroyed by earthquake, but its importance to the catholic church meant that it was always rebuilt.

After lunch in the town, they visited the Polish cemetery, another beautiful, tranquil place. Harry thought that the Polish soldiers who had fought so bravely deserved such a lovely place for their eternal rest. He and Audrey spent a long time quietly wandering among the gravestones.

"So much waste of young lives," said Audrey. Harry nodded.

When they were all gathered in the evening, Carla said, "I think you should have a break from graves tomorrow. Why do we not all go to Napoli and have a boat trip to Capri?"

"That sounds lovely," said Audrey.

They were up early and were soon on the train to Naples. It was a hot, sunny day and the streets of Naples were teeming with people. They were glad to get to the waterside and board the boat. There was a lovely sea breeze fanning their faces and arms as they sat comfortably enjoying the colourful scene as they approached the island.

"It looks quite hilly," said Audrey.

"Yes, the town is high, but there is a lift up to the centre of the town and the views from there are wonderful," said Alberto.

They went up in the lift and emerged into a quaint, narrow street. Most of the buildings were white or pastel colours; dazzling in the sun.

They wandered along the byways, every so often seeing spectacular views of the Bay of Naples between the shops and cafes. Coming to a wide square, they decided to have lunch at a cafe with outside tables. They had delicious sandwiches of crusty bread filled with mozzarella and tomatoes and pesto.

"What is the green sauce?" Audrey asked. "It's delicious, and I've never tasted such good tomatoes."

"Pesto; it is basil and olive oil. Very good for you," Alberto answered. He was in his element, showing Harry and

Audrey his lovely country. "The olives are the same as we grow on our farm," he added.

"Shall we have gelato to finish?" Said Carlo.

Carla laughed. "Carlo just loves gelato; you call it ice cream. They have many different flavours here. Would you like to go inside to choose?"

Harry smiled. "I'd like to just sit here and soak up the atmosphere; I'd be happy for Carlo to choose for me."

"Yes, me too," said Audrey. "I'm sure any flavour will be lovely."

Carlo was more than ready to choose for everyone, but his brother and sister went with him to choose their own favourites.

The waiter shortly appeared carrying a tray bearing glass dishes generously filled with ice cream and fruit.

"Gosh, they're enormous!" Audrey exclaimed. "I don't know if I can eat all that." But it was so delicious that she ate it all. "You Italians really know how to make good ice cream," she said.

Harry looked at her fondly, as she sat back with a contented smile on her face. He was so glad he had brought her to Italy. She deserved to be spoiled once in a while.

After a goodnatured disagreement over who would pay the bill - Harry insisted on paying - they made their leisurely way back down to the boat.

They were lucky to get seats in the bow of the boat. The sea was calm and the view of the whole bay, from Naples round to Sorrento, was extremely clear. Vesuvius was hazy in the distance. Harry and Audrey were entranced and Carla's family were delighted in the effect their country had on the visitors.

They slept deeply that night and awoke to another beautifully sunny day. They were getting the train to Salerno today. It would be a sobering experience, but Harry really wanted to go to pay his respects, not only to Jimmy, but to several more of his comrades who never left Italy.

Harry and Audrey travelled without the Italian family this time. Of course, Jimmy and the other casualties of the war in Salerno were unknown to them. Carla offered to go with them for moral support; Harry thanked her but assured her that they would be alright, especially as Alberto had given them invaluable advice on how to get to the cemetery.

A bus took them from the railway station to the cemetery. They entered an oasis of peace and gazed in awe at the rows of white gravestones. Over 18 hundred service men and women were buried here. The fighting in this area had been bitter and intense. Harry remembered it well.

They made their way to the grave of Audrey's first husband, Jimmy Bates. It was exactly where the commission had informed Harry, in plot 3, Row B, grave 22. Audrey knelt to place flowers on the grave and stayed there for several minutes, tears flowing freely. Harry stood with his hand on her shoulder, allowing her to give vent to her grief.

She finally stood up. "He would have been so proud of Johnny," she said. "I just wish he had been able to see him, just once."

"I know," Harry answered, holding her in his arms. "He was so proud when he heard that he had a son. We all went into Alexandria to celebrate, and he got so drunk we had to lift him into the jeep to get him back to camp. "

Audrey forced a laugh. "I can imagine him doing that. At least he knew that he had a son. I hope that somehow, he knows, wherever his spirit is now, that he has a son to be proud of."

"Yes, I hope, I believe, that we watch over our loved ones when we go on to something better at the end of our life on earth. "

Audrey looked up into his eyes. "You know, that's the first time I've cried for Jimmy. At first I couldn't believe it, and, of course, there was no funeral. Johnny was a baby, and I just got on with looking after him and helping everyone else to get through the war. Then, after the war, you and Bronwyn came home, and I could see she needed support, even before we realised she was ill. I got involved with bringing up the girls; I loved that, you know that I did, Harry. If I hadn't had you and Bronwyn and the children, my life wouldn't have been as happy. I am so lucky."

"And I am lucky to have you lovey," said Harry, and kissed her. "I love you," he simply said.

They didn't need to say any more. They understood each other completely. They wandered through the cemetery arm in arm for a long time, appreciating how well kept it was and reading some of the gravestones of these, mainly young, people; pondering on the futility of war.

They finally made their way back to the bus and spent some time in Salerno, having a late lunch before they boarded the train back to Cassino.

The rest of their holiday passed far too quickly. Carla and Alberto and their children were good hosts, showing them all the local sights and keeping them entertained. Two days before they left, Harry and Audrey took the family out for a meal. They went to a lovely restaurant in the centre of town, where they had the traditional four course Italian meal - antipasti, pasta, main course and dessert, accompanied by a delicious red wine. They were all merry on the way home, Alberto just sober enough to drive. There was much laughter and joking, and it was very late when they went to bed.

They spent the last day quietly at the farm. The three teenagers had gone out for the day, so it was just the adults. Harry and Audrey did their packing, and then they all sat on the dry grass, looking down on the town, Harry marvelling on all the changes since he was last here.

"We've had a lovely time," said Harry.

"I'm so glad," said Carla. "I hope you will be able to come often, and we will visit you. I long to see bambino, Michelle. The photos you gave us are so lovely. I am a grandmama!"

"Yes, it takes some getting used to," said Audrey.

The return journey went to plan, and they arrived home at teatime to cries of joy from Lynette and incessant questions from the other girls. They sank into chairs by the fire and enjoyed a proper cup of English tea.

"Ooh that's lovely!" Harry exclaimed. "The food and wine is delicious in Italy, but they don't know how to make a decent cuppa." Audrey nodded her agreement.

"I hope you don't mind having boring shepherd's pie for tea?" Carol smiled.

"Sounds sublime," said Audrey, and everyone laughed.

Twelve:

Careers and Anxieties

August 1967

All the girls were there when the O level results came through the post.

Rosalind was reluctant to open hers. "Will you open it for me?" She said to Carol, who smiled and took the envelope from her.

"You don't need to worry," said Carol as she opened it. "I expect you've passed everything. Yes, an A, three Bs and two Cs." Rosalind gave a sigh of relief.

"I've got exactly the same!" Nerys exclaimed, comparing her letter to her sister's. "We've even got the same grade in the same subjects!"

"Well, it's not surprising, as you did all your studying together," said Harry. "What have you got, Pamela?"

Pamela was opening her results nonchalantly. "The same; one A, three Bs and two Cs." She put the letter down, as if it was of no further interest to her.

"Oh, I thought you would get higher grades than that," said Carol.

"It's good enough!" Pamela retorted

"Yes, but if you had studied like we did, you would have got all As. You are the brainy one." said Nerys.

Pamela didn't bother to answer. She just picked up her library book and sat down to read.

Harry looked at Audrey, who was frowning. She moved towards Pamela, as if to say something, but Harry gave a slight shake of his head. He knew that it would be pointless to comment on Pamela's results now. They could only hope that she would work harder at her A levels in the next two years.

Harry's heart was heavy, but he smiled at his daughters and said, "Well, I think we should celebrate. South Pacific is on at the Pavilion. I think we should all go tonight, and have fish and chips afterwards.

"Oh that's great Dad!" Nerys cried, and everyone agreed it was a lovely idea. Even Pamela looked up from her book and smiled.

Grandmas Dorothy and Alice were delighted to babysit together. They saw each other every day, but they still enjoyed an evening together, knitting and 'putting the world to rights'. So Bill decided to have an evening with Fred, along with a couple of bottles of beer.

The family arrived home, singing "I'm gonna wash that man right outa my hair!" Harry was carrying a large, fragrant parcel of fish and chips, Audrey put the kettle on and Carol went next door to get the grandads. There was fish and chips for everyone.

They all sat around, eating straight out of the paper with their fingers, and talking in between mouthfuls.

"Grandma, you should go and see that film," said Nerys. "It's lovely, though there are sad bits too."

Alice looked at Dorothy. "Shall we go? It's ages since I went to see a film. I don't suppose Fred and Bill will want to go." She looked across at her husband.

"No, I'd rather watch telly," said Bill. "You girls go."

Rosalind and Nerys giggled at the thought of their grandmas being called girls. Alice laughed with them. "I quite like being called a girl now and again." She shared a smile with Dorothy.

"We'll go tomorrow," said Dorothy. "Are you 'boys' going to buy us a box of chocolates to take with us?"

"Oh, you've started something now," said Fred. "Is there anything else you'd like, while we're forking out for films and chocolates?"

"Ooh, well, now you mention it, I could do with a new hat," she joked. That set everyone laughing.

Harry loved it when the family got together like this and they had a laugh. He could put aside worries and anxieties for a while.

Nerys and Rosalind had been accepted as nursing cadets at Crumpsall Hospital. They started there on the second Monday in September.

Their first morning was a whirlwind of instructions from the assistant matron, uniform fittings, being shown various parts of the hospital and getting to know the small group of sixteen year old girls who started on the same day.

After lunch, in the small dining room in Delaunays Hospital, an annexe dedicated to care of the elderly, they were taken to the departments they had been allocated .

Nerys found her department was occupational therapy in Delaunays. There were two therapists who welcomed her and gave her an overview of her work, which seemed to be mainly finishing off craft work that the patients had been doing. There was a mountain of nylon material that had been knitted into strips. She had to sew these strips onto wooden coat hangers. Apparently the patients could knit the strips with big needles, but were unable to do the sewing. There was also basket work that needed to be finished. She was also responsible for keeping all the shelves and cupboards tidy. It seemed as though she would have little contact with patients in this department, which disappointed her, but she supposed, as new nursing cadets, her colleagues would be in a similar situation.

Rosalind had been allocated to the ECG [electrocardiograph] department in the main hospital. There were two ECG technicians and a second year cadet nurse in addition to Rosalind herself.

As it was afternoon, she and the other cadet, Beverley, were in a side room doing what Beverley Called 'licking and sticking', although Rosalind was relieved that there was actually no licking involved. The printed tape that measured a patient's heart activity on the ECG machine, had been cut into short lengths by the technicians. The cadets' job was to stick the pieces to A4 size card, with sellotape, and use a hole punch on the side of the card, ready to store it in the patient's notes. The most important part was to keep the patient's name with the correct set of tapes, and then to write the patient's name at the top of the card. When they had finished all the results from that morning, they then had to deliver them to the relevant wards. "That's my favourite bit of the afternoon," said Beverley. "It gets us out of this poky little room and, if we time it right, it's time to go home when we get back."

They visited the wards together that first afternoon, so that Rosalind could get used to the layout of the hospital. Beverley led Rosalind up several sets of stairs to various wards. "We're not allowed to use the lifts, but if you see someone getting in the lift with a trolley, or with a patient in a wheelchair, you can join them. It saves your legs a bit."

She showed Rosalind where the Sister's office was on each ward. "If there's no one in the office, you can leave the cards in the in tray on Sister's desk," she explained.

They got back to ECG at five to four. They reported to the technicians who, as Beverley had predicted, said they could go home.

Rosalind got to the changing room just minutes before Nerys. She was changing out of her yellow dress as her sister joined her.

"What was your afternoon like?" Nerys asked.

"Good; I'm working with another cadet, Beverley." She called over to Beverley, who was getting her coat on. "Beverley, this is my sister Nerys."

Beverley came over, looking at the two girls in surprise. "You are identical! I wouldn't have known which one was you, Rosalind, if you hadn't spoken. I suppose you've had comments like this a lot?"

"Yes," Rosalind replied, "but you can usually tell which one is Nerys, she's the one with a cheeky grin!"

"And Rosalind is the quiet one," said Nerys, "but if you see one of us alone, you have to guess which one you are talking to, and hope that we tell the truth. It's such fun confusing people!"

"See what I mean?' Rosalind laughed.

"Oh dear, things are going to get complicated, I can see," said Beverley. "Anyway, I must rush. See you tomorrow." She was out of the door before they could blink.

"Shall we take one of our uniform dresses home?" Nerys asked. "I know we're not allowed to wear them outside the hospital grounds, but it'd be nice if Dad could take a picture of us."

"Yes, let's do that. I can fit them in my bag," Rosalind replied.

They walked to the bus stop with two other cadets. They discussed their new departments.

Ellie was working in outpatients.

"I think I'm going to love it," she said. "I mainly run errands for the sister and the nurses, getting equipment from the store room and chasing up patient's notes from medical records. I'll also be helping to set up the clinics in the morning."

Sally had been allocated to X-ray. "My job is similar to Ellie's I think. Though there aren't any nurses in the department. We have two porters who bring the patients from the wards, but they tell me I may have to do that when they are busy. Only the ones in wheelchairs of course, the porters bring the ones who have to be on a trolley."

Nerys was a bit disgruntled. "Oh your departments seem a lot more interesting than mine. From what the OT therapists have told me, I won't have much contact with the patients. I'll be stuck in that room, sewing covers on coat hangers or finishing off basketwork. Running errands will be light relief!"

"I wouldn't mind that," said Rosalind. "I'm really nervous about tomorrow morning. Apparently, I'll be assisting the ECG technician on the wards. Beverley explained that she goes first to the patient and applies the arm and leg electrodes, so that the patient is ready when the technician arrives a few minutes later. She also has to explain the procedure to the patient, if they haven't had it done before. It sounds scary."

"I'd love that; I think they've allocated the wrong twin to the wrong department. Shall we swap? No one will know." Nerys replied.

Ellie and Sally were wide eyed with astonishment. Rosalind knew that Nerys wasn't completely joking.

"It's not like school sis," she said. "This is serious work; we're adults now and we can't be playing tricks. How could I go into your department and pretend I know what to do? The same for you. Beverley would have to explain the 'licking and sticking' again. She'd think I'm an idiot!"

They were at the bus stop now and Nerys turned to her sister. "I suppose you're right, but it would be good fun, wouldn't it?"

Rosalind laughed. "You're incorrigible! Anyway, we are only in these departments until the end of November. When the most senior cadets go into PTS on the first of December, we all change around"

"What does PTS stand for?" Asked Sally. "I remember Miss Green told us this morning, but there was so much to take in."

"Preliminary Training School," Rosalind explained. "There are three intakes of student nurses each year - April, August and December. We will go into PTS the next intake after our eighteenth birthday. That'll be August 1969 for Me and Nerys, as our birthday is in July."

"Oh, me too," said Sally. "My birthday is in June. When is yours, Ellie?"

"October; I'm 17 next month, so I'll be in December '68 PTS."

"Oh, you'll be two sets ahead of us then. You'll be able to tell us all about it." Said Nerys.

The number 7 bus came along just then, and they all piled on it. "All aboard nurses" said the driver. Even though they weren't in uniform, he assumed they were nurses. They swelled with pride.

The twins arrived home full of excitement, anxious to tell the rest of the family about their first day. Harry looked at the animated faces of his daughters. Their dark eyes were sparkling with happiness. He was delighted to see how happy they were.

"Dad, we've brought our uniforms home. We're not allowed to wear them outside the hospital, but we thought you could take a picture of us, for posterity," said Nerys. "Have you got any film in your camera?"

Harry laughed. "Yes, I've got a colour film in it, so those yellow dresses will show up really well. We'll do it after tea."

Audrey smiled indulgently. "I've done your favourite for tea; shepherd's pie with lots of red cabbage and apple pie and custard for afters."

"Ooh great, I'm starving!" Nerys was always starving.

"You wouldn't think that we'd had tea and toast this morning, and then Cumberland sausage with chips and beans, followed by rice pudding with stewed apples at dinnertime. Nerys even managed seconds of rice pudding!" Rosalind laughed.

"I don't know where you put it all," Audrey commented.

"She's got hollow legs," said Harry.

"That's grandma's saying," said Nerys. "I'll tell her you pinched it."

"She knows I pinch all her good sayings," Harry replied. "Now, let's have tea; I'm starving too."

"I'm starvin' too," piped up Lynette, who had been uncharacteristically quiet until now, sitting on Carol's lap in the rocking chair.

"Come on then little sis; let's eat." Said Carol, taking her to the table.

"Where's Pamela?" Rosalind suddenly realised that someone was missing.

"Oh she said she was going to Alan's straight from school. It's his first day back at university and she wanted to ask him all about it. His mum invited her for tea." Audrey replied.

"She didn't want to hear about our first day," said Nerys, sulkily.

"She's lost interest in nursing," Rosalind replied. "I feel sad about that. We used to do everything together. Now, if we didn't have choir practice on Fridays, we wouldn't be doing anything with her. At least she still likes singing."

"You're all growing up and you develop different interests," said Harry. "I expect she'll want to hear about your first day when she gets home."

"Well, if she doesn't ask, I'm not going to tell her anything," Nerys grumbled, but then forgot all about it when Audrey put a plate of shepherd's pie in front of her and handed her the dish of red cabbage. "Ooh thanks Auntie Audrey. It smells gorgeous!"

Pamela didn't hear about their first day, because the twins were so tired that they were in bed and asleep by ten o'clock. Pamela should have been in by ten, as it was a school day, but it was nearly half past when she arrived, with Alan in tow. Harry and Audrey were sitting by the fire, reading.

"Sorry Mr Roberts," said Alan. "We were doing a jigsaw and Pamela wanted to finish it before she came home. We weren't watching the time."

"That's alright Alan. Thanks for walking her home." Harry smiled at the young man but turned what he hoped was a stern profile to Pamela. He wasn't very good at disciplining his daughters, but this wasn't the first time that Pamela had come home late. He worried that, if he let it pass, she would think that it didn't matter how late she came home. He waited for Alan to leave.

"You know that you should be in by ten o'clock on schooldays Pamela. It's not good enough." He pinned her with his gaze, not allowing her to look away.

"It's only half an hour, and we wanted to finish the jigsaw," she argued, trying to look away but finding it impossible.

"It isn't the first time though, and you need your sleep. I suppose you had homework too?" She nodded, and Harry continued, "If it happens again I'll have to stop you going out on a weekday evening." His voice was gentle but firm, and he could sense that Pamela believed him. She didn't argue further, but just lowered her eyes.

"Sorry Dad, it won't happen again. I'll just go up to bed now. I can do that homework tomorrow. I'm not seeing Alan until after choir on Friday." Harry nodded ok.

"Would you like a mug of Ovaltine?" Said Audrey, feeling sorry for the girl, though she felt that Harry had dealt well with the situation.

"No thanks Mum, Alans mum made us a drink before we left."

Audrey was pleased that Pamela still called her Mum. Apart from her own daughter, Lynette, who called her Mummy, all the other girls called her Auntie Audrey. Though she knew they all loved her, she had a special bond with Pamela due to the fact that she had cared for her, almost exclusively, from birth, and continued to give her a lot of attention after the twins were born, so that she wouldn't feel left out. She smiled now, saying, "Night night lovey; get a good night's sleep."

"Night night Mum, Dad" she replied, and escaped up the stairs.

Carol came in at that moment. She had been next door, talking to Fred and Dorothy. She was very close to the older members of the family and enjoyed hearing their tales of the old days.

She took one look at Harry and said, "Was Pamela late again?"

Audrey wasn't surprised. She knew that Harry and Carol shared a special bond, seeming to be able to read each other's thoughts, though it wasn't exactly that. It was more that they could sense feelings.

"Yes," said Harry, "But I think she accepted this time that I meant it when I threatened to keep her in on school nights; and I do mean it, even if we have to endure her sulks."

"Good, it sounds like she's learning a bit of sense," said Carol. "I'm off to bed now. I don't have any lectures until afternoon tomorrow, but I'll have to be up fairly early, to work on my dissertation. Night, night." She kissed both of them.

"Night, night lovey," they replied.

Carol was now in her third year studying English at university, and she was planning to do a teacher training course next year and after that, secure a job as an English teacher in a secondary school.

She loved being a student and had many friends, though she still hadn't had a steady boyfriend. She didn't lack offers of a date, but she would only go out socially with a group of friends. That was how she liked it; no emotional ties; no chance of becoming too entangled in a relationship and then having to explain that she never wanted to get married or have children. Harry and Audrey wondered if she was doing the right thing, but agreed that they had to allow her to make her own decisions. They just hoped that she would be happy.

They got ready for bed; Audrey banked the fire down and put the fireguard in place; Harry took Flossie out into the garden to relieve herself and then settled her in her bed and locked the back door. All the girls were safe in bed, they had heard today from Sian and Roberto, who were deliriously happy with their baby girl, and from Johnny, who had a girlfriend up in Shetland. What more could they ask?

Thirteen:

A Worry and a Solution

January 1969.

The twins were enjoying their work as nursing cadets. They had worked in various departments over the past year and, at present, Rosalind was allocated to X-ray and Nerys was in theatre. Their work was still basic; Rosalind ferried patients to and from the wards, put clean laundry away when it was delivered and undertook any odd jobs.

Nerys worked in the 'prep room' attached to the operating theatres, along with another cadet, Sue, and a lovely lady orderly, called Marie. There was always lots of work to do in the prep room, mainly packing drums to be sent for autoclaving. These were stainless steel boxes containing everything, except instruments, that needed to be sterile; surgeon's gowns, green towels and drapes, different kinds of swabs. Everything had to be folded in a certain way and packed so that the items could be easily taken out of the drum using a pair of long handled forceps. They also had to fold and put away clean laundry, of which there were several large sacks every day.

The prep room looked out onto the corridor by which the patients were brought from the wards. The girls had to watch out for the trolleys coming by, as another of their jobs was to relieve the ward nurse and stand with the patient outside the theatre until they were taken into the anaesthetic room. This had been nerve wracking for Nerys at first, as each patient was, understandably, extremely anxious, despite often being drowsy, due to the medication they had been given. Nerys soon acquired the knack of putting the patient at ease and quite enjoyed chatting to them.

On the 26th of January Nerys and Rosalind were in the sewing room getting their caps and aprons, as this was the day that they were seventeen and a half. They admired themselves in the mirror, wearing the stiff, starched white apron, the bib pinned to the yellow dress with their name badge on one side and a fob watch on the other. The fob watches had been a lovely surprise present from Harry and Audrey. The starched cap was fixed to their dark curls with several white hair grips. They now wore their hair in braids, neatly pinned up. The cap was ideal for covering any loose ends.

Rosalind looked at Nerys. "You look like a real nurse now. The cap and apron make such a big difference."

"So do you," Nerys replied. Looking at her sister was like looking in a mirror. They were still identical to look at, although within themselves they were very different, the main difference being that Rosalind had inherited the gift

236

that Harry and Carol possessed. Nerys wasn't really jealous of the gift, in fact she worried that Rosalind may have difficulties as a nurse when she began to work on the wards. Nerys knew that, when someone was in pain, Rosalind could actually feel that pain, whereas Nerys could only sympathise. Until now Rosalind's interaction with patients had been minimal, but, now that they had their cap and apron, the next move would be to a ward, and they could only imagine what they would experience then.

On the first Monday in April, the cadets who had turned 18 since December went into PTS, proudly wearing their blue and white uniforms. Nerys, Rosalind and Sally, along with two of their friends, were allocated to wards for the first time. Sally was on a surgical ward, Nerys on orthopaedics and Rosalind was on E3, male geriatrics.

She was faced with a long ward full of elderly men, most of whom were sitting beside their beds, and all seemed to be staring at her. A male nurse with purple epaulettes on his white tunic came to meet her at the door. "Hello, I'm staff nurse Entwistle, but you can call me Fred, except when Matron is around; you are obviously our new cadet?"

"Yes, I'm Rosalind, most people call me Ros," she replied, nervously.

"Don't worry," he said, noticing her trembling hands. "We've all been in the same position, our first day on a ward. These old blokes are harmless, and you've missed all the hard work, getting them washed and out of bed. Starting at nine o'clock is a perk of being a cadet. Come on,

I'll introduce you to everyone." He took her up the ward, telling her the names of all the patients and the other members of staff. They were all friendly, welcoming her warmly.

"Right, everyone is up, so we now make the beds. You can pair with me," said Fred. "I'll show you how to do hospital corners."

The morning passed quickly. Bed making was followed by damp-dusting all the lockers, mid morning drinks for the patients and the inevitable job of putting away clean laundry. In between these tasks, Rosalind handed things to patients, brought urine bottles from the sluice, and took them back to be washed and sterilised. When the patients' lunches arrived, Fred and two other staff members went to lunch. Rosalind helped the remaining staff to give out the meals and feed the men who were unable to feed themselves.

The cadet nurses always went to second lunch, at one fifteen, as they started work an hour later than the other staff. By the time Rosalind went to lunch she was exhausted and hungry. She met Nerys in the corridor on the way to the dining room.

"I'm starving!" She complained.

"Hey, that's my saying!" Nerys laughed. "How did your morning go?"

"I loved it, but we never stopped, except for our twenty minute coffee break. I didn't see you in the dining room then. Didn't you get a coffee break?"

"Sister sent me on first break at ten o'clock, along with an auxiliary, because there was a doctor's round and she wanted the senior staff to attend that. It seems a long time since then. It was torture giving out patient's lunches when I was starving."

They giggled as they entered the dining room and saw Sally sitting at a table. She waved them over. "How was your morning?" She asked.

The three of them shared their new experiences, in between eating large helpings of roast beef, Yorkshire pudding, roast potatoes and carrots, followed by sponge pudding and custard.

Nerys sat back and gave a sigh of satisfaction. "That was delicious. I'm ready to face the afternoon now." She glanced at her watch. "Its five to two already; we'll have to get back!"

When Nerys had worried about how Rosalind would react to a patient in pain, she had no idea that she would find out that day, on their first day working on a ward.

On the female orthopaedic ward all the patients were nursed in bed, as the treatment for broken leg bones was to put the affected limb in traction. All the beds had complicated beams and pulleys holding the leg in place.

Nerys was assisting a student nurse to lift a patient onto a bedpan, when the Sister appeared around the curtains. "Cadet nurse Roberts, you're wanted on E3. Your sister has taken ill and Sister Hamilton wants you to take her home."

The patient was settled on her bedpan, so Nerys was able to go immediately, apologising to the nurse and Sister as she left.

"That's alright cadet nurse Roberts. We'll see you tomorrow. I hope your sister recovers soon."

Nerys rushed to E3 as fast as she could. She couldn't imagine what had happened to Rosalind. She had been in good spirits at lunchtime. Reporting to the Sister on E3 she was told that Rosalind was in the kitchen. She found her sitting in a corner, sipping a cup of tea and quietly sobbing into her cup. Fred was standing by her side.

"Ros, what happened?" She leaned to put her arm around her sister.

Rosalind sobbed even harder, unable to answer.

"She fainted," said Fred. "We'd just put a man into the bath, she went as white as a sheet, and the next thing, she was on the floor. She banged her head on the side of the hoist we were using, that's why sister wants her to go home."

"You've never fainted in your life!" Nerys exclaimed. "Do you know what happened to make you pass out?" Though she suspected that she knew.

"Is she premenstrual, do you know?" Fred asked.

"No!" Nerys flushed red with embarrassment. He was a nurse, but he was still a man, and she didn't expect him to ask something so personal. "No," she said again, more quietly. "It's not that, and she isn't pregnant either, before you ask"

"Sorry," said Fred, holding his hands up in defence. "Just trying to help."

"It was Mr Dando," Rosalind managed to say at last. "He was in so much pain as he was lowered into the bath. I couldn't bear his pain!" She dissolved into sobs again.

Fred looked at her quizzically. "He's got a nasty pressure sore on his bottom. I suppose it stings a lot as he gets in the water, but it soothes him after a while. We put Savlon in the water; it's a good antiseptic. I suppose if you haven't seen a bad pressure sore before it can send you a bit queasy. Don't worry about it Ros, we all do daft things at the start. I threw up the first time I had to clean up diarrhoea."

Rosalind's eyes begged Nerys to say nothing. She hadn't seen the sore, as Fred had taken the dressing off before she arrived to help him. Nerys knew as well as she did, that it was the unexpected pain that had affected her.

"You're probably right, she'll be ok by tomorrow." said Nerys. "Thanks for looking after her. Do you think Sister would allow me to use her office phone? I could ring my grandad to collect us in the car. He's called Fred too," she said, incidentally.

Fred smiled. "So is my grandad; that's where I got my name. Come on. I'll introduce you to sister Hamilton. She won't mind you using the phone."

By the time they got home Harry had arrived from work. He had left the school on the dot of 4 o'clock, knowing that there was a problem with Rosalind. Nerys wasn't surprised. Dad always knew when there was a problem with one of his daughters.

241

"She's ok now dad. She just had a funny turn when helping with a patient." She led Rosalind into the living room and settled her in the rocking chair. "I'll put the kettle on."

Fred had followed them in. Harry thanked him for picking up the girls. "It's ok lad, I'm glad I was able to help. I'll go and tell Dorothy that Rosalind is alright. Your Mum and Audrey and Lynette are with her, but I'll tell them to stay there for now. You don't want a crowd."

"Thanks Fred," said Harry, as he sat down opposite Rosalind. He looked at her sympathetically. "I think you felt someone's pain," he said; it wasn't a question.

She started to cry again. "It was so sudden! I'd been really enjoying the day. All the old men were lovely; they all had aches and pains, arthritis and that. I could cope with that, but this pain was so intense, just as we lowered him into the bath. I couldn't cope with it!" She dissolved into sobs again.

Harry knew that it wasn't the pain that was distressing her, or the fact that she had fainted. She was worrying about her future as a nurse. "You think that you can't continue as a nurse?" He suggested, gently.

"Yes, but I love nursing; I don't want to do anything else; it's my life!"

From anyone else this may have seemed overly dramatic, but Harry knew that she was sincere. She just couldn't think of any other career; she was a born nurse.

Nerys came in with the tea, closely followed by Carol, who immediately went over and knelt by Rosalind's chair. " I came as quickly as possible. Don't worry lovey, we'll think of something." She held Rosalind's hands in a warm grip.

Nerys was also in tears now. "You're not going to give up nursing are you? I don't want to do it without you."

"Don't get upset," said Harry. "I'm sure we can work out a solution to the problem. It was really the unexpectedness of the pain that affected you badly. I had a similar experience during the war. I didn't actually faint, but it was only the quick action of a nurse, who sat me down and put my head between my knees, that saved me from hitting the ground." He became quiet as he remembered the terrible experience of entering a hospital tent that was full of injured soldiers. He would never forget.

Rosalind stopped crying and looked up at her Dad. "You nearly fainted? I can't imagine that; you are so strong!"

"Not so strong, really. I always avoided situations where I might have to deal with the pain of others. That's one of the reasons I am a teacher, apart from the fact that I love teaching, of course. You and Nerys are strong. It takes a special person to be a good nurse. I think you will both become excellent nurses, and I'm sure we can find a way around your problem."

"We should ask Mymie," said Carol.

Nerys knew about Mymie, and she knew a little about the dream walking, because Rosalind had told her, although she didn't understand how they communicated through dreams. She looked from her sisters to her Dad, wishing she could take part in this fascinating thing.

"I can't contact Mymie like you can though," said Rosalind. "I'm like Dad; I have the dreams but I can't instigate them."

"That's ok," said Carol. "I'll contact Mymie tonight, and then she will contact you. I'll bet that she has a solution to your problem. Anyway, let's get tea ready; Nerys is starving!" Rosalind tried to laugh, but failed. She had little hope in Mymie solving her problem.

The twins and Carol all went to bed early. Nerys snuggled down into her covers. "Good luck sis," she said to Rosalind. She turned over and was immediately asleep.

"I wish I could sleep like you," Rosalind whispered. She admired Nerys' ability to sleep anywhere and any time. Rosalind always took a while to empty her mind of the days events, though she usually slept all night once she did fall asleep. She curled up in her blankets and tried counting from one hundred backwards, but she kept seeing Mr Dando being lowered into the bath and gasping with pain. "Why can't I stop thinking about it?" She asked herself.

After another few minutes Carol appeared, carrying a mug of Horlicks. "Here, sit up and drink this. I knew you were lying awake. I've spoken to Mymie already, and she is going to contact you as soon as you're asleep." She got on the bed and sat close to her sister. "Let's talk about something pleasant. Did I ever tell you about finding the orphan rabbit in the dunes of Swansea beach? It was before you were born. I was about four at the time. I thought everyone could sense animals like I could, so I was surprised when everyone was shocked at seeing the rabbit in my arms and I told them the mummy rabbit was dead. Dad understood, of course, and Sian was used to my strange ways. Gwynneth wanted to keep the rabbit, so Uncle Dai made a hutch for it. Gwynneth called him Bob the bunny. She had him for years,"

"I remember the rabbit," said Rosalind, sleepily. Her head nodded on Carol's shoulder; she was almost asleep. Carol took the mug out of her sister's hand and eased herself off the bed. "Lie down now," she whispered; Rosalind drowsily lay down, and Carol covered her up, quietly leaving the room.

Rosalind was in the small living room in Mymie's croft house, and the old lady was sitting in her usual chair beside the peat fire. She had been here before in her dreams. "Hello Mymie," she said, quietly.

"Hello dearie, I hear that you've had a bad day. Would you like to tell me about it?"

Rosalind told her about her day from the beginning, how she had loved 'real' nursing at last, how supportive the other nurses were and how sweet the old men were. She had sensed the aches and pains of old age from the men, and was able to cope with that, but the sudden, sharp pain that Mr Dando experienced was just too much to bear. "I was mortified, Mymie!" She sobbed. "How can I become a nurse if I can't deal with pain?"

"You can deal with it dearie. You were overcome because it was a surprise. I'm not a nurse, but I imagine that, most times, it will not come as a surprise like that. If you were on a ward where patients have had surgical operations you would expect a degree of pain, but they will come back from theatre under the effect of drugs, and the return of pain will be gradual and you will be ready to give them some pain relief. Isn't that so?"

"Yes, I suppose so."

"So, if you are expecting pain, you can prepare yourself, and you can prepare your patient, to a certain degree. I'll tell you first how I dealt with the pain of my ewes in childbirth. I would wake in the night and sense that a ewe was in labour. At a distance, the pain was bearable, but I knew that it would become more intense the nearer I got to the ewe. I would tell myself 'this pain is not in my belly, I must soothe it away' I would imagine a hot water bottle wrapped in a soft blanket, held to my belly. That would ease my pain a little. Then I would approach the ewe and look into her eyes. I would tell her that it wasn't really a bad pain, just a lot of pushing. She would calm down immediately, and so would both my pain and hers."

"But how could I do that with a human in pain?"

"Well, let's start with Mr Dando, his pain is in his bottom, yes?" Rosalind nodded. " You could try to imagine a warm pad just against the base of your spine, as I think that is where his pressure sore is. That will reduce the impact of the pain on you; but you can reduce his pain too. You remember how you dealt with the bully who was threatening your friend?"

"Yes, but I was very angry then."

"Carol has told you how to channel your anger. Do you remember?"

"Yes, but I wasn't angry with Mr Dando?"

"You need to be angry with the pain. Fix Mr Dando with your eyes and tell him that going into the bath will hurt, but only for a few seconds, and it will be just a slight sting. He will be convinced by your confidence, and it will only sting a little. It's called mind over matter."

Mymie's words were soothing and Rosalind realised that the words, and Mymie's confident manner, had increased her confidence in being able to deal with pain. "So I can help him in just the same way you've just helped me?"

Mymie smiled. "Exactly; now we need to talk about unexpected pain. When you help with Mr Dando again you will be prepared, but what if, in the future, you are taken by surprise again? You need to know how to prevent yourself from being overcome."

Rosalind was perplexed. "Is that possible?"

"Yes; there will be a second or so when you become aware of the pain and you need to act quickly. Imagine you are looking into your own eyes, in fact you are looking into yourself. Tell yourself 'this pain isn't mine, it's just an echo; it won't harm me'. You may have to close your eyes at first, and that may confuse people around you, but that's better than actually fainting, don't you think?"

"Yes, I suppose so, but I won't know if I can do it until it actually happens."

You can do this, and it will give you enough time to apply a virtual warm pad to the pain and then concentrate on the patient to reduce their pain. I know you can do it; you just need the confidence in yourself. Practice on your patients. See if you can ease their arthritic pains. Each success will increase your confidence, and then, when the bigger problem comes, you'll be ready. You can do it dearie."

"Thank you so much Mymie. I feel better already. I was thinking of taking tomorrow off sick; Sister Hamilton said I should take the day off if I still felt unwell. Now I want to go in and prove to myself that I can cope."

"That's good; now have a good sleep. I'll contact you again in a week or so. Good night dearie."

"Good night Mymie." As she drifted into a deep sleep, Rosalind was aware that Harry and Carol had been observing. Their love was palpable.

She told Nerys all about it on the bus to Crumpsall the next morning.

"Oh, I wish I could ease a patient's pain like that," said Nerys. "Wouldn't it be great if all nurses could do that?"

"I'll bet you could do it a bit," Rosalind replied. "You always know where I am and how I'm feeling. You're like Grandma Alice. She's always aware of us all, even though she doesn't have the dreams. I think we all have it in different ways. You could try, anyway."

"You're right," said Nerys. "I knew something was wrong yesterday before Sister came to get me. I was concentrating on lifting the patient without causing her pain, but I would have found a way to get to you after that, if Sister hadn't arrived." She gazed out of the bus window, musing. "I could try; what is there to lose?" She asked her reflection.

Rosalind nodded.

The rest of the week was uneventful. As they went home on the bus with Sally on Friday, Nerys said, "I'm looking forward to choir practice tonight. It'll be relaxing after all the new impressions this week."

"Do you go to choir practice every Friday?" Sally asked.

"Yes," Rosalind replied. "It's our favourite night of the week. Pamela comes too - we all love singing - and then Dad comes to pick us up and we get fish and chips on the way home.It's a lovely way to start the weekend."

"With no patients asking for bottles or bedpans, and no dramas," Sally added.

She wasn't to know that the twins were in for a drama of a different kind.

They came out of choir practice, singing 'Elizabethan Serenade', when Rosalind suddenly stopped. "Someone is upset!" She said. She could sense the same keening that had taken her to Mrs Watson's side on the coach to Cheltenham.

"It's round here, I think," she said, leading Nerys and Pamela round the side of the school. There were several bins in the angle of the wall here. Pamela saw it first.

"Its a dog!" She crouched down and coaxed the dog out from behind the bins. It was extremely thin and looked like a short haired whippet type, tan in colour.

"Oh, she's got puppies!" Rosalind cried. The dog had sent her a picture of several puppies crowded together on a pile of old newspaper. Pamela and Nerys pulled two of the bins away, and there were the puppies, five of them, all huddled together. They were very young, their eyes still closed. The mother dog looked up beseechingly.

"Oh, she's asking for help," said Nerys. "We can't leave them here. We'll have to take them home." They all turned suddenly, as they heard a movement behind them.

"Yes, we will take them home," said Harry. "I wondered why you were all mooching around the back of the school. He bent down to speak to the dog. "You'll come with us, won't you?" He offered. The dog wagged her tail. She understood that they were going to help her. They picked up the puppies and the mother dog followed them to the car. She didn't seem to know what to do when Harry opened the doors. She obviously hadn't been in a car before. He lifted her on to the back seat, where she sat between the twins. Pamela was in the front, cradling two of the puppies. The twins put the other pups next to their mother, so she could lick them.

"What on earth have you got!" Audrey exclaimed as they trooped into the kitchen.

"The girls will explain," said Harry. "I've just got to wash my hands and then I'll go for the chips."

Audrey knelt down to stroke the dog and Flossie came up for a sniff. The new dog backed away and started trembling when she saw the bigger dog, but Flossie backed her into a corner and started to lick her face.

"Look at that! She's not a bit jealous," said Pamela. "She's welcoming the other dog. Good girl Flossie!"

Flossie wagged her tail and went to Pamela for a pat. Then she saw the puppies. The girls had put them down on Flossie's blanket in the corner of the kitchen. The big dog went over to them and began to sniff and lick them.

Though she was still trembling, the mother dog gave a warning growl. She thought the other dog was threatening her pups. Flossie backed off, but she still leaned towards the pups, her nose active with their scent.

Rosalind knelt down and looked into the dog's eyes. "Flossie won't hurt your babies, she will help you." She sent the dog an image of the two dogs lying on the blanket, cradling the pups. The dog licked her face and then turned towards Flossie, still trembling but no longer showing any animosity. She cowered down and rolled over in submission. She was accepting the bigger dog as leader of the pack. Flossie licked her face and then turned her interest back to the pups. The mother dog also edged forward and soon the two dogs were busy cleaning and examining the babies.

Meanwhile, Audrey had opened a tin of dog food. She put half in each of two dog bowls and filled the water bowl. Both dogs immediately left the pups and went to wolf down the food. Flossie was a typical Labrador, in that she was always hungry. She had already had her food for the day, but she would never turn away an extra meal.

"That was clever, Mum," said Pamela. If you had just fed the new dog, Flossie would have been jealous.

"She needs more food than Flossie does, though," said Audrey. "When your Dad takes Flossie out for a walk later, I'll give her some more. She needs to make milk for her babies."

As if she had understood, the dog then settled herself on the blanket. The pups were soon happily feeding. The girls looked on fondly.

"We can't keep calling her the new dog," said Nerys. "We'll have to give her a name."

"Well, the colour she is reminds me of a dirty, rusty tin, though she could look a lot lighter when she has a bath," said Pamela.

"Why don't we call her Rusty, then?" Rosalind suggested.

"It's not a very feminine name," said Nerys.

Several other names were offered, but no one could agree on them.

"I think we should ask the dog," said Rosalind. She knelt down and said to the dog, "What do you think of the name Rusty?" The dog wagged her tail.

"There you are, she likes the name."

"She would have wagged her tail whatever you'd said!" Nerys complained.

The discussion ended when Harry came home with the fish and chips, and, by the time they had eaten, everyone was too tired to continue. The girls went up to bed while Harry took Flossie out and Audrey gave 'Rusty' another meal.

Rosalind was first up the next morning. She was delighted to see the two dogs entwined with each other and all the puppies snug in the middle. Flossie jumped up, causing all the pups to start mewling; their mother settled herself to feed them.

Rosalind opened the back door and followed Flossie down the back garden path to the gate. She leaned on the gate, looking out at the play park that had replaced the ollers a few years previously. It was good for the local children to have the play space, but Harry and his children missed the wildness of the ollers. It had been a wonderful place for them and their dogs to roam; full of wild flowers and grasses. Now it was a concrete area with swings and other equipment, edged with closely cut grass.

They returned to the kitchen and Rosalind put food out for both dogs. Mother dog jumped up, scattering her babies, and wolfed down the food, and then she went to the back door and looked up at Rosalind, who open the door to let her out. The dog relieved herself in the garden and then wandered around, sniffing and investigating her new environment. Rosalind let her wander around for a while, and then called, "Rusty!" The dog immediately turned and came to her. "I knew you liked the name!" Rosalind smiled with satisfaction. "Just let the others try to change it now," she said to the dog.

"Change what?" It was Nerys, who had just come downstairs, still in her pyjamas.

"Rusty's name. There's no way you can change it now, because she came to me when I called her name.

"I bet she would have come if you had shouted 'Dog'!"

"Well you try it then," Rosalind challenged.

Nerys looked at Rusty and said, "come here, dog." Rusty put her head on one side and looked puzzled, as if to say 'that's not my name'. So Nerys just said, "Rusty." The dog came up to her, wagging her tail.

Nerys stroked her and said to Rosalind, "Ok sis, you win, she's called Rusty."

After breakfast Harry suggested that they should bath Rusty, and wash the dog's blanket. "She's likely to have fleas, and if that's the case we'll also have to bath Flossie and check the pups."

Carol got the twin tub washer out. "I'll do an ordinary wash first, and then wash the blanket last. Good job it's a good drying day."

Rosalind took the old tin tub into the garden and Pamela and Nerys carried buckets of warm water to fill it. Flossie saw what was happening and sloped off to hide under the dining table. She hated having a bath, though she loved playing in muddy water. Rusty just watched all the activity with interest.

When they were ready Harry picked up the dog, and, speaking gently to her, he lowered her into the warm water. She didn't struggle, but just stood trembling while Harry held her and Rosalind rubbed her all over with carbolic soap. Then Nerys brought another bucket of water to rinse her. She looked desperately thin with her coat plastered down. "We'll have to feed her up," said Harry, as he lifted her out and let her free to shake off the water.

Pamela rubbed her with an old towel and then Rosalind brushed her with Flossie's brush. "I can't see any fleas," she said.

Harry took over and had a thorough look, parting her short hairs to see her skin. "I think you're right," he said. "I'll give Flossie a good brushing to make sure, but I'm amazed that a stray dog has no fleas. I wonder where she's originally from?"

"Perhaps she had an owner until recently. Maybe they were annoyed when she got pregnant, and threw her out." Said Pamela.

"Oh, how cruel!" Nerys exclaimed. "How could anyone do that?"

"I know, it's a horrible thought, but there are people who do things like that. They shouldn't have a dog in the first place," said Harry, angrily. "Anyway, we'll inform the police, in case anyone has lost her, but I'll be surprised if anyone comes forward. It's obvious that she gave birth to those pups alone. Well, they'll get looked after here, and we'll find good homes for them when they are old enough." He looked fondly at the dog, whose coat now looked much lighter.

"She doesn't look rusty now," said Pamela. When she said the name. Rusty came to her, tail wagging. "We can't change her name now, though," she laughed.

They checked the puppies after this, with Rusty hovering anxiously. There were three with cream coloured coats - two boys, one girl - and two with tan coats like their mother - a boy and a girl. It was easy to see on their tiny bodies that they didn't have any fleas.

As their blanket was now on the washing line, Carol found a couple of old towels for them to lie on. They laid the pups on the towels, and Rusty settled herself beside them. They immediately started to suckle. Everyone looked at the lovely sight and smiled.

"We've had a good morning," said Harry, "but we should get the soup on for when Audrey and Lynette get back from the market."

The vegetable soup had been made the previous day. It just needed heating up, and it would go well with the bread that Audrey was bringing from the market. It was simmering and giving off a delicious aroma when Audrey arrived.

"How are the dogs?" Audrey asked, as Lynette ran to the nest in the corner to see the puppies. She had been whisked away to the market early, so that she wouldn't be in the way of the bathing and possible de-fleaing of the dogs.

"No fleas, thankfully," Harry replied. "The girls have made a good job of bathing her and the blanket is washed and on the line."

"Can I hold a puppy now Daddy?" Lynette looked imploringly at Harry.

"Yes, just for a minute, and then you'll have to wash your hands. Be gentle and stay near Rusty - the mummy dog - so that she doesn't get upset. Her babies are tiny and she wants to be near them."

Lynette gently lifted one of the cream puppies and sat on the floor near Rusty. "Can we keep a puppy Daddy?" She asked.

"No lovey, but we'll keep them all until they are big enough to leave their mummy, and we'll keep Rusty. Two dogs is enough for us."

Lynette made a disappointed face, but she knew that it was useless arguing. Daddy was loving and generous, but his word was law. If he said that two dogs was enough, then she had to be satisfied with that.

Sunday was a busy day. The whole family arrived to see the new dog and the adorable puppies.

Susan and Bobby, Norma and Alf and their children came in the morning. Audrey had met her sisters-in-law at the market on Saturday and, of course, told them the news. Sian and Roberto, along with two year old Michelle, Jenny and George and six year old Colin, had been told by phone and they all arrived in the afternoon.

"Flossie's taking it all very well," said George.

"Yes, she thinks that she's the pups' auntie," said Harry. "She's given them all a good licking; their mother too. They're like sisters already. It couldn't have worked out better."

"We'd like to have one for Colin; it'll be a companion for Bob too. It'll have to be a boy though."

"Well there are three boys, so you have a choice."

"Can I choose, Dad?" Said Colin.

George nodded and Harry replied, "Yes, but the puppies can't leave their mum until they are eight weeks old. If you say which one you'd like, I'll get grandma to knit a little collar for him."

"Ooh thanks Uncle Harry!" Colin sat on the floor next to the dogs' bed and stroked each puppy in turn. Rusty seemed happy to let the children touch her babies, she had a gentle nature. Colin chose one of the cream coloured boys. Carol tied a piece of red wool around its neck as a temporary measure, as this pup was identical to his brother.

Michelle was looking on as Colin chose his pup. "Doggy for me Mummy?" She pleaded.

Sian looked at Roberto. "What do you think, lovey? We've talked about getting a dog, but you thought it may be too much, especially as . . ." She blushed.

Audrey picked up on Sian's confusion. "Are you expecting?" She smiled.

"We were going to keep it secret for a bit longer, but yes, we've only just found out ourselves. Our baby is due in December; a little brother or sister for Michelle."

"Don't want a sister, I want a doggy!" Michelle insisted.

"I think we could manage cara mia," said Roberto. "But Michelle has to help to look after the doggy," he said, with mock seriousness.

"I will Daddy, I will!" Michelle replied. She sat down next to Colin, who was still holding his puppy, and she chose the other cream boy.

"We need some more wool, Carol," said Audrey, laughing.

Rusty and the puppies continued to thrive over the next few weeks and, as Harry had predicted, no one came forward to claim the dog.

At the same time, the twins were getting used to their duties on the wards. Two weeks into her time on E3, Fred asked Rosalind if she would like to observe him dressing Mr Dando's pressure sore. She was delighted.

She had assisted with his bath on several occasions, and had followed Mymie's advice on dealing with the pain. It had worked well for both herself and Mr Dando. He had just been in the bath and was now in his bed, waiting for his dressing.

She followed Fred to the clinical room and watch him set up the dressing trolley. "Next time you can set it up for me," he said. "It'll be good practice."

They drew the screens around the bed and Rosalind took her place on the opposite side to Fred. Mr Dando was on his side, facing her. She looked him in his eyes. "You're used to this now, aren't you? It shouldn't hurt much."

"It's a lot better now lass," he said. "You nurses have done a grand job."

Fred uncovered Mr Dando's back and took off the gauze that was applied after his bath. Rosalind felt no pain at all. "Wow, it's doing really well!" Said Fred, surprised. "I've been off for two days, but I did your dressing the day before that, and it was much bigger then. Have a look at this Ros,"

She looked; there was a small, shallow ulcer, the size of a sixpence, with a wide area of pink, healing skin all around it. She didn't have the experience, but it looked pretty good to her.

"I've never seen one heal that quickly.' Fred continued, "I reckon it'll be completely healed in another two days. Then we've just got to stop it happening again. That means you keeping up with your physio, not sitting in your chair for too long, and eating a proper diet, Billy. You should be able to go home soon," said Fred.

Fred was still marvelling about the speed of Mr Dando's healing when they went to lunch together. "He's 84, had a terrible diet before he came into hospital and has had a stroke. His healing is nothing short of miraculous! I wish I knew his secret."

"Perhaps it's just the care he's been given," Rosalind ventured.

"I'd love to take the credit for it, but, somehow, I think it's more than that. I doubt if we'll ever find out though. Let's just be happy for the old bloke."

On the bus going home, Rosalind discussed Mr Dando with Nerys.

"Maybe you worked your magic on him when you were reducing his pain?" Nerys suggested.

"Oh no, I don't think so. How would reducing his pain also make him heal more quickly?"

"I don't know, but it's a thought. What about your other patients, have you seen anything unusual in them?"

"Well, I've been trying to ease their arthritic pains, and one or two of them have commented on how much better they feel, and they seem to be more mobile, and more confident. For example, one man always had to be helped to walk to the toilet, but he went by himself today. He actually refused help!"

"That's brilliant! Oh, Ros, I hope it is down to you. Just think how much good you can do."

"Well, it's not doing any harm anyway."

That night Mymie visited Rosalind in her dream. "How are you getting on with the pain relief dearie?" She asked.

Rosalind told her about Mr Dando, and also what Nerys had suggested.

"I think she is right," said Mymie. "I noticed that when I helped a ewe in childbirth, she seemed to get over the birth more quickly, and the lambs I delivered always thrived. I could see the difference between them and the ewes that gave birth alone. I think it is the element of mind over matter. When the body is relieved of pain it is able to put more energy into healing. Don't become too confident though. Remember that you are just adding to the medical and nursing care that the person is receiving. If you can help them to heal more quickly, that is a bonus, but don't expect it."

"I won't Mymie, and thank you for your advice. I know now that I'll be able to continue with my nursing career, and that means the world to me."

"I'm so pleased, and that is a bonus for me. Keep up the good work dearie. Goodnight."

"Goodnight Mymie."

Fourteen:

Another Worry.

The first Monday in August was a landmark day for the twins. It was their first day in PTS and the family were anxiously awaiting their return home at teatime. Audrey had iced a fruit cake to celebrate and had made their favourite shepherd's pie.

Carol was also celebrating, she had recently been offered a post as English teacher in a high school in the centre of Manchester. She would start at the beginning of September.

There were going to be many changes for the family. Lynette would be starting school in September, and Audrey had decided to go back to her old job of dinner lady, as one of her old colleagues had just retired. Pamela was awaiting her A level results and she had been given a conditional place at Manchester University. She had decided to study English and French, as she had gone off the idea of being a librarian and was now unsure of what she wanted to do. She had broken up with Alan a few weeks previously. When asked, she had said that he was 'boring'.

The dogs heralded the approach of the twins by standing at the back door with their tails wagging vigorously. The girls bounded in, full of energy, eyes sparkling and smiling widely.

They didn't need to be asked how the day went. Nerys was talking almost before she was through the door, stroking Flossie's head while at the same time taking off her navy gaberdine. "What a day!" She exclaimed. "We hardly stopped. Sister Tutor told us how hard we have to work, and that she expects us to be the best group she has taught; but actually, she said exactly the same to Ellie's group last December, so we shouldn't be too worried. She reeled off everything we will have to learn in eight short weeks. We've even got notes to write up tonight!"

"She's good at remembering names too," said Rosalind. "She asked everyone to introduce themselves and she had something to say to each person. You'll never guess what she said to Nerys?"

"What did she say?" Asked Carol, as she handed each twin a mug of tea.

Rosalind put on a haughty voice. "Nurse N Roberts, your reputation goes before you. We will have no practical jokes here. You are here to learn and to work hard. Remember that!"

"How did she know which one of you was Nerys?" Asked Lynette, wide eyed, when everyone had stopped laughing.

"She must have seen her initial on her badge, but I think it was the cheeky grin on Nerys' face that gave her away. She couldn't keep a straight face, even for Sister Tutor!" Rosalind laughed.

"She's a right tartar!" Nerys complained.

"I like her," Rosalind replied. "She's straight, so you know where you stand with her, and I could tell that she would be a good support if you needed her. She was laughing inside when she spoke to Nerys. I imagine that she was a practical joker in her youth."

"How can you tell if someone is laughing inside?" Asked Lynette.

"You can see it in their eyes," Carol replied. Lynette was satisfied with that explanation. She idolised her big sister, and thought that she knew everything.

"Is tea ready?" Asked Nerys. "I'm starving!"

When all the girls had gone to bed, tired from all the talk about teaching and nursing, Harry and Audrey sat by the fire, quietly musing.

"Our girls are doing well," said Audrey. "We can be so proud of them."

"Yes; I just wish that Pamela would make her mind up what she wants to do. She just seems to aimlessly drift through her days. She's confident about her A level results though, so that's something." Said Harry. "Did you notice that she didn't ask the twins anything about nursing? She obviously hasn't changed her mind about that. I still can't understand what happened with Alan. He's such a nice, steady boy. I thought they were made for each other."

"So did I. She's been going out with girls from school recently and she has missed choir practice twice for no apparent reason. I asked her if she had another boyfriend, but she became secretive and wouldn't answer. That's worrying in itself. She would always confide in me." Audrey's forehead creased with concern.

Just as they were thinking of going to bed they heard a light knock at the back door. The dogs stood up, wagging their tails, so it was obviously a friend.

Harry opened the door and a, seriously drunk, Alan staggered in. Harry led him to a chair.

"I'm sorry Mr Roberts," Alan sobbed, tears streaming down his face. "I had to come and tell you, cos Pamela hasn't been straight with me and she's not been straight with you either." He dissolved into noisy tears.

Harry put his arm around the young man, "Try to keep your voice down Alan, the girls are all asleep. Audrey will make you a coffee and you can tell us all about it." Audrey nodded and went into the kitchen.

Harry sat back and allowed Alan to compose himself.

"Sorry, sorry Mr Roberts," Alan continued more quietly. "I just can't believe how horrible Pamela has been to me." He got out a hankie to blow his nose.

"I don't know if she told you that I wanted us to get engaged. She seemed pleased at first, but then she said, 'let's get married straight away, and then I can have a baby.' I was amazed! I said that we couldn't afford to get married yet, and I certainly didn't want to have children for a few years. I've only just started as a librarian, as you know. I want to save up for a deposit on a house, and anyway, I thought Pamela would want to finish her studies first. That was when she said I was boring and she didn't want to see me again!" He took a large gulp of the coffee that Audrey handed to him.

"Oh, I'm so sorry Alan. She's been obsessed with babies since Michelle was born, but I was hoping she would tire of the idea."

"It gets worse though," Alan continued. "I went into the Blue Bell pub on Moston Lane tonight. You know, it's the one near the school where the girls go to choir practice?"

Harry nodded.

"I was sitting in a corner, drowning my sorrows when a lad I used to know from primary school came in with his mates. Tony Wilkinson, he's called. Loud mouthed bully. He came across when he saw me. 'You used to go out with Pam Roberts, didn't you?' He said. I just glared at him. 'Well, she's with me now, and she's a right goer, isn't she? I couldn't take it. I stood up, pushed him away and walked out. I went to the Ben Brierley and had three more pints before I decided to come here to see you." He sagged back in the chair, deflated now that he had told his story.

Audrey was devastated. "You don't think she's . . .?" She couldn't bring herself to say what she was thinking.

"It's very likely," said Alan. "She would think he is far from boring, and I don't think she would need much persuading to do - something stupid - with him. The rumours say he's

266

already got one girl pregnant and he just dumped her when he found out. He's a nasty piece of work!"

Harry had his head in his hands. He finally looked up and said, "Thanks for telling us Alan. I'll have a word with her as soon as possible."

"It might be better if I speak to her,: said Audrey. "We used to be close; maybe I can get through to her."

"Alright lovey; I'll leave you to talk to her. I hope . . . Well I just hope she's being sensible." He took a deep breath. "I'll give you a lift home Alan."

"Its ok, I'll walk. I don't want my mum to see me like this. She always waits up for me. She's been upset about our break up too. She thought the world of Pamela."

Audrey gave Alan a hug, and Harry saw him to the back door. "Good luck Alan, and thank you again." Said Harry, as they shook hands.

Alan just nodded and walked off into the darkness. At least he was walking in a straight line now. The strong coffee had helped.

When he returned to Audrey, she was staring into the fire and tears were rolling down her cheeks. "I've been too soft with her, haven't I?' She said, tearfully.

"We both have," said Harry. "We've tried to make up for them losing their mother at such a young age. It doesn't seem to have harmed the others, but Pamela has become more and more wayward. She's so clever, but she doesn't seem to have any common sense. I worry about . . ." He faltered, not wanting to voice his worry.

"I know what you're thinking Harry. You are worried that Pamela may have the same as Bronwyn." She couldn't say the name of the dreaded disease; that would make it too real.

Now Harry's eyes were full of tears. He nodded. "She is so like Bronwyn was at that age. Full of life but so gullible; and some of her mannerisms, her facial expressions . . . Oh, but I don't want to think about it!"

Audrey put her arms around him. "I know, I know lovey. Let's try and take each day as it comes. I'll talk to her and we'll take it from there. Let's go to bed now."

Harry didn't sleep for a long time. He lay, listening to Audrey's even breathing. At least she had eventually got to sleep. She needed her rest; she worked so hard making a comfortable home for their children. Even now, in the school holidays, she often refused help, saying that she'd rather see Harry working in his garden, or taking the dogs for a walk. The girls had their chores, but they were light compared to Audrey's workload. Harry treasured this lovely, gentle woman who had eased his grief and gave him so much love. Eventually, towards dawn, he slept.

He wasn't surprised to find himself in Mymie's little sitting room. "You always know when I need your counsel, Mymie," he said.

"You tell me in so many ways Harry. I feel your sadness, and also your happiness. You have so much to feel happy about; never forget that. You need to hold on to the happy times, to bolster you through the sad times. I don't know if what you fear for Pamela is true. I know nothing of illness and disease, but if it does come to pass, I know that you will be able to bear it with the help of your other children and your lovely wife. Keep hold of the joy that Pamela gives you; she is a lovely, generous girl and she cares very much for you and the rest of the family. Yes, she is being thoughtless, but she is still the same girl deep inside. Treasure that thought, and know that I am thinking about you, always. Goodnight dearie."

"Goodnight Mymie, and thank you." As usual after speaking to Mymie, Harry fell into a deep, restful sleep, and he awoke next morning feeling more optimistic.

The house felt very quiet when he woke up. He looked at the clock and was surprised that he had slept until ten am.

He quickly got shaved and dressed and went downstairs. There was nobody in, not even the dogs. There was a note on the kitchen table.

> *Dear Harry,*
>
> *Carol and Lynette have gone to Daisy Nook with the dogs and a picnic. Pamela and I are going shopping in town.*
>
> *Have a nice, peaceful day.*
>
> *Love, Audrey.*

Harry smiled; so Audrey was treating Pamela to her favourite thing - shopping and lunch in town. Hopefully that will encourage Pamela to talk. He had breakfast and then went out to work in his garden.

Audrey and Pamela were sitting in Woolworth's cafe, just finishing their fish and chips. Sipping her tea, Audrey ventured a question.

"I hear you have a new boyfriend lovey?"

Pamela looked up sharply. "Who told you that?"

"So, it's true then?"

Pamela looked down, shamefaced. "It was true, but I finished with him on Saturday. Well, that's not quite true. I should have met him outside the Fourways picture house, you know, the one at the junction of Moston Lane and Charlestown Road?" Audrey nodded. "Well, I was there on time, but he never turned up. So, as far as I'm concerned we're finished. I probably won't see him again anyway. He never comes to Newton Heath. He said he always stays in Moston."

"I'm sorry about that, but You're probably better off without him. What's his name?"

"Tony. I'm not bothered anyway. I've had it with boys; I'd rather have a good book!"

Audrey laughed at this, although Pamela looked serious.

"I'll tell you what, lovey. Let's go to the bookshop in St Ann's Square. We can browse through the books. You're bound to see something you fancy. I'll treat you."

"Ooh thanks Mum. They might have something by Monica Dickens. I love her books."

Later that evening, when they were alone, Audrey told Harry what Pamela had said.

"Well, that's a relief," said Harry. "I doubt if she'll be off boys for ever, but at least she won't be seeing that ruffian again. One worry shelved, hopefully for a long time."

Their worry was shelved just until December.

Sian gave birth to her second baby girl on her birthday, 22nd of December. The usual family party had been postponed until the New Year, due to this happy event.

The twins and Pamela went on the bus to Greenfield to see the new baby on Christmas Eve.

Roberto was out with Michelle, taking their dog for a walk. The girls settled down for a good gossip and a cuddle of the baby.

"Oh she is gorgeous!" Pamela exclaimed, as she held the tiny, dark haired baby. "What are you going to call her?"

"We've decided on Louise, though Michelle keeps calling her Lulu. I'm so pleased that she's not a bit jealous. She thinks the world of her baby sister."

"How does Roberto feel about her? Did he want a son this time?" Said Nerys

"He adores her, and he isn't bothered about having a son. He's already talking about having a vasectomy, as he is determined that two children are enough. I agree with him. We love this little house; it's just big enough for the four of us, and Snowy the dog, of course. The girls can share a bedroom when Louise is older. Roberto wants to ask the landlord if we can buy it."

"That's a great idea!" Said Rosalind. She turned to Pamela. "Come on Pam, it's my turn to hold her now."

Pamela reluctantly gave up the baby to her sister, and then she stood up. "I'll just use your loo, Sian," and she went upstairs.

"Has Pamela put on weight?" Sian asked the twins. "Or is it my imagination?"

"I hadn't noticed," said Rosalind. "But now you come to mention it, she seems to be eating more."

"And she is going to the loo more often," Nerys commented. "You don't think she's . . . ?"

"You don't think I'm what?" Pamela shouted, as she came back in the room. "Come on, don't talk about me behind my back!"

"Well, are you pregnant?" Nerys was never one for shying away from a difficult subject.

Pamela sat down and burst into tears. Rosalind went over and put her arms around her. "It's ok sis. We're here for you."

"Well, that's answered my question," said Nerys. "The next question is, who's the dad?"

Pamela recovered enough to say, "Tony Wilkinson."

"What! That detestable bully who threatened us on the way home from Choir? Are you barmy Pam? He's horrible!" Nerys was incensed.

Rosalind gently said, "You silly girl, when you could have still been with the lovely Alan."

"He's not that bad, well, he wasn't," she sniffed. "I only went out with him for two weeks, and then he stood me up. I haven't seen him since, and I don't want to. He was fun at first and then . . . he wasn't. It was too late then."

"Why didn't you tell us sooner, you could have had an abortion. It'll be too late now."

"I don't want an abortion! I want a baby. It's what I've always wanted. I'm keeping my baby!"

Sian was more shocked than the younger girls." Oh Pamela, what have you done? You're supposed to get a husband before you have a baby. You need the support of a good man. Why couldn't you wait?"

"I didn't want to wait, and I don't need a man telling me what to do. I'll look after my baby by myself!"

"Where will you live though? What if Dad and Auntie Audrey don't want the responsibility and throw you out? Have you thought of that?" She looked at Pamela's appalled face. "No, you didn't think of that, did you? I don't suppose you thought of the fact that there's no space at home. Carol and Lynette are in the small bedroom and there are three of you in the other room. Will the twins have to put up with sleepless nights because of a crying baby?"

Pamela stared at her elder sister, aghast, saying nothing while tears poured down her face. The twins could see that she hadn't thought of the possibility of her parents disowning her.

273

It was Rosalind who came to comfort her again. "I'm sure Dad and Auntie Audrey won't disown you," she said, giving her a hankie to dry her face. "They'll be shocked of course, but they'll stand by you, we all will," she glared at Sian as she said this, and Sian had the grace to nod and agree.

Nerys came and sat on Pamela's other side. "We'll work something out. The oldies have got spare rooms. Maybe Rosalind and I can move in with Grandma and Grandad."

"That's a good idea," Rosalind agreed.

"Would you do that, for me?" Pamela was looking more hopeful.

"Of course, We're still a threesome, even if you don't want to be a nurse, we've forgiven you for that. You can't help being an idiot!" Nerys laughed, defusing the situation a little.

By the time they left Sian's house they had the situation sorted in their minds. They just had to convince their parents, and grandparents, that it was a good idea. Of course, they had to break the news first. Rosalind had volunteered for that job, though she insisted that Nerys and Pamela had to be in the room to back her up.

They arrived home to be greeted by the delicious smell of mince pies. Carol and Audrey were busy In the kitchen, preparing the vegetables for the Christmas dinner. Dozens of mince pies and an enormous turkey were sitting prepared on the table.

"Oh sorry, we left all the work for you," said Rosalind. "But we couldn't wait until after Christmas to see the new baby."

"Thats alright," said Carol. "You two are working tomorrow; that's going to be really strange, but Pam, you can help in the morning."

"Fair enough," said Pamela. Her mind was on the coming confrontation anyway. She hardly noticed Carol's look of surprise.

"Where's Dad?" Rosalind asked, looking through into the empty living room.

"He's just gone over to Grandma Alice to pick up the Christmas cake. He took Lynette and the dogs with him, to get them out of our way. Lynette is so excited about Father Christmas coming, and the dogs were hovering, hoping for dropped food. I nearly fell over Rusty, twice," said Audrey.

The younger girls looked at each other and silently agreed to postpone the confrontation until after tea. It would be better after Lynette was in bed anyway. Carol noticed the look, but said nothing; she had a good idea of the subject they had to discuss. She would wait.

Audrey was oblivious to the atmosphere, as she finished the last of the sprouts. "There, that's done," she said, satisfied. "We've got the usual ham salad for tea; I just need to cut and butter the bread."

"You sit down now Auntie Audrey, you too Carol. We'll do the bread," offered Rosalind. "Pam, you can set the table. Come on Nerys, I'll slice and you can butter." Sliced bread was plentiful in the shops, but Audrey, and the two grandmas, still preferred the uncut bread from the bakery.

"Ok bossy boots," said Nerys, but she was smiling.

Audrey had put Lynette to bed and they were all sitting around the fire, drinking tea, the dogs sprawled across everyone's feet.

"Come on then, out with it," said Carol. "I know you three have something to tell us."

Nerys and Pamela looked at Rosalind. She cleared her throat and said, "You're not going to like this Dad, Auntie Audrey . . .." She didn't get any further.

Harry, his face as stern as it ever got, said "Pamela is having a baby, isn't she?"

There was a gasp from all three girls and Pamela looked down at the floor. "How did you know, Dad?" Nerys asked.

"I'm a father of seven, eight if you count Johnny. I know the signs. I was waiting for you to tell me Pamela, and you are a coward, getting Rosalind to do it." Pamela began to sob.

Rosalind wasn't surprised that Harry already knew, and that Carol had a good idea. She was just surprised that she, herself, hadn't realised before now. She was usually so in tune with her sisters.

"I don't know how I didn't notice," she said, wonderingly.

Carol smiled at her. "You've been getting to grips with your work. First it was intensive studying, and then it was shift work on the wards. It's not surprising that you haven't noticed what was going on at home." she looked accusingly at Pamela. "Also, Pamela has been avoiding all of us, haven't you? Going to bed early, supposedly to read your book; staying at a friend's house to study; going for a walk to 'clear your head' Hiding sanitary pads too, I imagine, so that no one would realise you aren't using them!"

Pamela held her head even lower, but nodded to agree with everything that Carol said.

"Oh Pamela," said Audrey, sadly. "When is your baby due?"

"I'm not sure; I think I'm about five months, so, about the end of April or early May."

"You haven't seen a doctor, have you?"

Pamela shook her head.

"Well, I'll go with you after New Year and get you booked into the ante natal clinic. You should have told us before now."

"I didn't want an abortion!"

Audrey was shocked. "I'm glad to hear you say that at least, but you should have known that neither I, nor your Dad would have asked that of you. Life is precious!"

"Sorry, I should have known." Pamela could still not look up.

Harry had his say then. "Yes, you should have known, but you were selfishly determined that you were going to have a baby, at any cost, and no one was going to stop you. That's why you've left it so long, isn't it?"

"Yes," she said, so quietly that the others could hardly hear her.

"Well, by leaving it so long you've put your own health and your baby's at risk. Let's hope that there isn't anything that should have been detected early on."

Pamela looked up, shocked. "I never thought. . . . "

"No, you didn't. I assume that the father is this Tony?" Pamela nodded.

"Does he know?"

"No, I haven't seen him since, and I don't want him to know!"

"I agree with you there. He sounds like a waste of space, but you will have to tell your child, at some time in the future, who their father is. They have a right to know."

"I suppose so," Pamela agreed, though she was horrified at the thought.

"What about your studies?" Carol asked.

"I don't think I'll go back after Christmas. Everyone will be able to tell soon, and the year end exam will be just when the baby is due."

"That's a shame, because, if you complete the year, maybe you can go back sometime in the future to finish your degree."

Harry intervened. "It would probably be better if you don't go back. You could repeat the whole course later, when you feel able." While saying this, Harry doubted whether Pamela would ever go back to her studies, but it was no use dwelling on that now. The main thing now was to ensure the best health for Pamela and her baby, and, of course, inform the rest of the family. At least, it being Christmas, most of the family would be together, so the news wouldn't have to be repeated too often.

Johnny came in just then. He had been having tea with his grandparents next door. He looked round at all the solemn faces. "What?" He asked

"Pamela is pregnant," said Nerys, with relish. Now that the news was out she was eager to see the effect it had on Johnny. She wasn't disappointed.

Johnny's face was a picture. "I don't believe it!" He looked at Pamela. "What about your studies?" As a teacher, that was the most important thing to him. He didn't even think to ask about the father, or when the baby was due.

Pamela just looked at him, not knowing what to say.

"She thinks that having a baby is more important than anything else," said Harry, bitterly. "Even more important than having a father for the child."

"There must be a father though; what does he think?" Johnny was wondering how he would feel if Rhona told him she was pregnant. He didn't like the way his thoughts were going. In fact he realised that he wouldn't like it one bit. For a moment he forgot about Pamela.

Carol looked at him, knowing somehow what he was thinking. She brought him back to the present. "The father doesn't know about the baby, and it's the general consensus of opinion among us that he wouldn't care if he did know. Apparently he is a nasty piece of work."

Johnny looked at Pamela. "So, why . . .?"

Rosalind answered for her. "He can lay on the charm when he wants to but, when he has achieved his ends, he doesn't want to know, and doesn't care about the consequences."

"Oh, I see," said Johnny. He couldn't think of anything else to say.

"Don't worry Johnny. We'll deal with it like we always do, as a family, and it'll be lovely to have another niece or nephew, won't it?" Nerys laughed.

"Well, let's hope that this time it will be a nephew," Johnny replied. "I've said it before, there are far too many girls in this family." He turned to Pamela, smiling, and said, "give me a nephew to play football with."

Pamela smiled wanly. "If nobody minds, I think I'll go to bed." It was only eight thirty, and they usually stayed up late on Christmas Eve, drinking sherry and wrapping last minute presents. No one complained though. The atmosphere was spoiled. it was a relief to let Pamela go.

"Does anyone want a sherry?" Said Audrey, after Pamela had gone upstairs.

"Actually, I wouldn't mind a cup of tea," said Rosalind.

"Me too," said Carol. "I'll go and put the kettle on.

oOo

Christmas morning started as usual with Lynette waking Carol at 5 am to tell her that Father Christmas had been. There was no getting back to sleep, so Carol took her little sister downstairs, hoping to give her parents another hour in bed.

The twins were up at six, as they were both on early shift, and Harry arrived downstairs soon after them, as he had promised to drive them to the hospital. There were no buses until noon. Audrey was up to see them off at 7 o'clock, but Pamela didn't emerge until after 9.

The grandparents were coming for Christmas dinner, which would be about 1pm; before that they would all go to church. Harry didn't want to talk about Pamela's news over dinner, so he went to tell his parents after breakfast, and then to Audrey's parents. To say they were shocked was an understatement. Being from a generation when unmarried mothers were hidden away in shame, it was difficult for them to understand that Pamela was determined to bring up her child alone. Harry managed to get them used to the idea, but he imagined that Christmas dinner would be a strained affair, with none of the usual jokes and laughter.

In the event, with everyone avoiding the subject of babies, it was the absence of the twins that dominated the conversation.

"I hadn't thought about the girls having to work bank holidays," said Dorothy. "They leave a big gap, don't they?"

"Yes," said Alice. "Especially as it's usually Nerys making the most noise, and Rosalind giggling at her antics."

Harry agreed. "It's not the same without them, but they are both on early shift, so I'll pick them them up at five o'clock and they'll be here for the evening. It'll be even more strange when they go on nights. They think that'll be towards the end of January. Apparently they have to do eight to ten weeks of nights each year of their three years training."

"I suppose it won't be many years before all the girls get married. That'll be another big change." Said Bill. He glanced sideways at Pamela as he said this. She seemed to Ignore this, but Harry could sense her disquiet.

The conversation petered out then, and everyone concentrated on eating.

By three o'clock the table had been cleared and the dishes washed and everyone settled in front of the television with their favourite drinks, for the Queen's speech, followed by a family film.

"Do you remember," said Fred. "When all the children were small and there was no telly. Everyone did a 'turn'. It's not as much fun watching a film."

"Yes," said Dorothy. "Remember when Pamela and the twins used to sing 'Sisters", pretending to be the Beverley Sisters. They were so funny. We asked them to do that every year, until they were about twelve, when they refused to do it again. They said they were too grown up!"

Everyone laughed at this and began reminiscing about other turns that the children had performed. "David and Billy sang 'What shall we do with the Drunken Sailor' one year. They were out of tune, but no one minded," laughed Audrey.

They talked and laughed so much that the film was ignored, and Harry eventually turned the television off. He left at four thirty to pick up the twins, leaving a lovely atmosphere of nostalgia. Even Pamela was smiling a little as she held her little sister Lynette on her knee.

The twins were in high spirits when they came in. "The patients had a lovely day," said Rosalind. "Everyone got presents and they had a turkey dinner with wine, for those who were allowed wine. Nerys and I had two hours away from our wards after dinner, as we are in the nurses' choir. We went round all the wards singing carols. Everyone was so happy."

"The day just flew!" Nerys exclaimed. "I don't suppose tomorrow will be as good, and I'm on late shift. I'll miss our usual Boxing Day party, but, never mind. I'm looking forward to our delayed party on New Years Day. We've both got the day off."

The rest of the week was unusually quiet for the family, but they made up for it on New Years Day. Family members started arriving at Fred and Dorothy's house in the morning, ostensibly to help with preparations, but really to catch up on the gossip. Everyone wanted to know the details of Pamela's pregnancy and to give their opinion on the matter. Pamela kept out of the way as much as she could, staying in her bedroom to avoid repeatedly answering the same questions.

By mid afternoon the party food had been set out in Dorothy's kitchen, the dining table having been removed to accommodate all the people. They were celebrating six birthdays now. In addition to Carol, Billy and Linda, who were now 23, and Sian - 26 David had celebrated his 21st birthday yesterday, and of course, the newest member of the family, Louise, had arrived on Carol and Sian's birthday.

The traditional small iced cakes had been made for each person. Louise's had a single candle, which was proudly blown out by her big sister Michelle.

After most of the food had been eaten, the older family members stayed in Dorothy's living room, while the younger people went next door to play records and dance.

Audrey played the piano for a good old sing song. Drinks were handed round and everyone became contentedly merry. They all agreed that it was the best party ever, and worth waiting for.

The morning after the party was an anticlimax. The twins, who were on late shift, Lynette and Pamela, stayed in bed until after nine, but Carol was up early and planning to take the dogs for a good, long walk.

Johnny came in as she was finishing her breakfast. "Are you taking the dogs out?" He asked. "Fancy some company?"

"Yes, if you can stand the cold." It was frosty and clear. Carol put on her winter coat, scarf, hat and gloves.

"It'll be refreshing," Johnny replied.

They set off for Brookdale Park, the dogs tugging enthusiastically at their leads. They walked for a while in companionable silence, then Carol asked. "Didn't Rhona want to come home with you?"

"No, she wanted me to go to her parents in Edinburgh for Christmas, but I really want to be with my family at Christmas. I asked her if she would come with me, and we would go to Edinburgh for New Year. As you know, the Scots make more of Hogmanay, so I thought she would be happy with that. I was even willing to forgo our New year party, but she said no, If I didn't want to spend all the holidays with her family, she would just go alone."

"Oh, I'm sorry," said Carol. "Are things not going so well between you?"

"I'm not really sure. She seems happy with me most of the time, but then she will stay away from me for a while. She'll be going out with her friends, or she will say that she needs some space. Then she will be back, being affectionate. I don't understand her."

Carol didn't know what to say. She could sense that Johnny wasn't broken hearted about being away from Rhona. In fact everything about him told her that he was relaxed and happy.

"I hope you get things sorted out," she finally said.

Johnny looked at her as though he was going to ask her something, but then changed his mind. "Thanks," he replied, and then said, "How is your job? I haven't really asked you about it. There's been so much going on."

"I love it," she replied. "The other teachers are so supportive, and the pupils are lovely. One or two are a bit moody, but then they are teenagers, so it's to be expected."

"I thought you would enjoy it. You're a natural teacher, Carol. I've noticed how you are with our sisters and cousins. You have so much patience, explaining things to them."

"I'd never thought about it, but you're right Johnny. I love seeing the look on their faces when they understand something I've told them."

"I'm the same. I can't see me ever wanting to be anything but a teacher. I love passing on my love of history to young people."

"What about staying in Shetland; do you think you'll stay there long term?"

"I'm not sure. I'm always eager to come home in the holidays. Maybe, if I could be sure of a post in a friendly school like the Anderson, I may be tempted to come back. I wouldn't like to lose touch with Shetland altogether though. I like spending time with Mymie; and now Andy and Maggie are married and living in Levenwick with Kirsty and peerie Carol, They are just like family. I would miss them."

Carol was aware that Johnny hadn't mentioned whether he would miss Rhona. It didn't seem likely that she would come to Manchester with him if he did leave Shetland, considering that she had refused to come just for Christmas. Deciding to change the subject, she said, "Hasn't Rusty grown into a lovely dog? She has a lot of whippet in her, but she has filled out. I don't know what other breed she is crossed with, but it suits her. She can run like a whippet though, watch this."

They had just entered the park, so Carol let Rusty off her lead and threw a ball across the field. Rusty shot off like a bullet. Flossie followed as soon as Johnny released her, but she couldn't catch up with the smaller dog. Rusty had grabbed the ball and was on her way back before the two dogs met. They both returned to the couple, with tongues lolling and tails wagging.

Carol produced another ball. "We'd better throw both balls together, or Flossie won't get a chance."

They threw the balls again and again, until the dogs flopped at their feet, obviously tired. "Come on," said Carol. "Lets have a slow walk through the dells to give them a chance to recover. I haven't been down there for ages."

The dells were pretty, despite the bareness of the winter trees. There were enough evergreens and lots of ferns to give a feeling of tranquility. The sky above was a clear blue. They didn't see anyone else until they were almost back to the park gates. It was as if they owned the park.

"Of course, it was a private park back in the nineteenth century," said Johnny. "Manchester Corporation bought it in 1900. Brookdale Hall was just over there, above the dells. It was only demolished about eight years ago. Such a shame. It was a magnificent house."

"I remember the house. I thought you would know the history," laughed Carol.

"It's what I do," Johnny replied, smiling.

They made their way back home, chatting about the party. Just as they got to the garden gate Johnny suddenly said, " Will you be coming up to Shetland soon?"

"I may come at half term, but it will depend on the weather. February weather can be severe., so I won't decide until nearer the time. I'll definitely be coming at Easter though." Was it her imagination, or did she have a strong sense of Johnny's pleasure at her intended visit?

"Mymie will be pleased to see you," *and so will I,* were his unspoken words.

Carol felt a warm glow that had nothing to do with the warmth of the kitchen as they came in from the back door.

In the event, February was far too wild for a trip to Shetland, but Carol went up for ten days in the Easter Holidays.

Johnny was waiting as the ferry docked. "I've got a car now," he said. "So I told Andy that I would pick you up. He's finished the new extension to his house, giving them two more bedrooms and another bathroom. Peerie Carol has her own bedroom now, and I'm staying in the other one for the Easter holidays."

"Oh, that's posh," said Carol. "I suppose Andy did most of the work himself?"

"Yes, his pals did the plumbing and electrics, and I helped him with labouring. It looks really good."

"I can't wait to see it."

"Well, Maggie has invited you and Mymie for supper, so you'll be able to have the tour."

"Lovely; I'm looking forward to seeing them all." Carol relaxed in the car and enjoyed seeing all the well loved sights of the South Mainland. It seemed no time before they were drawing up at Mymie's gate. She and Bess were waiting at the top of the steps. Carol greeted the dog before enveloping Mymie in a hug. "It's so lovely to be here again," she said, as Mymie led the way in and Johnny followed with Carol's case.

"I'll see you later then," said Johnny, as he deposited the case in the spare bedroom.

"Yes, thanks for the lift Johnny."

Carol and Mymie walked down to Andy's house in the early evening. Carol was carrying a bag of clothes and a gift for her goddaughter. Mymie's basket contained a large apple pie and a jug of custard. The custard would be cold by the time they were ready for dessert, but no one would mind.

Peerie Carol was jumping with excitement. "Auntie Carol, what have you brought in your bag?"

"Oh Carol!" Kirsty admonished her daughter. "That's not good manners. You should say hello and how are you. You haven't seen Auntie Carol since last year."

"Sorry Auntie Carol. How are you? Now can we look in your bag?" She said, without waiting for an answer.

Carol laughed. "You know I always bring something. Here's a new jigsaw for you." She knew that peerie Carol loved the jigsaws with big wooden pieces. "The rest is clothes."

Peerie Carol wasn't interested in clothes. She took the jigsaw and settled on the floor with it. Kirsty and Maggie came over to look at the clothes.

"My two grandmas knitted the cardigans. They know you have beautiful knitted clothes here, but you were so kind to say that you liked to see the different patterns, especially the cable ones. So they've made a dark blue one in cable and a pink one in a lacy pattern. They might be a bit big for Carol yet as they made them in age five size." Peerie Carol, at four and a half, was a dainty child.

"Also, Auntie Audrey has made two dresses to match the cardigans. She loves sewing."

Kirsty and Maggie were delighted with the clothes. "That's so kind of them," said Kirsty. "Carol will be the best dressed in the class when she starts school in September."

"We're sad that the Levenwick School closed last year. They've got a smart new school at Dunrossness. All the local children will be taken there by bus," said Maggie. "I suppose it's better for the children to have a new building and all the amenities, but the local school was more cosy, with just two teachers."

"Yes, That was my school when I was a peerie boy," said Andy.

"Mine too," Mymie agreed. "Everything is changing; we have to hope it is for the good."

They had a lovely evening with good food and conversation. Kirsty was very interested in Pamela and the imminent birth of her baby. Pamela's situation was similar, but not exactly like Kirsty's own, as it seemed that Pamela had deliberately become pregnant.

"She longed so much for a baby, you see," said Carol. "To the point where she finished with her steady boyfriend because he wanted to wait a few years to get married and have children. So she found a father for her baby, but she chose very badly. He had finished with her before she knew she was pregnant. She hasn't seen him since and she doesn't want him to know about the baby, as she has realised that he would make a very bad father."

"Isn't she frightened of bringing up her child alone?" Kirsty asked.

"Luckily, like you, she has a supportive family. She's been very silly, but of course we've forgiven her. So she won't really be alone. The twins are already debating whether they will be allowed to stay with her for the birth. They work at the hospital she is booked in."

"Kirsty isn't so alone now, apart from us of course," Maggie said, with a smile.

Kirsty blushed. "I have a boyfriend, Donald, and he loves peerie Carol."

"Oh that's wonderful news. Does he live nearby?" Carol asked.

"Yes, he lives with his parents here in Levenwick, though he works at the Gilbert Bain Hospital, in the kitchens. We met at chapel."

"Everyone is so supportive here," said Maggie. "Donald's parents are very fond of peerie Carol too."

"I'm so happy for you Kirsty. I'd love to meet him, while I'm here, if you think that would be alright?"

"Oh yes, I've told him all about you. I know he would like to meet you."

"Why don't you all come for supper; Saturday?" Suggested Mymie. "I know Donald slightly, but I haven't had the opportunity to talk to him."

"That sounds wonderful," said Maggie. "This time I'll bring the pudding."

It was raining when Carol and Mymie were ready to leave, so Johnny took them home in the car. As they left him, he asked Carol. "Would you like to go to Mousa tomorrow?

You too Mymie. They've just started the boat trips, and the forecast is good. I haven't been back there since the first year we were here. I'd like to see it again."

"Oh I'd love that," Carol replied. "I haven't been there since then either."

Mymie declined. "Thanks Johnny, but I promised Maggie I'd go into Lerwick with her. The two of you will get around the island much more quickly without me anyway." She smiled.

"I'll see you tomorrow then," said Carol.

"I'll pick you up at ten."

"Ok, I'll bring a picnic. Night night."

"Night night," Johnny replied.

Carol went to bed, wondering why Johnny was taking her to Mousa without Rhona. On previous visits to Shetland she had been invited to evenings with Johnny's group of friends, and Rhona was always with them. It was strange that Johnny hadn't even mentioned her. Maybe she would find out tomorrow.

It was a beautiful spring morning. The air was fresh and fragrant as only Shetland air could be. Carol stood at the front door with Bess at her side, watching Mymie walk down to Andy's house. She inhaled deeply and admired the scene spread out below her. The crescent of white sand was glittering in the morning sun and the wind sent waves across the blue-green of the bay.

Johnny parked the car and bounded up the steps to take the bag of picnic goodies off her hands.

"Gosh, you're energetic today!" Carol exclaimed.

"Well, I slept like a log and woke up to this lovely day. What could be better?"

"True, I was just thinking how lucky we are to be able to enjoy all this. I never want to live anywhere but Manchester, but I'm so glad that I can come here so often."

Johnny nodded his agreement. "Ready to go?"

"I'll just put Bess into the house." She bent down to talk to the dog. "We can't take you with us, Bess, because you don't like boats." She sent Bess a picture of a boat bobbing on the waves. The dog whined and turned back to the house.

"I wish I knew how you do that," Johnny said, as he watched the dog. "She seemed to know exactly what you said."

Carol smiled and said, "she's a clever dog."

It was only a ten minute drive to Sandwick, and they were in good time for the boat. It was a pleasant crossing; the wind wasn't too fierce and the sun shone through a gap in the clouds, giving them a little warmth.

They set off from the jetty to walk across to the broch. There were two couples with children walking in the same direction, obviously also making for the broch.

"Shall we go over to the other side of the island and have our lunch over there before we visit the broch?" Johnny suggested. "We may have it to ourselves later on."

"Yes, that's a good idea," Carol replied.

They walked over the rough grass to the east side of the island and found a pleasant spot sheltered from the wind, just above a small bay. They sat on a sun warmed rock, admiring the peaceful scene.

They were quiet for a while and then Carol asked, "Johnny, I hope you don't mind my asking, but, why didn't Rhona come with us?"

"Rhona isn't here any more."

"What do you mean, not here in Shetland?"

"Exactly. She never came back after Christmas. She sent a sick note to the head, but she didn't try to contact me at all. It was Angus who told me that she had suffered a bad bout of flu. I phoned her parent's number and her mother said that she was ill in bed and couldn't come to the phone. I asked her to tell Rhona that I hoped she would get well soon. She thanked me, but she seemed distant, almost unfriendly. I couldn't think what I had done to deserve that. I said I'd ring again in a week to see how she was getting on."

"But she still isn't back? That sounds serious!"

"She isn't coming back. I rang again a week later, and this time Rhona answered the phone. She then said that she hadn't been physically ill, but was depressed. Her parents had encouraged her to stay in Edinburgh with them and she could apply for a post down there when she felt up to it. She sent her resignation by post, giving a reason of poor health."

"Did she say why she hadn't told you about it?"

"Oh yes," he answered, bitterly. She said it was all my fault, that I didn't care enough about her. That I was always talking about my family in Manchester, and also that I spent far too much time in Levenwick with my 'adopted family' - her words. I was flabbergasted! Whenever I went to Levenwick I invited her to go with me, but she only came with me once. I invited her to go with me to Manchester, again she wasn't interested." He heaved a sigh and gazed out to sea.

"You can't help talking about your family. Didn't she talk about hers?"

"Yes; I always asked about her parents, and I got on well with them when I went with her to visit them. I really don't understand her. Perhaps she was right; perhaps I didn't care enough. She never said anything though. I told you that there were times when she didn't want to be with me, but she never gave a reason. I'm really sorry if her depression was caused by me; I told her as much, but she just told me not to phone her again. She wanted a clean break. I haven't told anyone but you. I feel so ashamed."

"Oh Johnny!" Carol leaned across and hugged him. "I don't think it was all your fault. How could you know how she felt if she didn't bother to tell you? Depression is a complicated thing There could have been many reasons for it, or no reason at all. I've heard of something called clinical depression, where the person suffering doesn't know what is causing it. Anyway, she said she wanted a clean break, and she's at home with her parents, being cared for. Maybe she'll contact you when she feels better."

"That's the trouble. I don't want her to contact me, and I feel guilty about that. I've realised that I feel relieved that she has gone away. I never truly loved her. I enjoyed her company, when we were together, but I never missed her when she went off with her other friends, and, when she said that she didn't want me to come to Edinburgh for Hogmanay, I was glad. I wanted to stay at home with the family. I can't believe that we were a couple all that time and neither of us realised it wasn't what we wanted."

Carol held his hand and asked, "what do you want?"

"I can't tell you that."

"Because you don't know what you want?"

Johnny turned and looked into her lovely, grey eyes. "No, because I can't have what I want."

His look was intense, and Carol didn't need to ask. His heart was overflowing with love, for her! She had known this for a few years, and had at first hoped that he would get over it, which was the reason she had encouraged his relationship with Rhona. She had hoped that his feelings for her would fade, but her own feelings had become stronger over time. She didn't want to love him, but had to admit that she did. She had convinced herself that she would never marry or have children, but now she realised that they had at least to talk about it.

"Johnny, I think we need to be straight with each other. I know you have feelings for me, and I have to confess I feel the same, but . . ."

"Why does there have to be a but? I've loved you for years, ever since you saved a horse and a rabbit in the same week."

"All those years?"

296

"Yes, I don't have what you and Uncle Harry, and Mymie, have. I don't have any gifts, but I can tell that you are a good and caring person, and I love you, Carol. Being away from you these last years has been terrible. I tried to love Rhona, but how could I, when I love you? I want to be with you for the rest of my life."

"But Johnny, you know that I can't get married and have children. I made that decision years ago. You know why."

"You're allowed to change your mind, you know? I know it's because you are worried that you might have what your mum had, but we could get married, and I would look after you if you became ill. We don't have to have children. Carol, I would still love you, no matter what."

"But surely you would want children sometime? You might come to resent me in the future, because I won't change my mind about that. I won't bring a child into the world who is at risk of such a horrible disease."

Johnny took her face in his hands and gently said, "I won't change my mind either lovey. I just want to be with you, and I don't want to bring an at risk child into the world either."

He kissed her then, tenderly at first, and then with passion as she responded. She couldn't help responding, as she finally gave in to the fact that she also wanted to be with him for always.

They finally parted and looked at each other, smiling.

"If I can get a post in Manchester from September, will you marry me this summer?"

"Yes," she replied. There was nothing else to say.

That evening as they sat by the fire, Mymie smiled and said, "So you are going to marry him, at last?"

"You knew, didn't you?" Was the reply.

"I knew that you couldn't stop loving him, but you had to realise for yourself. You've been dreaming about him, haven't you?"

"Yes, ever since he came to Shetland."

"Of course. Well, I cannot say that his time here has been wasted. He has been a good thing for the school, and he has been a good friend to Andy, Maggie and Kirsty, and me. I know that his time here has been good for him too. He has grown as a person and developed into a fine teacher. Whichever school takes him on will be very lucky. You will both come and visit often, I know."

"Of course we will. You and all my friends here in Shetland have been good for me too. I would miss you too much if I didn't see you regularly. Also, I hope you can come to Manchester for the wedding."

"I will definitely be there."

Fifteen:

A Baby, A Wedding and a Dream Come True.

Nerys was upset. "They're moving me to Ancoats, just as Pamela's baby is due! There's no way I can be there for her now, unless it happens on my day off."

Rosalind commiserated. She was moving to ward G4, which was immediately above the labour ward. She was hoping that the baby wouldn't be born on her day off. "Never mind Nerys. She's bound to have one or both of us with her. I'm sorry that they are sending you to Ancoats without me though. We've been relatively close to each other up to now. It looks like the next time we get together will be second year block."

At the beginning of their second year as student nurses the group known as 'August 69 PTS' would come together for a four week block of classroom study. They would receive their blue belt and, at the end of the four weeks they would sit a 'block exam'. Similarly, at the beginning of their third year they would receive their red belt and undertake another four weeks of study.

"You'd think they could have sent us both to Ancoats together," Nerys grumbled. "I'll bet it was that assistant matron who doesn't like me!"

"Well, you shouldn't have put that plastic spider on the counter in second office. She's never forgiven you for that!"

"How was I to know she was scared of spiders?" They both laughed.

Ancoats hospital was a smaller hospital, close to Town; part of the group of hospitals in North Manchester. The student nurses were expected to work there for a time. It was actually easier to get to from Newton Heath, as the number 25 bus that passed their house stopped right outside the hospital.

Apart from missing her sister, Nerys was looking forward to her time at Ancoats hospital. It would be a new experience, and she had only heard good about it from friends who had already worked there.

All the wards had names, rather than numbers. Nerys was assigned to Gaddum and Johnson - two small surgical wards run by one Sister. The Sister's desk was in the middle of the female ward, as these wards did not have a Sister's office. Nerys reported to the sister on her first morning and was assigned to the male ward across the corridor.

The two wards were extremely busy and Nerys was exhausted by lunchtime on her first day. She was disappointed to be told that she would have to go to second lunch, as Sister wanted the senior staff back on the ward for the doctor's round. Accompanied by two auxiliaries, Nerys left the ward at one fifteen, only to find that the auxiliaries were part time workers, and were going home. Feeling lonely, she made her way downstairs to the dining room.

As she walked along the ground floor corridor she heard a male voice shout, "Ros, Ros!"

Realising that someone had mistaken her for her sister, Nerys looked round, grinning, to see a tall, dark haired young man, who had the brightest blue eyes she had ever seen. He was vaguely familiar. She thought that she must have seen him in Crumpsall hospital at some time.

As he approached her, she remembered. "Fred, sorry, I can't remember your surname." She didn't enlighten him yet, but continued grinning.

He looked puzzled, and then smiled widely. "You're not Ros, are you? I remembered now, you are identical twins." He shook her hand. "Fred Entwistle, at your service ma'am." His amazing blue eyes were twinkling.

What a lovely man! Thought Nerys. She gazed into his eyes for too long. "Sorry, Nerys Roberts, Ros's alter ego; She's the quiet one, I'm the joker."

"Pleased to meet you, Nerys. Are you on your way to the dining room?"

"Yes, I'm starving. I believe it's just down here?"

"Yes, that's where I'm going. Do you mind if I join you?"

"I'd be delighted."

The dining room was almost empty. Those staff members on the early shift had been to first lunch, and those on a split shift - working the morning and evening and having the afternoon off - had obviously gone into town, shopping.

Fred and Nerys sat at a corner table and talked in between eating.

Fred was a staff nurse, now working in Casualty. "I love it; there is always something happening, so there's never time to get bored." He described some of the gory cases that came through the doors. Luckily, Nerys had a strong stomach and she continued eating steadily through all his descriptions.

"I think I'd enjoy Casualty," she replied. "I Like to be busy, and you must feel as though you're making a difference to someone's life when you're patching them up after an accident."

"Exactly, that's why I love it." He looked at his watch. "Gosh, it's time to go back! I've really enjoyed chatting, Nerys. What shift are you on tomorrow?"

"Split shift," she replied.

"Me too. You'll be on second lunch again. Do you fancy going into town for lunch? We can take our time, and I know a nice little cafe in Spring Gardens. My treat."

"Oh yes, that'd be great, thanks Fred."

Nerys returned to the ward, wondering what had happened. It seemed she had a date! She couldn't wait to get home and tell Rosalind all about it.

"You never told me how lovely he is," Said Nerys.

"Well, I must have said he was nice. He taught me loads of things while I was on E3."

"You know I don't mean nice in that way. He's gorgeous!"

"I don't think I noticed that. He was just a great colleague. Anyway, you met him once or twice. Did you fancy him then?"

"I didn't say I fancy him. I'm just pleased to be going out for lunch with him. I've not had a date for ages. In fact I've never had a really serious date, with someone that I . . ."

"Someone that you fancy. That's what you were going to say; admit it!" Rosalind laughed.

"Ok. I do fancy him. Did you never notice his gorgeous blue eyes?"

"Can't say that I did."

"Probably just as well. It wouldn't do for us both to fancy him. That would be really confusing."

Harry and Audrey were listening to this conversation and chuckling. The twins were so lively and happy.

"So, you don't mind being at Ancoats now, Nerys?" Harry asked.

With a big grin, Nerys answered, "I think I'll be able to put up with it. I'm still sad that I might miss the birth of Pamela's baby, though."

Pamela looked up from her book at the mention of her name. She was looking huge, as her baby was due any day now; she was also looking contented. "I may have my baby on your day off. Anyway, they may not let you be there at the birth. They are only just allowing husbands in, and some of the older midwives are not very happy about that."

"Well, I've already asked my ward Sister if I would be allowed some time off to be with you, as you don't have a husband," said Rosalind. She's really nice, and she said I could go down to the labour ward for a while if our ward isn't too busy, but I would have to go back if I'm needed. Hopefully you'll be admitted just as my shift finishes. I'll keep my fingers crossed."

In the event it was Saturday the 2nd of May, mid afternoon, when Rosalind felt pains in her abdomen. She immediately knew that Pamela was in the labour ward below. It was visiting time, and Rosalind was in the laundry room, putting clean laundry away while the patients were busy with their visitors. She wondered how she could let Sister know about Pamela's labour, without telling her how she knew.

She started her mental preparations for dealing with the pain, just as Mymie had taught her. She was getting quite practiced at it now. She was just getting ready to speak to

Sister when she heard Audrey's voice in the office next door.

"I was wondering, Sister, whether nurse Roberts is free to go down to the labour ward. Her sister is asking for her."

Rosalind approached hopefully.

"Oh, nurse Roberts, there you are. Have you put all the laundry away?"

"Yes Sister."

"Right, well you can go to your sister now. If they let you stay, you don't need to come back, as you finish at five. I imagine you'll be there half the night, as it's her first baby. They always take ages to arrive. What is your off duty for tomorrow?"

"I'm on a late, Sister."

"Right, so you don't need to be here until 11. I'm on early tomorrow, so ring me if you feel unable to work, and we'll sort something out."

"Oh thank you Sister, that's really kind, but I'm sure I'll be fine to do my shift."

"Yes, well, off you go then."

As they went down the stairs, Rosalind asked, "how is she?"

"Remarkably calm," Audrey replied. "She's been in labour since this morning, but she didn't want to come into the hospital too soon. The pains are coming about every ten minutes now. Your dad is in the waiting room. He'll take me home. We already asked the midwife if you could stay with her. She's one of the younger ones, so she's quite happy to let you stay."

Harry was standing at the door of the waiting room. "Oh good, can we go now?" He said, while rubbing his abdomen. "I think they're every five minutes now!"

Rosalind could sense how agitated he was. "That's ok Dad. You two go home now. I'll ring you as soon as there's any news." She saw the midwife at the door to Pamela's cubicle and went towards her.

"Are you Ros? Your sister is asking for you. Here, wash your hands and put this gown on."

Rosalind did as she was told and went in to see Pamela, who was gasping with the pain. Rosalind pictured her hot water bottle and told herself it wasn't her pain; it was just pushing. She felt it ease a little."

"Ros, don't stand there with your eyes shut!" Pamela gasped. "Come and hold my hand; this is horrible!"

As Rosalind went across and took her sister's hand, she felt the contraction fading. Now was the time to prepare Pamela for the next one. She put her hands on each side of Pamela's face.

"Look at me Pam," her words were gentle, but firm as she gazed into her sister's eyes. "When the next pain comes, it'll be strong, but it won't hurt as much. Just keep looking at me and concentrate."

The next contraction seemed to arrive more quickly. The midwife gave Pamela the gas and air to breathe and Rosalind stood back slightly, holding her hand and never taking her eyes off her sister. "It's strong lovey, but not as painful, is it?" Pamela nodded, still puffing at the gas and air. They both relaxed as the contraction faded again.

"That was brilliant!" Said the midwife. "Keep that up and you'll have a reasonable labour.

They continued like this for about two hours and then the midwife examined her. "You're fully dilated! It shouldn't be too long now; you're doing so well, both of you!" She smiled at Rosalind.

The contractions became more intense and almost continuous, but they were coping well and Pamela was now pushing.

"Come on lass, I can see the head; another big push now!"

The baby's head was delivered, and very soon after, Pamela's baby boy was crying lustily as the midwife cut the cord and placed the little boy in her arms.

The look of adoration on Pamela's face made Rosalind cry.

"Don't cry; you've got a lovely nephew," said the midwife. "And he's a big baby. You've been an excellent assistant. I could do with your help more often. Do you fancy doing midwifery after you qualify?"

"I don't know, maybe," she replied.

Mark Roberts was born at six thirty pm and weighed exactly nine pounds. Rosalind phoned home to tell everyone, and asked Harry, "Can you pick me up Dad. I'm shattered!"

"Of course I can lovey. You've done a grand job!"

The house was crowded when Harry and Rosalind got home. The grandparents were all there, along with Carol, Nerys, Audrey and Lynette.

Lynette ran to Rosalind shouting, "I'm an auntie again! Ros, did you know that I'm an auntie?"

"Yes lovey, I did know, and I've seen your new nephew."

"Oh, what does he look like?" Lynette wasn't the only one wanting more details.

"Well, he's called Mark and he weighs nine pounds. He's got black curly hair and his eyes are dark blue, though I think they'll change to brown as he gets older."

"Oh, do babies' eyes change colour then?"

Audrey answered for her. "Yes, most babies are born with blue eyes, but they change after a couple of months, usually to a colour like one of their parents. As you have grey eyes, like Daddy's."

And like Carol's?"

"Yes, and your other sisters have dark brown eyes, like their Mummy."

"I know, she died, didn't she? Daddy told me. It's so sad. We all have the same daddy, but you're my Mummy, and you are Johnny's Mummy, but his Daddy died in the war, and that's sad too."

Audrey, with tears in her eyes, cuddled her daughter. "Yes, that's right lovey."

"Shall we have a cuppa?" Dorothy suggested.

"Yes," Carol smiled. "I'll put the kettle on and get Rosalind and Nerys' tea out of the oven."

"We'll eat in the kitchen," said Nerys. She had only been home for half an hour. "Come on Ros, I'm starving!"

When the twins were settled at the kitchen table, Nerys asked, "how did you get on with the pain, could you cope?"

"Yes, I was really pleased with myself, and with Pam. She was amazing, especially giving birth to such a big baby. I found it all fascinating, and rewarding. I'm seriously thinking of doing midwifery when I get my State Registration."

"Well, I find that amazing, considering all the pain involved. Are you sure?"

"I think so. It'll depend on my experience over the next two years. I may find something I prefer, but it was so rewarding, helping Pam to deal with the pain. If I can do that for every woman in labour, that would be fantastic!"

"Yes, I imagine it would."

"Anyway, back to the present. When shall we move into Grandma Alice's?" Said Nerys.

"She's already had the room redecorated for us, and the grandads have moved the double bed out of there into the little room, so we just need to move our beds and clothes. Maybe tomorrow would be a good day, being Sunday. Dad and Uncle Bobby said they will dismantle the beds and take them over."

Sunday was busy for everyone. The twins sorted their clothes out, made a pile for the jumble sale and took the rest across to Alice's house. Harry, Bobby and Alf moved the beds and the girls made them up with clean bedding. Alice had already polished the wardrobe and bedside tables and made a new rag rug to go between the two beds. She was delighted to have the twins staying with her and Bill. They would be having most of their meals, when not working, with Harry and Audrey and their sisters, but Alice had insisted that she would make breakfast for them.

"It will give you a good start to your working day, and I'll enjoy doing it."

Meanwhile, the men got the cradle down out of the loft and Audrey gave it a good clean. The bedding for the cradle was put ready for washing, and Pamela's bed was made up with fresh bedding.

Sunday afternoon found everyone back in Harry's, drinking tea and eating fruit cake.

"I'm just going to phone Johnny," said Carol. Harry and Audrey were smiling fondly. She had told them about her and Johnny's plans and they were delighted. The rest of the family didn't know yet. They wanted to wait until Johnny at least got an interview near home.

"Hello Johnny, I've got some news. Pamela has had a baby boy. Are you pleased to get a nephew to play football with?"

"Oh that's good news, give Pamela my love. I've also got some news. I've had a reply from that high school in Bury that I told you about. I've got an interview at the end of June, after term ends here. I am going to give in my notice tomorrow, because, even if I don't get the post, Uncle Harry said I should come home anyway, and I can do some supply teaching until the right post comes up. We can get married in the holidays and we can live with my grandma and grandad until we get a house. I can't wait to see you again lovey."

"Same here Johnny; I've missed you so much. I'm sure you'll get the post in Bury. They won't get a better history teacher than you."

"Ah yes, but you are biased my love."

She laughed; loving the way he called her 'my love'. "We've wasted so much time, haven't we?"

"Maybe not exactly wasted. Maybe we were meant to wait until now. We are both mature and sure of what we want. I'm glad I had this time in Shetland, but I'm ready to come home now, and so happy that you'll be waiting for me."

"Shall I tell everyone now, or would you like to be with me when we drop the bombshell?"

"I think you should tell everyone, then you can tell them about my interview at the same time. I'm sure Mum and Uncle Harry are desperate to talk to the grandparents about it. Let's give them something good to talk about."

"Ok lovey. Ring me on Wednesday evening and I'll tell you how everyone reacted. Bye bye, I love you."

"I love you too. Take care and I'll speak to you on Wednesday."

Carol's cheeks were red and her eyes sparkling when she got back in the living room.

Harry smiled. "Good news lovey?"

"Yes, Johnny's coming back home this summer. He's got an interview in Bury."

"Oh that's lovely!" Dorothy declared. "We'll have our grandson back living with us."

"There's something else," Said Carol, slowly. She had everyone's attention.

"Johnny and I are getting married." She looked around at her family. There was a stunned silence at first, and then everyone started talking at once.

Dorothy was loudest; she screamed, "Carol! That's wonderful. Oh you lovely girl. What a lovely surprise!" She jumped up from her seat and enveloped Carol in a tight hug.

"I'm glad you approve, Grandma," She returned the hug.

Fred said, "Good job we've got a double bed in the spare bedroom. You won't want to sleep in the bunk beds in Johnny's little room, lass." He gave her a hug too.

Alice, with tears in her eyes was next to hug her. She didn't speak, she was so overcome, but Carol could sense the happiness. After that everyone joined in with the hugging. It seemed that no one was surprised.

"We knew that you two were made for each other," said Nerys. "It's about time you realised it too. Well done sis. Can we be bridesmaids?"

"Can I be a bridesmaid too?" Lynnette asked. "And can I have a pink dress? It's my favourite colour."

"Yes, of course you can lovey. The twins can be big bridesmaids, and you and Michelle can be the little ones." Carol replied.

The news called for another pot of tea and lots of animated talk. Everyone was happy and Carol was relieved.

Johnny came home at the end of June, bringing all his possessions in his Ford Cortina. He piled all his boxes and books into his little bedroom and slept in the bunk bed. Fred and Dorothy were busy getting the double room ready for after the wedding.

The interview went well and Johnny got the post in Bury. "I knew you would lovey," said Carol. She kissed him and gave him a small oblong box. "A present for your new job," she said, with a smile.

"Oh, I love it!" He exclaimed, when he saw the smart fountain pen with his name engraved on it. That deserved another kiss.

The next few weeks were full of preparations for the wedding, which was to be on the second Saturday in August. Audrey made Carol's wedding gown and Dorothy and Alice made the bridesmaids dresses, pale pink for the little girls and cerise for the twins.

When they were being fitted for their dresses, Nerys asked Carol, "Can I bring a guest to the wedding?" She blushed as she said it.

Rosalind laughed. "It must be Fred, the man with the bright blue eyes. I knew you were serious about him!"

"Ok, yes I am. We've been seeing a lot of each other, when our shifts coincide. I haven't asked him, but I'm sure he'd love to come."

Carol smiled, "of course you can bring him. What about you Rosalind, have you got someone you'd like to invite?"

"No, there isn't anyone serious, and anyway, I'd rather get my studies out of the way before I find Mr Right."

Nerys laughed. "She's very picky," but Carol looked closely at Rosalind. There was something she was holding back, Carol could sense it, but Rosalind obviously wasn't ready to talk about it, so she said nothing.

Nerys met Fred in the dining room the next Monday. She was feeling down, as she was leaving Ancoats on Friday and going back to Crumpsall for second year block. She would be with Rosalind and all their friends, and they would have every weekend off, but she would miss seeing Fred.

"We'll still see each other," he reassured her. "Let's make a definite date. For a start, I can pick you up at Crumpsall, if I am on early shift, or on my day off." He had a red mini that was five years old and very handy for 'nipping about', as he termed it. "Then we can go to the pictures, or to our house." He lived with his parents in Moston. "Or, if you are tired, or have some studying to do, I can just run you home. Also, if I can get a weekend off, we can have a drive out, or something."

Nerys smiled. "If you can get the Saturday off in two weeks time, my brother and sister are getting married. I'm a bridesmaid. Would you like to come? There's always lots of fun when our family get together."

"I'd love to come. So it's a double wedding?"

Nerys was wearing her habitual grin. "No, they are marrying each other!"

"You are such a joker Nerys. How can they marry each other if they are brother and sister?" He was waiting for the punch line.

"Didn't I tell you that I come from a strange and complicated family?"

"I don't think you did. I think you said that there are eight of you, six girls and two boys. Is that right?"

"Yes, well; My eldest sister, Sian, is my half sister, we have the same mother. Her husband, Roberto, is my half brother, we have the same father, so they are not related to each other. They fell in love and got married and now they have two little daughters."

"Right, I've got that so far, I think, but what about the two that are getting married now?"

"Right, Carol and I are full sisters, but our mum died young and then Dad remarried Auntie Audrey - who isn't a real auntie, but a good friend. She was a war widow and

Johnny is her son, but he was brought up next door and was always like a brother to us. So therefore he and Carol are not blood relatives either. He is our stepbrother. Do you get it now?"

"Whew! You weren't kidding when you said your family is strange and complicated. Any more complications?"

"Not really, unless you take into account that our littlest sister is related to all of us. Oh, except she isn't related to Sian, but that's a whole new can of worms that I think I'll leave to another day."

"Oh wow, I think I'd love to meet this wacky family!"

"Why don't you come for tea tomorrow then? We're both on early shift, so you can just come home with me. You'll meet some of us then."

"That's a great idea. Thanks for the invite. Won't your parents mind my coming at short notice?"

"No, Auntie Audrey is used to catering for extra people, and I'll tell her tonight. She's a great cook."

Fred got on well with the family, especially Lynette, who thought he was wonderful. "You've got bluey, blue eyes, just like Auntie Jenny and my cousin Colin, and your eyes are always laughing."

That made Fred laugh and his eyes twinkled all the more. "I didn't know my eyes could laugh!"

"Oh yes, Carol told me. She said to look at people's eyes and you can tell if they're laughing inside. It's true!"

"Well, I've learned something new today. I'll have to take more notice of eyes," Fred couldn't help laughing at Lynette's earnest little face.

Nerys walked to the car with him when he was going home. "I hope you don't think my family is too wacky," she said.

"No, I've really enjoyed meeting them, I'm looking forward to this wedding now. I'll see you tomorrow; we are both on split shift, so, shall we go to our favourite cafe?"

"I'd love that." She looked up into his impossible blue eyes and he leaned forward to kiss her.

She floated back into the house on a cloud.

The weather was glorious for the wedding. Harry waited fondly at the church entrance while the twins arranged Carol's veil. He was so happy that she and Johnny had finally decided that they were made for each other. He had known since they were children. He looked down the aisle to where Audrey was sitting in the front pew, and he knew that she was just as happy. All around were the members of their joint family. Sian and Pamela were sitting in the left front pew, cradling their babies. Alice and Bill were with them. In the pew behind were Mymie and his friends from Shetland - Andy, Maggie, Kirsty, Donald and peerie Carol.

Bobby and Susan and their family were on the right; Alf and Norma sat with Jenny and George on the left. It didn't matter which side of the church they were on, because everyone was connected with both the bride and groom.

317

Harry was also pleased to see Mrs Watson, the old lady befriended by Rosalind, sitting with her best friend in the last pew. He gave them a friendly wave.

The only person conspicuous by her absence was Auntie Elsie. She could have been brought in her wheelchair, but she had refused to attend, saying that she was disgusted that yet another brother and sister were getting married. No one missed her.

The organ started to play 'here Comes the Bride' and Johnny stood, with Roberto at his side, and watched, his eyes full of love, as the woman he had loved for years came towards him. Carol's beautiful smile shone from beneath her veil.

This was the happiest day for both of them.

Nerys, with her twin at her side, saw Fred, sitting on the right hand side with his namesake, grandad Fred, and grandma Dorothy. Fred gave a dazzling smile as blue eyes met brown. Even though the twins were identical, Fred knew which was his twin. Her smile was unmistakeable, and full of love for him.

A year later; almost a year to the day, Carol and Johnny were having a joint anniversary and housewarming party in their new home, a semi detached house on Assheton Road, just about half a mile from their families' homes on Amos Avenue.

"Ooh, this is posh!" Nerys exclaimed. "I hope Fred and I can have something like this when we get married." They had been engaged for six months and were planning to get married next year, after Nerys became State Registered. Fred was now a Charge Nurse in Casualty, back in Crumpsall hospital. Nerys and Rosalind were in third year block, their last time in the classroom before their final exams next year.

There was ample room in this house for the family to get together, as it had a front room, known locally as a parlour, as well as a living room and a large kitchen.

The older family members were settled in the comfortable chairs in the parlour. The double glass doors through to the living room were open, making one big room. The dining table, laden with food, was pushed into a corner and the younger people were filling plates to take through to their parents and grandparents. Sian and Pamela had also found seats in the parlour, and were watching their toddlers, who were in danger of being trampled underfoot.

The twins and Carol were making sure everyone had drinks. There was wine and beer and sherry as well as fizzy pop for the children. Rosalind went into the parlour with a wine bottle to see if anyone wanted a top up.

"I'll tell you what lovey," said Dorothy. "I could murder a cup of tea."

"Of course, Grandma; I'll put the kettle on. Anyone else for tea?" She ended up making a big pot of tea for all the ladies. The men, apart from Harry, were happy with beer. Harry was drinking a glass of red wine; he would only have one, as he was still unused to alcohol.

As Rosalind gave a cup to Pamela, her sister grabbed the cup clumsily and spilt some of it on the floor. Pamela just laughed, but a suspicion that had been at the back of Rosalind's mind made itself known. She went to get a cloth, and wondered if she should share her worries with her twin. In the end she decided to say nothing. It was no use making Nerys worried as well. Nerys was so happy with Fred. She knew that Nerys had told Fred about Huntington's Chorea, and he still wanted to marry her. Rosalind hoped that she would one day find someone as caring.

Back in the classroom on Monday, Rosalind was still distracted. She couldn't concentrate on the lecture, and thought that she may have to borrow Nerys' notes later. At lunchtime Nerys said, "I'm just going to nip into casualty to see if Fred is free. "I'll see you in the dining room."

"Ok," Rosalind replied, and watched Nerys rushing down the main corridor.

She waited for the other students to go, and then walked down the corridor, alone, looking down at the floor and not really noticing where she was going. She was so deep in thought that she turned into the corridor that led to the dining room without looking up, and bumped into someone coming the other way. She looked up at the tall young man and her heart pounded.

"I'm sorry," he said, catching her hands as though he thought she might fall. "Are you alright?"

She took in the sight of him. He was in the uniform of a physiotherapist and was tall and muscular looking. His skin was a beautiful shade of brown that should have gone with brown eyes, but his eyes were green. Rosalind couldn't take her eyes off him.

"Are you alright?" He asked again, as she was still staring at him. He looked puzzled. "Have we met before?' He had a delicious Caribbean accent.

"Yes, I'm alright," she managed to say at last. "I don't think we have met before." She held out her hand to shake his. "Rosalind Roberts. Pleased to meet you."

"Carl Peters. Pleased to meet you too, Rosalind." His smile was magnetic.

She hadn't met him before - physically - but she knew him as intimately as she knew her family, because she had been dreaming about him since she was five years old!

Sheila. R. Kelly

Acknowledgements

This third novel in the 'Harry's Dream' series has been the hardest to write. Partly because I had several main characters - Harry's children, rather than concentrating on Harry himself; Partly because I moved house just as I started to write it, and then we were thrown into lockdown due to the pandemic of Covid-19.

I may never have completed my story if it hadn't been for the encouragement of my family and my many friends, who were anxious to read the next instalment. So my heartfelt thanks go to everyone who encouraged me.

I would like to thank Jimmy and Irene Davidson of Lerwick, who answered my many questions and gave me valuable information about Shetland in the 1960s, for the chapters based in Shetland.

I also learned about the Viking influence in Shetland from the book, 'Egil's Saga', written by Leifur Eiriksson. The couple who eloped and spent the winter in Mousa Broch - Bjorn and Thora - were actual characters from Egil's saga. Bjorn's cousin, Haki, is a figment of my imagination, but, as Bjorn had a crew on his longship, we can imagine that there was a crew member called Haki, who became the ancestor of Harry's family.

Thanks also to Wikipedia. I could always turn to this invaluable site to keep me right on the history. Particularly, I found the details of the World Cup Football Final in 1966, so I could describe Harry's family getting together to watch the match.

Heartfelt thanks to my three proofreaders; My sister, Karen and my two sons, Michael and Stephen, and finally, I couldn't have managed at all without the encouragement and endless cups of coffee from my loving husband, John.

About the Author

Sheila Kelly was born and raised in Manchester as part of a close knit, working class family. She worked as a nurse, and then as a podiatrist in various areas of the NHS.

She has always been an insatiable reader, and enjoyed writing from an early age, so it was a natural progression, after retiring from the NHS, to write her memoirs. These were published in two volumes in 2017, and their modest success led her to write her first novel, and the following two sequels.

The story of Harry Roberts, very loosely based on her father's life, had been in her mind for many years. It was a great feeling to transfer her ideas to paper, and to discover that many people enjoyed the story.

Sheila now lives with her husband in Oldham, and is planning a fourth novel in this saga.

Harry's Children

Sheila. R. Kelly

Harry's Children

Sheila. R. Kelly

Harry's Children

Sheila. R. Kelly

Harry's Children

Sheila. R. Kelly

Harry's Children

Sheila. R. Kelly

Harry's Children

Sheila. R. Kelly

Sheila. R. Kelly

Harry's Children

Sheila. R. Kelly

Harry's Children

Sheila. R. Kelly

Harry's Children

Printed in Great Britain
by Amazon